ERICA LUCKE DEAN

Eve
versus the
Apocalypse

Eve Versus the Apocalypse
Red Adept Publishing, LLC
104 Bugenfield Court
Garner, NC 27529
https://RedAdeptPublishing.com/

Cover Art by Erica Lucke Dean[1]

This is a work of fiction. Names, characters, places, and incidents either are the product of the author's imagination or are used fictitiously, and any resemblance to locales, events, business establishments, or actual persons—living or dead—is entirely coincidental.

---

1.   https://ericaluckedean.com/

To Mike, for promising to help me survive the apocalypse

Chapter 1

The Stuff Nightmares Are Made of

The lime-green paper clip holding my denim waistband together snaps apart in my hands. "Aw, crap."

Once upon a time—in a world *not* torn from the pages of a dystopian novel—the tattered Hollister jeans were my favorite. Chad Whitaker had ripped off the button with his teeth at a post-homecoming kegger sophomore year at Georgia Tech. We were trying to recreate some stupid viral internet stunt on the frat house lawn—a drunken dare, of course. Even now, I have no idea why I let him talk me into it... but like Coach always said, "Never underestimate the determination of a color guard." And as squad leader, I had a reputation to uphold. If the whole world hadn't gone to shit half a year later, I would probably *still* be the talk of the campus.

I glance down at my current state of hobo-chic and choke back a laugh. I wonder what my TikTok followers would say about me now.

With one last grunt, I give up on the broken paper clip and whisper a silent prayer for the zipper to hold. Back when I was attempting aerial acrobatics while dangling from a lacrosse player's teeth, I couldn't imagine parting with my favorite jeans—missing button or not. Now, I would give almost anything for a new pair—and a hot shower. It's been weeks since I've done more than wash up in random puddles or streams. I don't even want to think about how gross my hair is. Or how far my highlights have grown out.

"Quit whining, Eve," I mutter, dragging the greasy strands into a loose ponytail and securing them with a frayed rubber band. "Dirty hair and dark roots are the least of your worries."

Before exiting the stall, I use my foot to flush. The roar of the toilet echoes off the walls, and my heart kicks into high gear as I realize what I've done. I know better than to draw attention to myself. Especially so close to nightfall. "*Shit...*" The word slips past my lips at the same instant a bone-chilling shriek cuts through the air.

Instinctively, my hands shoot up to cover my ears. The sound, like sharpened claws on a giant chalkboard, sends a wave of tremors down my spine. For an instant, the cloyingly sweet odor that surrounds *them*—like sticky molasses or maple syrup burned to the bottom of a pan—floods my senses. I know it's impossible to smell them from here, but even through thick concrete-block walls, I can *hear* one. Another shriek turns my blood to ice.

It can't be dark yet, can it? Damn it, why did I wait so long to find a safe place for the night?

This *can't* be how I go down—in a dirty gas station restroom on the edge of some town I wouldn't be caught dead in under normal circumstances. I'll stick out like a sore thumb—or a tasty treat—out in the open, but staying put isn't an option. I can't afford to be trapped in a small space with only one exit—and no weapon.

With my hands trembling and my pulse pounding in my throat, it takes me way too many tries to unhook one of the rusty safety pins holding my ratty black leather jacket closed and frantically use it to secure my waistband. There isn't a chance in hell of making it out of here with my pants around my ankles.

Why did I have to flush? And what are the odds I'd flush the one toilet that actually still works? My bladder picked the absolute worst moment to need attention. I should've held it until I found shelter, or even an old soda cup. It wouldn't be the first time I've had to use one of those. Delivery drivers used to pee in empty bottles all the time—back when we still got packages. And without question, dropping my pants on the side of the road would've been a lot faster but would've also left me vulnerable to more than one evil.

Shaking off the internal berating, I cringe at the whine of metal on metal as I slide the lock free and crack open the door. Crimson streaks etch the sky as the sun creeps farther down the horizon. I have no idea where *they* hide until after dark, but I've got maybe an hour before this place is swarming with them. *Like hornets in a nest.* I need to get out of this death trap before the stragglers get to me first.

Outside, the high-pitch squeals are twice as loud... and three times as terrifying. Where the hell did it come from? Before panic sets in, I dig into my pocket for a pair of battered AirPods and stuff them into my ears with a shudder. I would gleefully trade my last pack of gum for a pair of real earplugs or a charging station. There isn't much I wouldn't give for an hour's worth of electricity. My iPhone battery has long since crapped out—along with the soles of my favorite boots—but at least the lifeless buds somewhat muffle the sound. I can't afford to be paralyzed by fear, not now.

Fighting back the terror clawing at my insides, I mentally calculate the distance between me and the closest gas pump, where my stolen motorcycle waits, key still dangling from the ignition. Thirty feet maybe? Fifty? I have no idea. I only hope the distance between here and there is shorter than the one between me and *it*.

How could I be so stupid? I chastise myself for leaving my only means of escape—and my weapon—so far away.

"Better run fast, Evie," Coach's gruff baritone barks inside my head. Even when he isn't here, his is the only voice of reason.

My heartbeats count out the seconds as I suck in a lungful of cool air and dig in my heels to make a break for it.

Another bloodcurdling screech shatters the air like an ax cutting through plate glass—this one coming from the opposite direction—and my stomach drops to my toes. Then the first wisp of cold fog hits the back of my neck, like a Dementor's icy breath, I imagine, and I know at least one of them is directly behind me.

Run!

My lungs burn as I pour every ounce of adrenaline into closing the distance.

The creature's long, bony fingers rake through my hair, and my steps falter. A scream catches in my throat. I'm this close to losing it as I lock my eyes on my sharpened saber still strapped to the back of the bike.

"Focus, Eve!" I hear Coach again, as if he's standing beside me, pushing me like he always did. *"Go through the routine, step by step."*

My eyes fog over as I let my mind drift just long enough to pretend I'm back on the field doing drills. I practiced the routine with a blunted saber so many times I could do it in my sleep. Only now, I carry a sword that could slice through a truck tire—or a thick-as-hell alien exoskeleton. And after six months of listening to the same soundtrack over and over—the only one I bothered to download before a fucking alien spaceship vaporized the cloud—Justin Timberlake continues to loop inside my head.

If I concentrate really hard, I can almost hear JT drowning out the cries of the monster bearing down on me. And with my eyes laser focused on the glint of metal looming in front of me, I can almost *feel* the leather warm as my fingers itch to wrap around the handle. I lengthen my strides until my thighs burn and my heavy boots slap the pavement, raising dust clouds from the loose gravel.

Spindly gray arms reach for me, and I hit the ground, sliding the rest of the way to the bike as if I'm scoring the winning run at the World Series. I coil my fingers around the smooth leather grip and unsheathe the blade in one fluid motion, somehow managing to scramble back to my feet while whirling the saber around me to the beat of the imaginary track.

JT may not be able to stop the feeling, but I can damn sure stop ET where he stands. It takes every drop of courage I can muster to face the beast towering over me—a nightmare-inducing cross between a giant praying mantis and the thing that tried to kill Sigourney Weaver in half a dozen *Alien* movies. The weight of the saber in my hands gives me a false sense of security as I stand toe-to-toe with seven-plus feet of drooling alien.

It stares me down like a snake, trying to hypnotize me into submission or whatever it is they do. As soon as my brown eyes meet its huge milky-white ones, the creature's mouth gapes open, and it lets out another earsplitting cry, blowing my hair back in the process. I don't breathe for at least half a minute. Its breath may not be toxic—the jury's still out on that—but the smell alone, a horrifying cross between rotting meat and death, is enough to bring me to my knees.

As far as I know, there are only two ways to kill one. The first is to trap it in the sun—I'm not sure if it's the light or the heat, but the bastards dry up like a time-lapse video of raisins on a hot day. The second is to separate its head from its shoulders, like video game zombies or movie vampires. Since the sun is going down fast, I'm left with only one option. And with a second alien hunting me, I won't get more than one crack at this one.

With Justin Timberlake singing in my head, I whip the saber around me one more time before bringing it down and around, using stored-up momentum and the element of surprise to slice a path through the air and its narrow neck, dropping the alien like a bag of rotting fruit. I don't have even a second to celebrate before ET's even uglier brother pounces, and I pirouette out of the way, swallowing back the half a bag of stale Doritos I scarfed down for dinner. Years of practice drilled into my head has my feet moving before I even think of where to place them. I dance around the monster with my saber flying like a ribbon in my hands and my heart hammering against my trembling ribs.

The alien lunges again, and a quick sidestep has my feet sticking to the syrupy "blood" seeping out of the first one, slowing me down just enough to bring the second creature too close for comfort. With its face just inches from mine, a blast of icy death washes over me.

This is it.

My eyes flood with unshed tears. Any second, I'll be dead—like Mom and Dad. Like my little brother Zack, my best friend, Serenity, and literally everyone else I've ever known. An odd sense of relief sweeps through me, instantly followed by regret. I haven't killed nearly enough of them. I'm supposed to live to see the aliens suffer, if not fall, before I die.

With a primal scream working its way up my throat, I tighten my fingers on the grip of my blade. I may not get to see them all burn before I go, but I can at least leave this one a few scars to remember me by.

My muscles twitch as I raise my arm, ready to go down swinging, when something in the alien's peripheral vision draws its attention for a split second.

What the hell? I can't be this lucky, can I? I'm paralyzed for what seems like forever but couldn't possibly be longer than a single heartbeat. Without wasting another second, I whip the saber around again, lopping off its head and dropping its twitching carcass right beside the first one.

Eve: 2 - Aliens: 0

A loud whoop of excitement from behind catches me off guard, and I almost drop the sword. I spin toward the sound to see three muscular guys standing in the back of an open-top Jeep parked across the street. They're young—maybe not as young as me but midtwenties at the most—and they're gaping as if I just pissed wine into a barrel.

Dressed in makeshift tactical gear pieced together from what looks like football equipment stolen from a high school locker room, each with a shotgun tucked at his side, any one of them could take me out in the blink of an eye. The biggest of the three guys hops down, and I catch sight of a fourth leaning against the roll bar. Instead of focusing on me, the tall, dark-haired guy has a bow and arrow trained on the alien at my feet. In head-to-toe black leather, he looks like he belongs in a superhero movie... or on a runway, modeling Calvin Klein's new assassin line.

The ridiculous thought knocks a shaky laugh out of me, and the archer's intense gaze snaps up to fix on mine. My muscles lock tight, and a flutter of fear swirls low in my stomach as I suddenly wonder if I'm his next target. Like a rabbit caught in a snare, I can't tear my eyes away. Even from across the road, I can almost *feel* the heat of his stare. In another lifetime, his attention would have elicited a completely different response in me. But gorgeous or not, the guy is one itchy trigger finger away from releasing an arrow straight into my racing heart.

Still out of breath from my last battle, I raise the saber again, mirroring his offensive stance. Without relaxing his arm, he lowers the bow, cocking his head to the side as if trying to solve a puzzle. Then, pulling his eyes from mine for an instant, he says something to the driver, and the Jeep jumps to life, making a U-turn in the middle of the road to cut a path toward me.

Shit! I quickly sheathe my blade and hop on the bike, firing it up before they get close enough to block my escape.

"Wait!" the stocky blond leans over the side to shout at me. "It's not safe out here!"

Understatement of the century, buddy. If I've learned anything in the past several months, it's to trust no one but myself. I may crave human companionship with every fiber of my being, but the other humans I've run across since being on my own have been just as dangerous as the aliens. If not worse...

The Jeep growls behind me, but by the time they've made it to the gas station, I'm already half a block away, gunning the engine as I head north—far away from everything I left behind in Atlanta.

Chapter 2

Ghost Town

———◦———

What used to be a quaint little tourist spot only a few hours north of the city has turned into a ghost town. With broken windows and abandoned vehicles as far as the eye can see, it's as if I've wandered onto the set of *The Walking Dead*. All that's missing is a tumbleweed rolling down Main Street... and a horde of zombies. But as I pass through the town square, there isn't a zombie in sight. And the people who lived here year-round are either hiding or gone. I try to tell myself they all managed to get out, that maybe the national guard showed up with buses to take everyone to safety, but I'm a terrible liar. Most are likely dead. And honestly, that's probably for the best. This is no kind of life.

With my hair whipping around me and the fading rays dappling through the treetops in a kaleidoscope of color, I accelerate past what used to pass for civilization and head up the mountain. Above me, sunlight glints off windows like winking stars. Somewhere up there, amongst the countless other cabins dotting the ridge, is the place I used to call the Treehouse. It's been several years since the last time I made the trip, but thankfully, I still remember the way.

The two-story timber-frame chalet belonging to my grandparents has always reminded me of a fancy owl's nest, perched on the side of a cliff, tucked among thick tree branches and almost totally hidden from view. My parents used to bring us in the fall to catch fish and watch the leaves change colors while we bonded as a family. As a teenager, I hated being away from my friends for even a few days.

Now, I'd give anything to sit around the table and try to catch my brother cheating at Monopoly. Hell, I'd even let him win, if it meant he wasn't dead.

Speaking of dead...

That's exactly what I'll be if I don't reach the cabin before the last rays of sun slip behind the peaks.

The higher I climb, the brighter the sky, but it won't be long before the sun completely slides below the horizon. Less than a few miles away, in the town below, where shadows block what's left of the waning light, I can hear the baleful cries of the creatures coming out of hiding to feed.

The aliens don't seem to be particular about what they eat. Whatever happens to be in their path. Human... wildlife... vegetation. And if I've learned nothing else in the past few months, it's that humans aren't equipped to be at the bottom of the food chain. Those without survival skills make for easy prey. The young, the old, the sick—they got picked off first. But before long, almost everybody else was gone too.

Sometimes, I wish I didn't know how to defend myself, wish I didn't have a blade I could unwrap, that I'd been taken out in that first wave that took nearly everyone I loved. And I feel like I'm betraying my family with every regret. The last thing my mom said to me before the line went dead was "head to the cabin." Her words echo in my brain, and I'm glad I can still remember the sound of her voice.

Minutes tick by like hours as I wind my way to the top of the summit. After a few wrong turns, I finally reach the Treehouse. To avoid drawing any more attention than I already have, I push the bike the last hundred yards or so and stow it around the back, tucking it under the deck, where it'll be hidden from view behind the thick trunk of an ancient oak. I take the back stairs two at a time, hoping the key's still in the same place.

The rusted bird feeder hanging from the covered deck is coated in a thick layer of fresh pollen. The seeds have long since run out, so it doesn't take me long to retrieve the key and unlock the back door. Eerie silence greets me as I step inside.

Heavy beams crisscross the soaring ceiling, casting matching shadows in the dying light. Mom would've immediately opened the windows to air out the place, but instead, I quickly slide the deadbolt into place, locking myself in with the stale mildew and dust. I lay the bike keys and my sword on the primitive console table by the door and tick off the seconds along with my pounding heart. I know I'm being paranoid, but I won't relax until I'm sure no one followed me.

My stomach chooses that moment to rumble loudly, reminding me how long it's been since I last ate. Even longer since I've eaten anything of substance. Gran used to keep the place stocked for any occasion, and I'm fairly sure Mom did the same. Unless someone got here before me, there should be something worth salvaging. Checking the shadows along the way, I drag my battered carcass toward the kitchen. Every inch of me aches from my last alien smackdown. *Killing takes a lot out of a girl.* I snort, the unladylike sound too loud in the quiet.

With a passing glance at the fridge—anything left in there would be toxic by now—I head straight for the pantry. Rows of assorted canned goods and glass jars line the first shelf. Boxes of sugary cereal, crackers, and baking mixes line the next.

"Jackpot!" I grab an unopened jar of peanut butter, a sleeve of Saltine crackers, and two cans of tuna.

Dipping the crackers directly into the peanut butter, I slap together a few little sandwiches. Like a savage, I lay waste to each one before making the next, licking the salty remains from my fingers as I go. Once the crackers are gone, I pop the top on the tuna and devour one after another, straight from the can like a feral cat.

Sated and thoroughly exhausted, I drop into the old leather sofa, sending a puff of dust into the air. The last glow of daylight has finally disappeared below the horizon, and the normal sounds of the forest fade away as the otherworldly shrieks of the aliens fill the night air. Despite the late-summer temperature hovering close to eighty, I shudder. I can't seem to shake the bone-deep chill taking root in my soul. A neat stack of wood piled beside the hearth calls out to me, begging me to start a fire, but fear of drawing the creatures—or anyone else—to my hiding spot keeps me rooted in place.

"At least you're safe, Evie," Coach's voice reminds me. And for now, that's almost more than I could hope for.

Chapter 3

End of Days

"Eve!" My roommate, Serenity, nudges me. Her frantic whisper strikes like a percussion blast in my ears. "Wake up."

"*Noooo.*" The word comes out on a groan. Whatever she wants can wait till morning, when I'm not in the middle of a good dream. "Go to bed. Talk tomorrow."

She shakes my shoulder violently, and I catch a whiff of cinnamon candy on her breath. "Damn it, Eve. Get. Up!"

The dream version of Harry Styles waves a sad goodbye, vanishing into the mist as I blink open my eyes to find Serenity hovering over me. "What the hell, Ren? I was just about to kiss—"

"Something is very wrong." Her face is so close I can see every clogged pore across the bridge of her nose.

"No shit. You just ruined a really good—"

"Forget about Harry Styles." She rolls her eyes as if she's heard enough of my fantasies already. "I just watched this video—"

"Are you kidding me?" I scoot back and sit up, putting some much-needed distance between us. "You woke me up to look at some stupid *Tik Tok*—"

"Damn it! Just shut up and listen for two seconds." She stands, pacing the short distance between her bed and mine, and her panic-stricken expression roots me in place. "You know how people have been posting about UFO sightings a lot lately?"

Curious, I nod.

"Well, some guy in Arizona just livestreamed—"

A loud rumble shakes the walls, knocking books and empty liquor bottles off the shelves, and the sound of breaking glass echoes through the small room. "What the hell—"

Serenity turns toward the window, the color draining from her already-pale complexion until she looks like a corpse. "They're here..."

Another crash cracks through the fog of my dream, dragging me into the present, and Serenity fades away as quickly as Harry Styles had in another lifetime. For half a second, I catch myself thinking about that morning again, and I shudder. Now isn't the time to re-play bad memories. Staying low, I roll off the sofa and grab my saber from the console table. Melting into the shadows from the beams overhead, I focus on what's happening inside the cabin.

The sound of muffled voices tells me I'm dealing with my own kind, and I cautiously follow the sound to the open pantry to assess the danger. I haven't survived this long by jumping indiscriminately into the fray. Taking on a lone alien—or malevolent human—would be doable. Taking on more could cost me more than my life.

A soft cry and a muffled *shhh* cut through the silence, and I risk a peek. In the dim light, I can barely make out the slender figure with an even smaller one tucked behind it, but in the months since the world I knew ceased to exist, I've seen enough to know size alone isn't a fair indication of danger.

When the smaller of the two—*a child?*—breaks into a coughing fit, I make my presence known. "Who's in there?"

A muffled scream sets my nerves on edge. The last thing I need is to draw the monsters to us.

Holding out my saber in front of me, I pull myself to my full height and step into a shaft of light. "Come out where I can see you."

"Please don't hurt us!" The dark-skinned woman's voice cracks as she inches into the light, tucking the child behind her. "We're just looking for something to eat."

Lowering my saber, I glance down at the dark curls of the little boy peeking around her. The kid's pupils stretch impossibly wide as he gapes up at me in the wash of moonlight, and I imagine the gears in his tiny brain spinning wildly as he sizes me up.

Shifting my focus back to the woman, I let months of anger and frustration wash over me as I scold her in a heated whisper. "Are you crazy or just stupid, bringing a kid outside after dark? Those *things* could be anywhere. You don't even have a weapon!"

"I didn't bring him out in the dark!" she snaps, as if I'd insulted her parenting skills, and a sliver of guilt works its way under my skin.

"Then how did you get here?" I pop an eyebrow, planting a fist against my hip. "You sure as hell didn't teleport."

"We..." She glances toward the open basement door, dislodging a fleeting memory of a dark, rarely used lower level. "We've been in the basement."

My mouth falls open. "You've been down there this whole time?"

"Since just before dusk. We needed a safe place to shelter for the night, and a secluded cabin tucked into the trees looked as good as any."

"Why didn't you tell me you were here?"

She rolls her eyes as if I'd asked the dumbest question ever. Maybe I did. I know better than most how dangerous it is out there. "We heard you come in and hid. If it hadn't been so long since Theo's eaten, we would've stayed hidden and slipped out at dawn. I didn't dare put the lights on, and... well, I dropped a jar of sauce. I'm sorry about the mess."

"I don't care about the damn mess. How did you even get here? This place isn't exactly easy to find."

She lets out a slow breath. "We have a small cabin a few miles away... farther up the mountain."

"So you live here full-time?" I catch the kid watching me and tuck the saber behind my back.

"No... ours is just a weekend place, not nearly as nice as this." She nods toward the spacious great room. "But when the first wave arrived, my husband packed up the car with everything we could carry, and we headed north. James figured, with enough meat to fill the freezer and a whole pantry's worth of canned and dry goods, we could wait it out until the military took care of the monsters. We'd seen all the disaster movies... we knew the drill. All you need is plenty of food, water, and a safe place to hide. But they just kept coming..."

Her breath hitches, and the desperation in her eyes hits me like a gut punch. None of us had been prepared for what had come next.

"We spread our rations as thin as we could without starving to death, and we *still* went through most of our provisions in a few months' time. It got so bad that my husband decided to go out for supplies." A tear rolls down her cheek, and I know what she's about to say before she says it.

"He didn't come back." I swallow the lump in my throat and blink back tears. Pain lances through me as I think of my own family, lost to the same fate.

"I've known James since I was fifteen years old... nothing would stop that man from coming back for us if he was able." She lowers her chin to stare at her feet as her tears flow freely. "I waited until we ran out of food before I stole from the cabin next door. Those people hadn't come back, either, and I'd be damned if I'd let my baby starve."

The kid coughs again, and I point my chin toward him. "Is he sick?"

"He has a weak heart." The woman tucks the boy under her arm and smooths back his curls. "Gets tired faster than most."

Wave after wave of guilt and remorse flood my senses until my skin prickles with the overwhelming emotions. "You're welcome to anything I have. Help yourself. But I'm not sure how long it'll last with three of us—"

"We'll only stay long enough to eat, and maybe trouble you for a place to sleep for a spell. As soon as the sun's up, we'll go."

"You can't go back out there… it's not safe. Even with this"—I glance at my lowered saber—"I can't handle more than one or two of them at a time."

"We'll be fine." She hugs the boy tighter, as if to reassure herself as much as me. "We'll keep moving during the day… find shelter by dusk. But staying put is as good as being dead. We need to make our way toward the safe zone."

I tilt my head to the side, and her eyes light up.

"You don't know? One of the last news broadcasts we heard urged anyone listening to head for North Carolina. Fort Liberty set up a camp for survivors. We would've gone then, but James thought for sure the military would burn those sons of bitches to the ground before we made it to the state line."

A safe zone. My thoughts race at a thousand miles an hour as I process the new information. Fighting against the urge to run out the door and jump on my motorcycle, I shift my focus to the small boy clinging to her side like a sock straight out of the dryer. "You can't walk all the way there."

The woman lifts her chin in defiance. "We won't be walking. I have a car, an old map, and enough gas to get me at least halfway there. If you can spare a meal, and maybe a few snacks for the road, we'll be on our way at dawn."

Safe zone…

The thought continues to percolate in my brain until that's all I can think about. I can't help but wonder if any of my friends made it to safety. As Theo and his mom help themselves to my peanut butter and a sleeve of crackers and settle into my spot on the sofa, a faint whisper of hope sparks deep in my soul. *Mom and Dad.*

Fresh pain lances through me as I stare out the window at the pitch-black forest. Memories of those first days after the invasion flash through my brain like fireworks—a recurring nightmare I can't seem to wake from. The ghost of my mom's voice tells me to run. In our last phone call before the signal was forever lost, she begged me to head for the cabin, to leave the city and not look back. But despite the waves of paralyzing panic willing me to curl into a ball in a corner, I couldn't turn my back on them. I refused to abandon my family for dead.

It took me almost a week—walking all day until my bones turned to jelly and my feet blistered and hiding in abandoned buildings at night—but I somehow managed to make my way from campus to our ravaged neighborhood in the suburbs.

The deserted streets and the house I grew up in were almost unrecognizable. Uprooted trees lined the driveway. The front door had been ripped from the hinges and tossed aside like a discarded candy wrapper. Inside, eerie silence replaced the laughter that once permeated every inch of the place. Every piece of furniture we owned had been snapped in half like a matchstick, the debris scattered from one corner to the next, as if a tornado had swept through the rooms. Bloody trails led in every direction, smearing the walls and floors, but I never found their bodies.

I lick the salty trail of tears pooling in the corner of my lips and grasp onto that tiny flicker of hope with both hands. At the time, I assumed the worst—assumed they'd fallen prey to the monsters. But maybe they *didn't* die. Maybe they took Zack and fled for the safe zone in North Carolina.

"Maybe..." I clear my throat, forcing myself back to the present. "Maybe I'll go with you."

"Oh no." My uninvited house guest—I still don't know her name—shakes her head vigorously, making her tight curls bounce. "We don't need an escort. We've done all right on our own."

I let out a dismissive grunt. "From your cabin to mine, maybe, but do you have any idea what's out there waiting for you?" A shudder rolls through me as the vivid memory of my last alien encounter resurfaces. No way would one unarmed woman and a sick little boy be able to fight off two full-grown ETs. *Let alone the Jeep full of strangers with dubious motives.* I brush off the thought and fix my gaze on hers. "Because I do. You'd be safer traveling with someone who can at least fight if it comes to that."

"No, thank you." She laughs as she sizes me up. "You have the stink of them all over you. You'd only be a magnet, calling them straight to us."

The urge to sniff myself gets the best of me. "So I'll wash it off... I'm sure I have some old clothes I can change—"

"Changing your clothes and washing your hair won't erase the mark on your soul!" Her voice climbs until it slices through me like a sharpened saber, and I can almost feel the blood pooling inside.

Focusing on my ragged reflection in the dark window, I rein in the thunder brewing below the surface when all I want to do is let loose and scream. With a steadying breath, I turn to face her. "And you think the aliens can see inside my soul? You think *you* can?"

"You don't understand..." She exhales slowly. "Do you really think these *creatures* are here by happenstance?"

Every alien movie I've ever seen flashes before my eyes. "M-Maybe they destroyed their planet and they're after our natural resources."

"Or maybe"—she fixes me with a piercing stare—"they're the harbingers of death, the four horsemen from the Bible."

I choke back a laugh, but the thought chills me to the bone. "So you're saying this is Biblical end-of-days shit we're dealing with here?"

"Who said Hell had to come from below? It would make just as much sense for it to come from above."

"Well, I hate to burst your bubble, but I've killed a handful of those suckers all by myself." *Exactly five, to be precise.*

The woman rests a hand on my shoulder, and the sudden gesture reminds me of my mom. "Because you're an avenging angel doing God's work, striking them down where they stand. But that marks you—puts a great big target on your back—you and anyone around you."

My mouth falls open as I struggle for the words to convey my shock. I may be a speed bump in the aliens' road to complete domination of our planet, but I'm no avenging angel.

"Don't get me wrong." She tucks a crocheted afghan around her son's delicate shoulders, and the little boy is fast asleep before she turns back to me. "I really do appreciate your hospitality—and your generous offer—but me and Theo, we don't stand out. We'll be safer traveling under the radar, where we can blend into the background, where no one will pay us any mind."

With another nod, I plop into my grandfather's favorite recliner, breathing in what's left of his scent along with the dust. *Are avenging angels allowed to rest?* "I hope you're right."

"I know I am." Theo's mom slips under the afghan to lie beside him. She closes her eyes, and the deep grooves etched across her forehead smooth out. "I know God is protecting us. He must be for us to have made it this far."

The cabin descends into silence again as she drifts off to wherever her dreams take her.

I let my thoughts wander back to the safe zone. For the first time in months, I have hope—hope that my family may still be alive, hope that I might see my friends again someday, and hope for the future of humanity. I let my eyes drift shut, eager for the sounds of the forest to lull me to sleep.

The metal roof creaks and pops, groaning as it releases the summer heat stored within its bones. The sound that used to terrify me as a child comforts me with its familiarity. I listen for the call of the screech owls or the droning song of the katydids in the trees, but they don't come. In fact, nothing comes—no buzzing, no chirping, no anything.

I sit bolt upright, focusing my attention on the woods surrounding the cabin. In the hundreds of times I've visited over the years, I've never known the forest to be so completely devoid of sound. My skin prickles to attention as the eerie silence sends a chill down my spine. I suddenly wish I'd asked the woman for her name as I creep forward to where she and her son lie sleeping.

"Wake up." I can barely hear my own whisper over the pounding of my heart.

I lightly touch her arm, and she jerks awake, flinching from my touch as if I burned her.

"Wh—" Her eyes go round as I lay a hand over her mouth.

"Something's wrong," I whisper, pointing to the wide expanse of glass across the back wall. "It's too quiet out there."

To her credit, she doesn't question me and doesn't hesitate even an instant before scooping Theo into her arms. She carries the sleeping boy to the pantry, tucking him into the shadows where I'd first discovered them earlier that evening. "Is it them?"

I shake my head, but I grab my saber from where I'd left it and tuck it close. In truth, I'm not sure what we're hiding from, maybe just my overactive imagination, but much like she has her God, I have my gut. It's protected me this far, so I'm not about to ignore it now.

Chapter 4

Monsters at the Gate

For a long moment, none of us so much as breathes, and the eerie quiet spreads until the only sounds in the cabin are the combined beating of our hearts and a persistent ringing in my ears. With my focus locked on the vast nothingness of the dark forest beyond the windows, I relax the grip on my saber just enough for blood to flow through my fingers again, wondering if I've let my imagination get the best of me.

"Maybe—" A loud shriek vibrates the glass, and my muscles go on total lockdown. "Shit."

Theo's mom springs into action, pushing him farther into the shadows until he all but disappears under the shelves in the pantry before snatching the broom from behind the door to stand shoulder to shoulder with me in the kitchen.

My stomach tightens as I eye her useless weapon. "Are you planning to sweep it out the door?"

She exhales through her nose, straightening her spine as she balances the wooden handle in both hands. She's obviously trying to put on a good show, but her arms are visibly shaking. "It's not exactly a bo staff, but it'll do in a pinch."

Doubt clouds my vision as I quickly size her up. She looks nothing like someone trained in martial arts, but then again, no one would've mistaken me for some kind of alien slayer, let alone an avenging angel, walking around the Georgia Tech campus before the shit hit the fan. Not even me.

"You know how to use a bo?"

"In theory?" She lets out a nervous laugh, and a bead of sweat slips down her temple. "I took a six-week class at the Y, but Theo's a huge Donatello fan."

I cock my head to the side, but before I can ask, she continues.

"We watched a lot of Ninja Turtles before... well, before."

I gape at her, unable to hide my shock. "Are you seriously staking your life on skills you learned watching a kids' cartoon?"

"You have any better—" A loud crack cuts her off as a huge tree crashes through the picture window, sending glass and broken limbs everywhere.

"Hide." I shove her hard toward her son's hiding place before diving in the opposite direction, tucking my saber at my side as I belly crawl under the heavy slab dining table.

"That's right, Eve! Flank those sons of bitches. They won't know what hit 'em," Coach's voice barks in my ear.

Divide and conquer isn't exactly the color guard motto, but even my hallucinations learned to adapt a long time ago. For half a second, I let myself believe Theo's mom will back me up when the time comes, but the growing knot in the pit of my stomach warns me not to get my hopes up. It wouldn't be the first time someone left me holding the bag.

Another bone-chilling shriek—this one way too close for comfort—interrupts my walk down memory lane, and I quickly focus on the crunch of pine boards and broken glass. From my vantage point, I have a clear view of the destroyed wall and the single alien making its way over the fallen tree into the cabin. Its lanky gray body nearly fades into the shadows, but there's no mistaking the rancid odor.

The first whiff of rotting meat reaches me, and every fiber of my being—from my dark roots to my unpolished toenails—vibrates with tension. I pull the neck of my T-shirt over my nose to block the smell while I formulate a plan. Imaginary Coach may be right. Again wishing I'd bothered to get her name, I send up a silent prayer for Theo's mom to come out of hiding just long enough to draw the alien toward her. The last thing I want is to put anyone else in danger, but if she can capture its attention long enough for me to get into position, we might have a fighting chance.

As if she heard my thoughts—or maybe her divine protector whispered in *her* ear—she pops out of the shadows, waving the stupid broom like a white flag.

"Hey, you!" She takes a few steps to the side, luring him away from the pantry. "This way, you big dumb alien. Stay the hell away from my baby!" Once she has its undivided attention, she drops the broom and darts down the hallway toward the main bedroom with the alien in pursuit.

"Shit! Shit! Shit!" I spit the words under my breath and scramble to my feet. She picked the absolute worst place to run. Even if she clears the narrow hallway before it gets to her, and that's a big if, there isn't a chance in hell of me having room to wield my saber if she gets trapped in a tight space.

Her scream pierces my eardrums, making my blood go cold as I take off after her, racing into certain death. I really hope she's right and some higher power is actually watching over us, because if not, we're dead meat.

I follow a dark, sticky trail from the bedroom into the adjacent bathroom, where she somehow managed to wedge herself between the sink and the toilet and wields a full rack of antlers that used to hang over the dresser. Using the horns as a weapon, she jabs the points into the alien while it takes lazy swipes at her with its spindly claws like a cat swatting at a shadow. Judging from the thick amber fluid dripping from the tips, she got in a few good hits.

Locking my focus on the monster's exposed neck, I plant my feet and raise my saber, letting the blade sail through the air and straight through skin and bone. Syrupy blood squirts everywhere, coating the walls and the floors... and Theo's mom.

She lets out another scream and kicks the severed head out of the way to climb to her feet. "That's it. I'm getting my son, and we're leaving." Wiping her face with her shoulder, she pushes past me, making a beeline for her little boy.

As soon as he sees her, Theo rushes forward, slamming into her hard enough to knock her back a few steps. "Momma! Are you okay?"

"I'm fine, baby, just a little dirty." She spears me with a look that reaches all the way inside to twist the knife in my gut. I can't decide if I'm more hurt or angry at her insinuation. I wasn't expecting her to fall at my feet, but I did just save her life. A little gratitude would be nice.

"We can't stay here any longer." With a quick glance toward the faint glow growing on the horizon, she reaches for a pair of empty backpacks hanging on a hook behind the pantry door.

"You're leaving?"

"It'll be daylight soon." Without another word, she starts filling the bags with canned goods and bottled drinks until the seams stretch to their breaking points.

I set my saber on the counter and wipe my gory hands on the front of my ruined jeans. "Are you sure you wouldn't rather travel with someone who can watch your back? Someone who knows how to fight?"

She lets out a breath, and the weight of the world seems to come out with it. "No offense, but avenging angel or not, you're bad for our health. We'll be better off taking our chances out there."

"If you're sure that's what you want."

"It is."

With nothing left to say, I help her load the overstuffed bags into her dirty green Subaru and watch in silence as she buckles Theo into the back.

Then, with the sun coming up behind her, she climbs into the driver's seat and rolls down the window. "Take care of yourself, Angel."

The urge to hug her is strong, but I'm stronger. "You too."

I wave goodbye as they pull away, and for a fleeting second, I feel a pang of guilt for letting her go without trying harder to convince her there's strength in numbers. I may not be the avenging angel she thinks I am. Hell, I may only be a color guard with a weapon, but that isn't nothing. *I'm* not nothing.

The moment the low rumble of her engine fades into the distance, I bolt back inside and tear through every closet until I find another, smaller duffel bag, and I fill it with as much food and water as it'll hold. I even find the remnants of a first aid kit and a dusty box of tampons in the linen closet and tuck those away for later. I can't remember the last time I had actual tampons, since the world went to shit. My pack brimming with supplies, I make my way back to the great room for one last look around.

So maybe a saber-wielding color guard isn't the best escort for a kid and his mom. That wasn't my decision to make. I respected her wishes. I let them go. But with or without them, I'm heading to North Carolina.

Chapter 5

Buffy the Alien Slayer

With dawn cresting the horizon, and Theo's mom's words echoing in my brain, I hop in the shower. Mark on my soul or not, I can wash the stink from my skin. Barely more than a quick rinse, it's easily the best damned cold shower I've had in weeks, and I use every last drop left in the well's pressure tank. With an amber-tinged trail still swirling down the drain, I scour the cabin for something fresh to wear. Piecing together an outfit from the few things I manage to dig up in my size, I pull on a pair of what I assume is Mom's underwear, a pair of skintight black leggings, a black sports bra I haven't worn since puberty, and an old *Buffy the Vampire Slayer* T-shirt that's seen better days. The underwear is a little loose, and I'll be lucky if the sports bra doesn't cut off the circulation to my boobs, but at least I'm clean.

My hunt unearths a brand-new LifeStraw water filter, and I hug it to my chest as if it's the last brownie on Earth. Mom gave it to Dad for his birthday several years ago, and I remember him being so excited to drink from the creek. I guess he never got the chance. I shove my new prize along with an unopened pack of baby wipes, a few snack-size bags of peanuts, and a bottle of aspirin I found in my grandmother's sewing bag into the already overstuffed duffle bag.

With my saber strapped alongside the pack on my back, I climb onto my motorcycle and kick the bike to life. Ignoring the urge to take one last look at the cabin, I gun the engine and wind my way down the mountain, following the rising sun through a canopy of trees. Filtered light splashes my face in waves, and I eagerly soak up the vitamin D. With not another soul on the road and the aliens hiding in their dens, or wherever they go during daylight hours, these few minutes of solitude may be the last ones I get for a while.

Six months ago, if anyone had told me I would be flying down the highway on the back of a vintage motorcycle, I would've called them a liar. I guess I owe my little brother a huge debt of gratitude for asking for a dirt bike for his sixteenth birthday and again for letting me take turns riding it. And I kind of wish I could thank the guy next door for restoring the Triumph... and for leaving the keys in it. Sometimes I wonder if he misses it, *if he's even still alive.*

"No time for guilt, Eve... gotta get to getting," Coach whispers in my ear as I hit the intersection at the bottom of Scenic Drive.

"Good advice, Coach." With tires squealing, I make the turn onto the highway before changing gears and accelerating again. I can't be more than an hour behind Theo and his mom, and thankfully, I'm all fueled up, so unless she has a lead foot, I might actually be able to catch up to them before nightfall.

Abandoned vehicles litter both sides of the four-lane highway weaving through the countryside. A little voice says to check for survivors, but instinct tells me to keep moving. The aliens may be bad, but they're not the worst things out here. Even the good people lost their minds when the first wave arrived in spaceships that looked straight out of Star Wars. But by the third wave... a thick knot forms at the pit of my stomach. I've come face-to-face with enough survivors to know there aren't many *good* people left.

A flash of light catches my eye, and I follow it to the sunlight reflecting off the gunmetal-gray pickup rolling up to the next intersection. Keeping the vehicle in my peripheral vision as it does a slow crawl forward, I whisper a silent prayer for the driver to just mind their own business. But in the back of my mind, I know better. Nobody minds their own business anymore. Especially when they see what might be a helpless female on the road alone.

Focusing my attention on the road ahead, I hold my breath and whip through the intersection. I don't get far before the truck guns the engine, kicking up rocks and dust as it gives chase. *Shit.* I guess quiet time is over. Locking my muscles, I give the Triumph more gas, pushing the bike's limits. I'm confident I can outrun them, but if they have weapons, all bets are off.

The pickup manages to stay close on my heels for several miles, but I know this road, and the next section of highway is a series of giant curves, winding north toward another peak. If I can make it that far, I'll lose them for sure.

A loud crack pierces the air, making me flinch. I hazard a peek in my mirror to see a denim-clad figure leaning out the passenger window with a shotgun. They fire again, coming close but not close enough to hit me.

That son of a bitch is shooting at me!

I've watched my brother play *Grand Theft Auto* enough times to know you need to bob and weave to avoid getting hit. And that'll slow me down. But maybe that's their goal—slow me down and intercept. All things being equal, I would rather be facing down a few aliens right about now.

Up ahead, the burned-out wreckage of a toppled 18-wheeler clogs the middle of the road. Huge chunks of steel and rubber cover almost every inch of pavement, blocking my path like a giant beaver dam and forcing me onto the loose shoulder. Now is the worst possible time to slow down, but I can't afford to lose control of the bike, not with the truck barreling through the rubble like a wrecking ball.

Shit. Shit. Shit!

With my pursuers gaining ground, I hit the gas, skidding a little as my back tire connects with the pavement again. The driver takes that opportunity to rush me, forcing me back to the loose shoulder, and this time, the bike comes out from under me, throwing me into a shallow ditch.

Pinpricks of bright light cloud my vision as I lie on my back on the soft ground beside the capsized Triumph, trying to catch my breath. My head aches, and I can clearly feel the saber's sheath pressing into my spine, but other than my throbbing pinky toe, I don't think anything's broken. I know I'm damn lucky to be alive. But I also know I would be better off dead if I'm still lying here when they get to me.

Where are they? Reaching for my saber, I stagger to my feet, inexplicably remembering how drunk I was at the last frat party Serenity and I went to before everything went down.

I crawl up the low embankment, but before I can fully unsheathe my saber, a dusty brown steel-toed boot catches me off guard, hitting me square in the stomach and taking my unsteady legs out from under me. My teeth come together with an audible *clack* as I hit the bottom of the ditch again. Miraculously, I manage to maintain the grip on my saber, and I swing it wildly in front of me, sending the sheath flying as I slice through the air. I make light contact once or twice but not enough to do any real damage, so I don't fully understand when my attacker takes off running for the pickup, clutching his bloodied hands as if Satan were snapping at his heels.

As soon as the truck peels out, I melt into the hillside and do something I haven't allowed myself to do in weeks. I cry. Full-on body-racking sobs that leave me shaky and drained.

"Are you all right?" A pair of strong hands grips my shoulders, helping me to my feet and holding me steady as if I were a toddler yet to fully grasp the whole walking thing.

I lift my head and lock onto *his* gaze... the same intense, *unyielding* gaze I'd connected with yesterday. From a distance, his eyes looked almost black, but up close, they're the prettiest shade of green.

"You."

His smile is breathtaking but short-lived. "Are you hurt?"

Ignoring the throbbing in my little toe, I quickly catalogue the rest of my limbs before giving a weak shake of my head.

"Good." He drops his hands and turns to stalk away.

"Wait!" I call after him. "Who are you?"

He locks his intense gaze on mine again, the threat of a smile teasing his lips. "They call me Archer."

Mr. Tall, Dark, and Clearly Disinterested stalks away without another word, leaving me to figure out how to drag my motorcycle out of the ditch myself.

"Nice to meet you, Archer!" I shout at his retreating back. "Don't worry about me. I've got this."

He's lucky I didn't lop off his fingers with my blade after he startled me like that. Kicking a few stray pine cones out of my way, I re-sheathe my saber and set it down with my pack before tugging the handlebars. Straining my already-bruised muscles and using every bit of strength I have left, I still only manage to move the heavy piece of machinery a few inches farther up the embankment before it rolls right back to where it started. *I so do not have this.* For half a second, I contemplate calling him back over, but my wounded pride won't let me. This is the second time in two days he's had to swoop in and rescue me, and I would really rather not make it three.

"Need some help?" A stocky blond guy I immediately recognize as part of the crew in the back of Archer's Jeep the other day jogs toward me. "I wondered when we'd cross paths again."

"Were you following me?" My mouth hangs open while the implications swirl around my fuzzy brain.

"No." He laughs as if the mere suggestion is ridiculous. "Why would you think that?"

Searching for clues to his motives, I study his open expression and relaxed body language. "You seem to have a habit of showing up at exactly the right moment."

"Lucky for you. But no, we aren't following you. We were out scouting for supplies and heard shots."

While his explanation sinks in, I make another unsuccessful attempt at pushing the Triumph up the little hill.

"Here, let me…" He nudges me out of the way and hauls the bike back onto the pavement, barely breaking a sweat. Then wiping his hands on the front of his jeans, he nods toward my Buffy tee. "Nice shirt."

"Thanks." I force myself not to stare across the road at Archer's well-defined forearms as he helps one of the other guys load supplies from an abandoned minivan into the back of the Jeep. He catches me stealing glances, and I quickly drag my gaze away as my face goes up in flames. "What's his problem?"

The blond follows my errant gaze and scratches his head. "Don't take it personally. He's just pissed off. The pair who ran you off the road did the same thing to a couple of our scouts last week. They, uh, didn't fare as well as you. Arch took it pretty hard."

My bruised stomach twists into a knot. "They died?"

"No, but they were pretty banged up. A few broken ribs, a split lip, a concussion. They'll live, but they won't be doing the Macarena anytime soon."

I scan the deserted countryside, seeing nothing but spindly pines framed by the peaks and valleys of the blue-tinged mountain range in every direction. "You guys live around here?"

"Not exactly." Blondie chuckles. "A bunch of us came up from Athens right after those *things* arrived."

My ears perk. "University of Georgia?"

"Yup." He helps me out of the ditch then hops down to grab my bag and saber, placing both on the pavement beside the bike.

"Lemme guess..." I eye his bulging muscles and hulking size. "You guys played football?"

He beams, eyes dancing with unabashed pride. "The best UGA has—" The light in his eyes dims, and his smile falters. "*Had*—to offer. Bulldogs through and through." He catches me checking out Archer again and laughs. "Not him. He was captain of the archery club. State champion. Olympic-bound... well, he would've been. At least his skills come in handy in an apocalypse."

Archer punctuates the point by taking down a stray woodchuck with his fancy bow and arrow, and the blond shrugs.

"They don't look like much, but if you cook them just right, they're actually pretty good."

The thought of freshly cooked meat has me salivating. Once upon a time, I would've happily starved to death before eating groundhog, but now that I know what it feels like to go hungry, I'm not nearly as picky. If I weren't in a hurry, I might try to swing an invitation to dinner. Instead, I grab my pack and saber from where he placed them, wincing as I sling the bag across my tender back. "Thanks for your help, *again*, but I should really get going."

"What's the rush? Sun doesn't go down for hours. We've got a camp set up a few miles from here. Safety in numbers and all that." He pauses for me to respond, but when I don't, he leans a little too close for comfort, setting off red flags.

Operating on pure instinct, I unsheathe my saber and bring it within a few inches of his throat in a single fluid motion.

"Whoa!" He takes a quick step back, raising his hands, palms out in surrender. "We're good. I wasn't making a move, I swear."

Across the road, Archer snaps to attention as if he's been quietly observing us the whole time. He laughs at his friend's defensive reaction, giving me a quick, approving nod before turning back to his task. Relief washes through me, and I relax, letting out a low chuckle with my next breath.

"Look, you don't know me. I get that, but it's dangerous out here. Why don't you stick with us? We've got plenty of room for one more."

"Thanks, uh…" I realize, once again, I never asked for his name.

"Thor."

I pop an eyebrow, making him laugh.

"Obviously not my real name, but that's what everyone calls me."

"Okay, Thor." I extend my free hand. "I'm Eve."

Ignoring my outstretched hand, he roars with laughter, drawing the attention of the rest of his crew across the road. "No shit."

"What's so funny?" I lower my hand while his eyes follow the length of my saber before returning to my face.

"Not a thing, alien slayer. But since we don't use our real names around here, how about we call you"—his grin widens, and he nods to my shirt again—"Buffy."

Six months ago, I probably would've been offended, but these guys just saved my skin for a second time, so I figure he can call me anything he wants. I'm not planning to be around long enough for the name to stick anyway.

I shrug and shove the saber back into its sheath before strapping it to my back. "I always did like Buffy. But I really have to go. I'm trying to catch up to a… *friend*." The fib tumbles off my tongue easily. "She and her son headed north, and we, uh, got separated. Maybe you saw them. They should've come through here just ahead of me in a green Subaru."

"No. Sorry. We got here just after you did." He shoots another glance toward Archer, as if the two of them are engaged in a telepathic conversation, then turns back to me with even more urgency in his expression. "Listen, we're gearing up to head north too—as soon as we have enough fuel and supplies to make the trip."

"The safe zone?"

"In Fort Liberty? Yeah." He looks surprised I've heard of it. "You should come with us. I know you've got mad skills with that sword, but you're only a—"

My fierce glare cuts off whatever he was about to say, and he clears his throat before starting again.

"I'm just saying, you'd have a way better shot of finding your friend if you have backup."

Hadn't I just made the same argument to Theo's mom a few hours ago? "I appreciate the offer, I really do, but like you said, the world is a dangerous place, and I hate the thought of *them* out there without any backup, especially after what almost happened to me."

"Are you sure?"

"I am." I pause before climbing onto the bike, and he jumps on my hesitation, resting his hand beside mine on the handlebars.

"If you change your mind, head toward the dam on Highway 129. We're holed up at the old flea market warehouse just past the lake."

"Maybe I'll see you at the safe zone." It isn't until the words are all the way out that I realize I actually mean them. I sneak another peek at Archer. I really hope I see them again.

He pats the bike's fender. "Be careful out there, Buffy."

I crank the engine, my throat constricting as I nod. "You too."

As I pull away, he jogs back to Archer, and I watch the two of them have what looks like a heated exchange in my mirror until the road curves and I lose sight of them.

Chapter 6

Marked

O nce Archer and Thor disappear from view, I turn my full attention to the road in front of me, cranking the gas and flying down the highway like a woman possessed. If I have any hope of catching the Subaru, I need to make up for lost time. Without a game plan—or a map—my only option is to rely on my instincts and what little I know about Theo's mom to guide me.

My traitorous gut twists as I pass the turn for the dam, as if trying to steer the bike itself. Thor's words—*safety in numbers*—echo in my skull. I know I'm being stupid, but I can't shake the overwhelming feeling that I'm needed somewhere else. Maybe Thor was right. Putting myself in danger to search for people I barely know isn't the smartest decision I've ever made, and lately, I've made some doozies. But the crazy idea that I may have marked them somehow has taken up space in my soul like a living, breathing thing with a mind of its own.

Ignoring the voice of reason whispering for me to turn back, I follow the sign pointing toward Asheville, sticking to the route I think Theo's mom would most likely follow—the *safest* route for someone trying to fade into the background. If I was truly destined to cross paths with Archer and Thor when I needed them most, then I have to believe we'll run into each other again someday.

Eyeing the thick line of clouds forming ahead of me, I shove thoughts of Archer to the back of my mind. With the road switchbacking through the forest, now isn't the time to daydream. Between the towering trees and the dense cloud shelf blocking the sun, I quickly lose track of where I am. I'm not sure if I'm still heading east or if I've circled back the other way again. The farther up the mountain I go, the thicker and lower the cloud cover becomes. And with every rise in elevation, the temperature drops a few more degrees until it feels like I'm driving into a cold, wet sponge. Icy air whips through my hair, tangling it around me like seaweed.

The first drop of rain splashes against my cheek just as a loud boom of thunder cracks the sky. Dread prickles under my numb skin, and my grip on the accelerator falters. The absolute last thing I need is to drive into a storm. Nightfall isn't for hours, but the aliens don't exactly have watches. If it gets much darker, the impending rain won't be the worst of my worries. With warning bells going off in my brain, I scan the path in front of me, looking for any means of escape, should the need arise.

"Don't slow down, Evie!" Coach bellows in my head, and I can almost feel his calloused hand resting on my shoulder. *"Stay the course, but keep your eyes peeled."*

Squeezing the handlebars until my knuckles go white, I give the bike as much gas as I dare, shooting forward into the oncoming storm. Another crash of thunder has me hoping like hell I'll be able to hear the aliens coming before they're right on top of me.

As I cross the state line into North Carolina, the road finally widens and levels out, stretching in front of me like a runway leading to the outskirts of what was once a small town. With my tires skating over the slick pavement and rain pelting me in the eyes and mouth, I speed past a deserted Prius and a powder-blue pickup that had been towing an open hay trailer before its driver left it on the side of the road to rot. I ease off the gas to swerve around the first of what has to be dozens of cars haphazardly parked across the road as if a massive tornado swept through and scattered them like Hot Wheels. As I roll through the steel graveyard, the wail of a horn catches my attention, and I instinctively follow the sound to the faint red glow of taillights in the distance.

With my heart hammering in my ears, I zigzag my way through the remaining cars, heading for the dark-colored vehicle parked along the shoulder at least a half a football field from me.

My subconscious tries to conjure Coach again to remind me to be cautious, but every fiber of my being screams to hurry. *It has to be them.* Terrified of getting my hopes shattered, I inch closer, running every possible scenario through my head for why they're parked along the highway with the engine running and the horn blaring. Maybe they stopped to wait out the storm. With all the debris scattered the length of the highway, she could've gotten a flat tire... or run out of gas.

What if it's not them at all? The thought pops into my head, and despite the very real possibility, I shake it off and continue forward as cautiously as my pent-up emotions will allow. For reasons even I don't understand, I feel responsible for them being alone out here to begin with. I don't want to believe the whole thing about having a mark on my soul, but what if she was right? I shove the thought aside and gun the engine to close the distance.

As soon as I get close enough to see the star emblem on the back of the hatch, I hop off the bike to jog the last few yards. Nervous laughter bubbles out of me as I approach the driver's side. "I know you said you didn't need a chaperone, but—" The words die on my lips as I notice the door dangling from a single hinge. "Hello?" My voice cracks as I creep closer and shove the door the rest of the way open, careful not to touch the bloody handprint beside the handle.

Before the sound draws every alien in the state to me, I yank the broken seat away from where it presses against the horn, and my ears ring in the sudden silence. With no signs of life anywhere, I begin to wonder if maybe this isn't even their car. For all I know, dozens of green Subarus could be lying abandoned along this same stretch of highway.

My breath catches as I glance into the back and glimpse the familiar black nylon bag behind the seat. *How many of them would be carrying backpacks embroidered with my little brother's initials?* With my insides clenching hard enough to double me over, I stumble away from the car, desperate to find the little boy and his mother.

Half blinded by tears, I comb both sides of the embankment and every empty vehicle in a hundred-yard radius until I've run out of places to search. Lightning etches across the sky, and I catch a flash of something white wedged behind the Subaru's front tire. Soaked to the bone and shaking hard enough to rattle my teeth, I reach under and pluck out a small sneaker with what appears to be a smear of blood across the toe.

"Theo!" I scream his name into the abyss, over and over, until my voice gives out, and I slide to the ground beside the deserted car, clutching the sneaker to my chest.

Apparently, not even a good hard rain can wash that mark from my soul.

Another flash of lightning etches the gray sky, almost immediately followed by a bloodcurdling shriek. The inhuman sound manages to shock my wounded heart back to life. The involuntary reaction sends my pulse racing, but the rest of me stays firmly riveted to the side of the green Subaru, still clutching Theo's bloody sneaker.

"Get up, Evie!" Coach frantically shouts in my head. *"Get your ass on that bike and get out of here before it's too late."*

My ears buzz with the ghost of his voice, but instead of following my gut and leaping to my feet the way I always do—the way I know I should—I can't seem to muster the strength to give a damn anymore.

"Leave me alone."

"You need to face your fears head-on. That's the only way to defeat them."

"Bullshit," I mutter into the mist. Why do people always say that?

That advice might've worked when I was five and a spider crawling across the floor had me in hysterics. Dad had scooped it in both hands, showing me how not scary it was before letting it loose in the backyard and telling me that the tiny spider was way more afraid of me than I was of him.

Well, that might have been true about spiders, but it certainly isn't true now.

Another cry pierces the air, and I don't even lift my head to scan the perimeter. I don't need visual confirmation to know the monster is getting close.

"What the hell are you doing? Color guards don't quit!"

"Don't you get it?" Covering my ears to block out his voice, I scream into the steady downpour. "Theo and his mom are dead because I failed them!" My voice cracks, fading into a faint whisper. "I don't even know her name." Tears mixed with rain streak down my face as the last threads of my will break, and I collapse into body-racking sobs.

"There she is!" Thor's familiar voice precedes his heavy footsteps quickly closing the distance between us. "Jesus, Buffy, are you okay?"

Cold and numb, I flick my gaze to Thor's blurry face then back to the cracked blacktop. "Go away."

"Come on, let me help you." Gently resting a hand on my shoulder, Thor crouches beside me.

"Don't touch me!" I jerk out of his reach, stubbornly refusing to move from the wet ground. "You don't understand... I'm marked. Just let me die in peace before I get you killed too."

"Sorry. No can do, not after Arch tracked you this far."

His revelation surprises me, and I lift my eyes to his face again.

"Yes." His sad chuckle does nothing to ease the tension in his large frame. "*This* time we followed you."

"Why?"

"I'll tell you after we get the hell—"

Another shriek, closer this time, cuts him off.

"Go." I squeeze Theo's shoe until the hard rubber sole digs painfully into my sternum. "Save yourself. I'm already dead."

"You just had to make this difficult, didn't you?" Thor stands and cups his hands around his mouth. "Arch! Over here."

Moments after Thor bellows his name, Archer marches through the storm like a damn wraith. The two exchange a quick look, then Archer wordlessly slings my bag and saber over his shoulder. "We need to go."

"Then go." I jut out my chin in a weak show of defiance.

"I don't have time for this." Archer exhales loudly before scooping me off the ground and cradling me to his chest as if I weigh nothing.

"Let me go!" My thrashing only manages to spur his determination, and his grip on me tightens, bringing our bodies impossibly closer. Too broken to put up more of a fight, I lay my head on his shoulder and melt into his warmth. It's been a long time—*too long*—since I've felt anyone else's heartbeat this close to mine, and I would be lying if I said I didn't crave it like my next breath.

"Get her bike!" Archer's chest rumbles as he barks the order, and Thor wastes no time following it.

For someone so intimidating, Archer is surprisingly gentle as he carries me toward his waiting Jeep. He stiffens as the shrieks get closer, seeming to come from every direction. Shifting my weight in his arms, he breaks into a jog, zigzagging through the maze of cars. He carefully places me in the passenger seat before tossing my belongings into the back and climbing behind the wheel.

"Buckle up."

With his words still echoing in my brain, he hits the gas, and I barely get my seat belt fastened before he does a one-eighty in the road to head back the way we came. Any other time, I would've had some smart-ass comment ready—some diatribe about his poor communication skills or broody antihero demeanor—but I'm having a hard time finding my voice with my heart lodged firmly in my throat.

A streak of milky gray shoots out of the tree line to our right, and Archer lets loose a string of obscenities as the spindly creature runs straight for us.

"Hold on," he barks, jerking the wheel and sending us off-road to avoid impact.

The alien barely brushes the rear bumper as it darts past, and Archer overcorrects, making the Jeep pitch sideways as we connect with the pavement again.

"Grab the wheel."

With his abrupt command ringing in my ears, I whip my head toward him. "What?"

"I need you to take the wheel." He's halfway out of his seat before our gazes collide. "I have to grab my bow."

Operating on pure instinct, I do as he says, grabbing the wheel and sliding into the driver's seat before he's all the way out. He braces the front of his muscled thigh against my shoulder as he lines up his bow and fires, striking the alien in the throat. The impact doesn't kill it, but the wound slows it down enough for us to get away.

Archer taps my arm, signaling for me to switch places with him again, and we quickly swap seats without slowing down.

"You did good."

"Thanks." It takes every bit of my remaining self-control to tear my gaze from his when I can still feel his warmth penetrating my skin. Promptly shutting down that dangerous train of thought, I clutch Theo's shoe and refocus on the retreating storm.

Thor roars alongside us on my bike with a loud whoop.

Archer flips him off with a chuckle. "Thanks for the backup, asshole!"

"I was ready to jump in if you needed me!" Thor yells over the growl of the engines before speeding up to take the lead as we work our way back down the mountain toward the dam.

Archer clears his throat, keeping his eyes fixed on Thor in the distance. Despite being too big for my bike, the former football player looks as though he's having fun leading us down the winding highway toward their temporary home near the dam.

"I'm sorry about your friends."

Squeezing the shoe to my chest, I blink back the tears threatening to fall and swallow the lump in my throat so I can answer him without falling apart. "Thank you. We weren't exactly *close*, but I felt responsible for them."

"I get that." He nods but doesn't elaborate.

Other than what I've seen with my own eyes—his skill with a bow and his almost-scary confidence—I don't know anything about him. But based on my brief conversation with his friend, I assume Archer takes his responsibilities seriously. Official leader or not, he seems to look out for everyone in his group, so maybe he does understand how I feel.

A dozen questions run through my mind, but the desire to find out more about him loses out to my grief, and I throw up a wall between us and stare out at the world flying past the window.

"You have some mad skills with that sword," he blurts, ending the awkward silence.

I keep waiting for him to add "for a girl," but he doesn't, and when I cut my eyes to his, he's gazing at me with what can only be described as awe.

His reaction surprises the hell out of me, and instead of saying thank you, I snort. "It's a saber."

"Okay. Fair enough." He chuckles and shakes his head. "Where'd you learn to use a saber like that?"

"I was a color guard at Georgia Tech."

"A color guard?" He bites back a grin. Above us, sunlight streams through the breaks in the clouds, and he seems to brighten right along with the sky. "You mean, like waving flags at football games?"

"Flags. Sabers. Rifles. But we didn't exactly twirl them around like little girls at a dance recital. It's about agility, physical strength, and balance."

His mouth drops open at my little tirade, and despite the deep ache in my soul, I can't help but laugh.

"I dare you to try spinning a blade in the air without cutting off a few of your fingers in the process."

His smile disarms me. "How do you go from spinning blades to badass warrior? I'm guessing a lot of fights broke out at Tech?"

The twinkle in his eye tells me he doesn't believe that for a minute, but he's obviously fishing for more than I'm willing to divulge to someone who's essentially a total stranger. "Not exactly..." Trying to block out the unpleasant memories of my last moments on campus, I turn my attention back to the forest outside the window, but the memories keep coming. As if someone pushes me from behind, I go tumbling down the rabbit hole, landing back in my dorm room with Serenity, shattered glass at our feet.

"What are you talking about?" My eyes fixed on her ashen face, and fear coiled itself around my insides until I could barely take a breath. "Who's here?"

Her pupils dilated as she refocused her attention on me. Her pale-pink lips moved, and I heard her voice, but the word she spoke was all wrong. "Aliens."

Impossible.

Another explosion rocked the building, shaking Serenity out of the spell she was under, and she leaped into action, grabbing her backpack and stuffing it with whatever she laid her hands on. "We have to get the hell out of here."

My thoughts scrambled as I stared through the jagged shards of glass that used to be our window. The scene below reminded me of a disaster movie—the kind where dinosaurs jumped out of bushes to eat unsuspecting tourists. Terrified people scattered like roaches under the streetlights, pushing and shoving each other as they fled the shadowy monsters coming from every direction. "What's happening?"

"Get dressed"—Serenity scooped my favorite jeans and T-shirt from where I'd dropped them beside the bed and shoved them into my chest—"and grab whatever you can carry. We need to go!"

My head buzzed as I followed her instructions, blindly grabbing the only things I knew I couldn't live without. With my phone, charger, and AirPods shoved into the pockets of my brand-new leather jacket, I grabbed my saber—not the blunted one I used in competitions, but the sharpened one Coach had gifted me for leading the squad to victory. I wasn't sure why, but clutching the sheathed weapon to my chest made me feel safer.

Serenity laughed as I locked the door behind us. "I don't think we need to worry about anyone stealing my chem book."

"Probably not." The words had barely crossed my lips when the lights in the hall flickered and went out.

Serenity pulled me into a quick hug, squeezing the life out of me. "In case this is the last time I see you."

"It won't be," I promised as we clung to each other for longer than we probably should have under the circumstances.

Not even half an hour later, as we crossed Eighth Street on our way to the Curran Street parking deck, seven feet of drooling alien snatched Serenity from her feet, tearing into her as if she were nothing more than a snack. The light in her eyes dimmed as I pulled my saber from its sheath with trembling hands. She took her last breath as I swung the blade, slicing through the creature's spindly neck in a single life-changing motion. Then I turned and ran, with Serenity still bleeding out at the feet of the first alien—the first *anything*—I'd ever killed. But it wouldn't be the last. Not if I still had breath in my lungs.

My heart racing from the memory, I turn to face Archer. "I learned to fight out of necessity."

Chapter 7

Dixon House

Serenity's memory is like a two-ton elephant sitting on my chest, and the weight drags me under. Silent tears streak down my face, all but drowning me in a well of grief, but to his credit, Archer doesn't attempt to rescue me. His knee bounces restlessly, but he doesn't say a word as I study every thread and groove in Theo's sneaker.

We ride in uneasy silence for several more miles until the Jeep jerks to the left, bouncing over rough terrain and shocking me back to the present.

Mentally chastising myself for being stupid enough to get into the car with strangers after everything I've seen over the past six months, I grip the door handle and fumble for the seat belt release. Visions of chainsaws and skin suits flicker through my thoughts as we follow Thor deeper into the thicket, and I quickly calculate the odds of reaching my saber versus leaping from a moving vehicle. Neither one is an appealing option under the circumstances, but neither is being flayed alive.

As I coil my muscles, preparing to jump, we pass a rustic sign swinging from a weathered post. Primitive letters carved into the wood advertise the Chattahoochee Craft Market. Just beyond the marker, the woods open to a clearing, and the overgrown gravel road turns into a crumbling parking lot.

Relief floods me, and I release the death grip on the handle, blood rushing back to my fingers as I melt into my seat. When Thor had told me they were holed up in an old flea market, I'd let my imagination fill in the gaps, envisioning every leaky pole barn wrapped in rusty corrugated sheet metal my mom had dragged me to as a kid. I could almost smell decades of stale tobacco, smoked meat, and caged poultry permeating the walls.

Boy, was I wrong.

The run-down brick building looks more like an abandoned safe house—*or secret government lab*—than a craft market. Chipped white paint curls away from the bricks in coils, like an albino snake shedding its skin. Leggy weeds sprout through cracks in the crumbling sidewalk. Both of the tiny windows flanking the glass door—the *only* windows from what I can tell—have been completely boarded up and painted to look like a pair of closed, bedazzled eyes. And a rustic sign—the twin of the one I saw back on the road—hangs over the entrance.

Despite the dozens of open parking spots, Thor squeezes my bike between a blue minivan and a silver SUV at the far end of the only occupied row while Archer takes the handicap space at the opposite end, directly in front of the door.

Leaving the engine running, Archer hops out and marches over to where Thor waits. As the two of them share a few tense words, I reluctantly leave the safety of the Jeep, wishing I could read lips. After their brief conversation, Archer retrieves my things from the back seat, placing them on the cracked sidewalk in front of me before climbing behind the wheel again.

"You're leaving?" Still clutching Theo's shoe, I wrap an arm around my midsection, attempting to hold myself together. I don't want to admit the obvious, that I've grown somewhat attached to him in the short time I've known him, but ignoring the truth doesn't make it go away.

"I have to do something. Thor will introduce you to everyone." He lowers his voice, piercing me with his jade eyes and studying me as if he can see directly into my ruptured heart. "You'll be safe here."

Swallowing the lump in my throat, I nod, but in the back of my mind, I know none of us are truly safe anywhere for long.

Archer's jaw flexes as he eyes his friend. "I'll be back before night-fall."

Thor gives an exaggerated salute, making Archer laugh as he backs out, then he slings his arm over my shoulder. "Come on, Buffy. I'll show you around." He gives me a quick squeeze then releases me to open the door.

An old brass plaque embedded in the wall beside the door catches my eye. With several layers of dirt obscuring the inscription, all I can make out is the name. "Dixon House?"

"Home sweet home." Thor follows me into the narrow lobby, where rickety tables cluttered with hand-painted crafts still take up every inch of space along every available wall, and a dark hallway leads to a single closed door.

My hands tremble as I pick up a misshapen clay pot from the nearest table. "What was this place?"

Thor takes the pot from my shaky hands and puts it back on the table. "According to Chuck... you'll meet him a little later. He played ball with me at UGA, but he's a local boy. Knows all the dirt. He's the main reason we ended up here in the first place. He said there were lots of places we could lie low on our way to Fort Liberty. Chuck says Dixon House was a home for unwed mothers back in the forties and fifties, but..." Thor lowers his voice reverently. "Legend has it, Dr. Dixon was actually doing illegal adoptions out of the back room. Supposedly sold the babies right out from under their unsuspecting mammas."

"That's..." My mouth drops open as the ramifications of his allegation swirl through my brain.

Lips pursed, he bobs his head. "I know."

"Who *does* that?" I scan the room again, unsure of what I'm searching for in the crackled paint or dusty cobwebs. "And who turns an illegal adoption clinic into a craft market?"

"Oh, you haven't heard the worst of it." His eyes sparkle with mischief, and he leans in as if sharing a secret. "Sometimes at night, you can still hear the babies crying."

"Shut. Up!" I smack his bicep so hard my hand stings.

He tosses back his head in a full-blown belly laugh. "You should see your face."

"Who is this?" A girl who looks to be a few years younger than me steps out of the dark hallway. Her auburn hair glints in the fading light as she studies me.

"Oh, hey, Calico." Thor puts a protective arm around my shoulders. "This is Buffy. Archer invited her."

The girl looks me up and down with a sneer. "Since when is Archer taking in strays?"

"Aww, don't be like that. You'll like Buffy. She's a fighter."

Her frown deepens as she crosses her arms over a vintage Led Zeppelin tee. "We have plenty of fighters."

"True." He grins, squeezing me to his side like a stuffed toy. "But Archer isn't sweet on any of *them*."

The redhead huffs, and heat rushes to my face.

With a chuckle, he releases me to approach the girl. "I mean it, Callie. Behave."

"Fine." Her shoulders droop, and the rest of her deflates along with them. "Come on. You missed dinner. Canned tuna with canned beans."

"My favorite." He beams. "Oh, wait. I almost forgot." He fishes in his back pocket and hands me a blue-and-red quilted wallet. "Found this beside the Subaru."

My hands tremble as I unzip it and pull out the worn driver's license inside. Theo's mom stares up at me from the tiny image, and I scan down to her name.

Andrea Mitchell.

Is it ANN-dree-uh or Ahn-DRAY-uh? The question clatters around inside my head like a penny caught in a vacuum.

Thor frowns as he peers down at me. "You okay?"

I nod, but I think we both know I'm as far from okay as I could possibly be.

"Are you coming or not?" Callie snaps. "It'll be dark soon, and we need to lock this place down unless you want company tonight."

"Yeah, yeah. You don't have to tell me twice." Thor grumbles, grabbing a flashlight from inside a wicker basket on the far table. He switches it on and leads us through the darkened doorway. "Come on, Buffy. Let's get you something to eat, then Callie can show you where you can bunk for the night."

Callie glares at me over her shoulder before marching into the darkness ahead of us, and I wonder if she got her nickname for being catty.

"Don't mind her," Thor whispers. "She puts up a tough front, but she's harmless."

Declawed or not, if I have to bunk anywhere near Callie, I'll be sleeping with one eye open.

Thor leads us down the dark corridor into a large cafeteria-style room. Instead of the typical fluorescents illuminating the space, rows of mini LED string lights hang from the ceiling like dozens of fireflies floating through the air. A rowdy group of guys eats at the long wooden table running down the center of the room, every one of them as big as Thor.

We step into the room, and the laughter comes to a screeching halt. One by one, the guys stand, loudly greeting Thor with chest bumps and handshakes.

Out of Thor's shadow, I catch the attention of a tall, dark-skinned man I immediately recognize as one of the guys from the back of Archer's Jeep.

"Hold up. I know you!" He snaps his fingers and points. "You're the chick with the motorcycle... and the big-ass sword."

"That's her!" Thor beams like a proud papa. "She knows how to use that sword, too, so watch yourself."

Laughing, the guy holds both hands in front of him like a shield and takes an exaggerated step away from me. "Consider me warned."

"Smart man." Thor slaps him on the back then turns his attention to me. "This is Raptor. You may remember him from the first time we almost met."

"Nice to meet you."

Raptor gives me a polite nod.

Thor continues around the room, introducing me to what has to be the rest of the UGA defensive line. "Supes... Lancelot..." He rests both hands on the fourth guy's shoulders. "And Chuck."

"I thought no one uses their real names?"

The room breaks out in loud laughter.

"We don't." Raptor snorts and flicks a piece of Chuck's flaming-red hair. "He's Chuck because he looks like a life-size Chucky doll on steroids."

"Guys." Thor presents me with a flourish. "This is Buffy."

"Welcome to Casa Dixon." Chuck flashes a toothy grin. "Where the food tastes like shit."

The dark-haired guy called Supes grabs his tray and heads to the stove. "The beds are as hard as rocks."

"But at least the company sucks," Lancelot finishes with a booming laugh, tossing his head back and making his scraggly blond beard bounce.

"Nice welcome, assholes." Thor snickers, pulling out a chair for me. "Have a seat. I'll get you some dinner."

"I've got it," Callie snaps, giving me the evil eye as she stalks toward the stainless steel pot on the stove.

The grin fades from Raptor's lips. "Where's Arch?"

Thor spins the closest chair around backward and straddles it, facing the table. "Bonnie and Clyde didn't show up for check-in after the storm."

"I'm guessing Arch went looking for them?" Supes raises his dark eyebrows.

Thor nods, and his stiff body language tells me all I need to know.

"Those idiots will get us all killed one of these days." Supes stabs a forkful of loose meat and shoves it into his mouth before saying more.

"But it's daylight." I dart my gaze between them. "So it shouldn't be dangerous, right?"

Lancelot coughs out a dry laugh. "Everything out there is dangerous to someone, blondie."

"Hey." Thor locks his gaze on me. "Arch doesn't take unnecessary risks."

"Only with his own life." Raptor gives me a pointed look and takes a swig of his drink.

Tension slithers around the small space, wrapping around my throat like a thick vine. First Andrea and Theo, now Archer. Is anyone safe from my curse?

Callie drops a small rectangular tray on the table in front of me with a loud clatter, making me flinch. "Eat up. We don't waste food around here."

My empty stomach turns as I glance at the watery mound of waxy green beans and flaked tuna slowly spreading across the center. As hungry as I am, I'd rather skip dinner and sleep for the next twelve hours, but the last thing I want to do is insult my hosts. With a pasted-on smile, I pick up the cheap metal fork. "Thank you."

"Where's mine?" Thor asks.

She grunts a reply, stalking back the way she came. The waves of ice rippling off her add to the sense of foreboding already invading my senses.

Keeping her in my peripheral vision, I lower my voice. "Is Callie the only girl in your group?"

"No." Thor steals a bean from my tray and shoves it between his lips. "There's Winnie—Chuck's girl. She's pregnant, so she's probably sleeping. The main reason we haven't headed out yet is because she's been as sick as a dog for damn close to a month."

"Is she gonna be okay?" Concern for the stranger has me sliding to the edge of my chair.

"The further along she gets, the better she seems to feel." He lowers his voice further. "But we need to go soon because the bigger she gets, the harder it'll be to travel."

He doesn't say it, but the word *safely* hangs between us in the subtext.

"So just her and Callie?"

"And Bonnie. That girl has almost as crazy-good skills as you, but her weapon of choice is a pistol. And she won't let Clyde out of her sight. Or it's the other way around. Either way, the two of them are inseparable."

"Does Callie have a—"

"Skill? Other than sarcasm and opening cans? No, but she's Chuck's little sister."

"I meant a boyfriend."

"Oh. No." He laughs, and his voice drops again. "Though, not for lack of trying."

"That's the last of it." *Speak of the devil.* Callie appears behind us with another tray of slop and drops it in front of Thor with a grunt.

"Thank you, Calico." Thor puckers up and kisses the air in front of her.

"I suppose you want me to find your *friend* a blanket next?" She pops an eyebrow and glares at him.

He flashes her a dazzling smile. "If it's not too much trouble."

Callie grumbles before crossing the room and disappearing through another door.

"Is it me?"

He sighs. "You want me to lie?"

"I'd rather you didn't."

"Then, yes. It's you. More accurately, what you represent. She's jealous."

I stare at the closed door, waiting for her to come flying through it with a sharpened can opener. "That's kind of obvious. But why? I haven't spoken more than a few words with him. We just met. He was kind to me. That's all."

"You keep telling yourself that, sweetheart." He follows my gaze with a chuckle. "She's just a harmless kid, caught in a shit situation."

"You mean, like the rest of us?"

"Yeah." He turns back to his food, exhaling through his nose. "Exactly like that."

Chapter 8

Calico

———◆———

"**H**ere's your blanket."

Moth-eaten and covered in splotches of dried paint and crusty bird droppings, the tattered canvas tarp Callie hands me has seen better days. It looks like something she dragged out of the trash and reeks of animal piss and mildew. The rancid odor reaches me, and I almost hand it back, but with everything that's happened in the past twenty-four hours, I've had the fight beaten out of me. Half-dead on my feet, all I want to do is sleep for the next decade.

I ball up the nasty "blanket" with a sigh. "Uh, thanks?"

"You're lucky to have anything at all." She straightens her spine and locks her bitter gaze on me. "It's not like we knew you were coming."

"Look, I'm tired." My shoulders droop under the weight of my bag and saber. I get that she doesn't like me, but I don't have it in me to argue. "If you could show me where I can crash for the night, I'll be out of your hair."

"Yeah, sure." She eyes me cautiously then nods to the dirty sneaker clutched in my hand. "What's with the shoe?"

Until she pointed it out, I almost forgot I still held tight to Theo's tiny sneaker. "It's nothing." Or everything. I dig my fingers into the soft leather, letting it ground me to my new reality. I can never allow myself to forget.

"It's a little weird," she mutters, winding through dark hallways to the back of the old building.

We finally stop, and she grabs the knob, using her hip to bump the door open when it sticks. Stale air and a cloud of dust pour out as if she unsealed a tomb.

"It's not much, but it'll be nice and quiet." She shines her tiny penlight into the cramped space, highlighting an antique walnut dresser in the center of the room. Covered in dust and cobwebs, the dresser reminds me of a giant changing table with a padded top... and stirrups.

I gape into the old examination room. "Is this...?"

"Home sweet home." Her teeth flash in the dim light. "Well... I guess I'll leave you to it. Better rest while you can. Things around here are pretty crazy come morning."

"Wait!" I stop her hasty retreat. "This place is huge. There has to be another room I could use. Where does everyone else sleep?" Shoving me into what was essentially a torture chamber doesn't seem like something Thor would do.

"We sleep on the other side of the building. I figured you might want some privacy. I certainly wouldn't be able to sleep in a room full of strangers. The guys are great, but they're still guys, if you get what I mean."

"Believe me, I've dealt with worse."

She exhales impatiently. "Full disclosure? I don't trust you. So I'd really rather you weren't within striking distance of me while I sleep."

"Right." My gut twists uncomfortably. I'll take my chances with the aliens before I plead with this petty little girl. "Got it."

"Glad we understand each other." She turns on her heels and heads back down the hallway, taking her light with her.

Darkness settles over me, and the sour scent of mildew floats through the stale air like dense fog rolling in. I scramble to pull the penlight Thor gave me from my pocket and click it on to do a quick sweep across the room. Thick cobwebs stretch from every corner to every surface and across the ceiling, and long shadows dance around them as if the ghosts of Dixon House are preparing for a ritual sacri-fice.

Fuck my life.

Something scurries around my feet, and I drop the musty blanket and scream.

Nice, Eve. You've faced down aliens and crazed survivors, and you're afraid of a little rat.

My bag and saber slung over my shoulder and Theo's shoe still clutched in my other hand, I shine the pitiful light around every nook and cranny while my pounding heart slowly returns to its nor-mal rhythm. Tiny footprints surround mine on the dusty floor, but there's no sign of the creature that made them.

"Why couldn't I find a nice group of survivors holing up in a Marriott?"

"Suck it up, buttercup," Coach barks in my ear. *"You've slept in worse places."*

"Yeah, well, I didn't like it," I reply as if he's actually here.

My snarky subconscious has nothing more to say, so I grab the shitty tarp and use it to wipe the dust from the antique gynecologist table. In an effort to keep them off the floor, I hook my bag and saber on the stirrups and climb onto the table. Curling into a ball in the center, I let my thoughts drift back to Archer and wonder if he's safe wherever he is. After everything I've been through in the past twen-ty-four hours, it doesn't take long for sleep to claim me.

"Eve?" Mom's worried voice crackles down the line. "Honey, are you okay? Are you safe?"

"Mom?" I can barely hear her through the ancient landline, but she's alive. "I'm okay... I'm on my way home."

"No! Don't come here. It's not safe. They're everywhere. Do you remember how to get to the cabin? Go there. Go to the cabin. I love—"

My pulse races as I jerk awake, nearly toppling off the narrow table.

"Oh, good." Callie shines a bright light in my face, blinding me. "You're awake."

"What do you want?" I snap, blocking the light with my hand.

"Come with me, and bring your sword."

"After how you've treated me?" I let out a hollow laugh. "I don't think so."

She huffs, fidgeting with the little flashlight. "I'm sorry I was mean to you, okay? But you can be mad at me later. Right now, your help is needed."

Gaping at her, I sit up and dangle my legs over the side like a kid in a booster seat. "Why should I do anything you ask?"

"Because it's not about me. It's..." She lowers her voice. "It's Archer."

Theo's shoe slips from my fingers, tumbling into the shadows as Callie's words sink in. I hop off the examination table and step into her personal space.

"What about Archer?"

"He—" She flinches under my stare. "He's in trouble. Everyone keeps going on about your mad skills, so I-I thought you could help. But hey, if you'd rather cower in here, where it's safe, I get it. You don't owe us anything."

Her words hit me like a slap in the face. Even before the aliens invaded, I never backed down. No matter how difficult the challenge.

Still sleep drunk and half-delirious from hearing Mom's voice in my dreams, I grab my saber from the stirrups and sling it over my shoulder. "Where is he?"

"Follow me." She lowers the light, directing it to the floor as she turns and walks out.

I stick close to her heels as we wind our way through the labyrinth of hallways in the darkened building as if wandering through a funhouse maze. I almost expect something to jump out around every corner, but we don't pass a single soul the whole way.

"Where is everyone?" I whisper reverently, as if the ghosts of the Dixon House are listening.

She stumbles but keeps moving, picking up her pace. "They... they're doing what they do. Fighting aliens. Trying to keep people alive."

"Is Archer back? Did he find the others?" Questions I hadn't thought of when she first woke me pop up like Facebook notifications in my head. "Is he hurt?"

"I don't know." She shakes her head. "I only know he needs your help. Now be quiet before you call every alien in the tri-state area to our door."

"Where are we going?"

Callie stops at a metal fire door with several deadbolts running up and down the left side.

"You want to help Archer, right?"

"Of course I do."

She pulls a wad of keys from her pocket, jangling them as she uses trial and error to find the one that fits the top lock. "He's on the other side of this door."

She repeats the process, using a different key in each of the remaining three locks. After several tense moments, she turns the last one, leaving the key in the slot and the rest of them dangling. As if finally realizing the graveness of our situation, she eases the door open.

The hollow cries of aliens far in the distance pierce the night sky, and she flinches, falling in behind me.

"Y-You have the weapon. You go first." She urges me forward with gentle pressure on my spine.

Doubt clouds my vision, and I hesitate for a second. Despite Thor's confidence in her lack of claws, I don't trust her as far as I could throw her. But her attachment to Archer is obviously strong, and she seems genuinely worried about him, so against my better judgment, I nod and inch into the open.

Shadows creep from the back of the building, stretching into the trees and around every corner. A large dumpster—the industrial kind used at construction sites—sits rusting in the tall weeds. Between that and the building, someone had set up a picnic area—just a few wooden tables and benches at the center with a rickety barbecue grill nearby.

But I don't see Archer anywhere. "Where is—" I turn toward her.

Eyes wide, she shrinks away from me.

"Callie?"

Before I can react, she slips farther into the shadows, slamming the door behind her.

I dive for the door and slam both palms against the thick metal, shoving against it as hard as I can to keep her from closing it all the way. Even with all my weight behind me, the latch clicks, the lock sliding into place, and I realize I've been played.

"Callie!" I plead through the heavy door. "Please let me in!"

"It's all your fault!" She hurls the accusation at me. "If you hadn't come here. If you hadn't distracted him, he'd be back already."

Her words tear open the fresh wounds festering beneath my skin, and I lay my forehead against the cool metal. Visions of Theo and Andrea, Serenity and my parents, dance through my thoughts. I should've been there for them when they needed me. But I wasn't strong enough or brave enough or *good* enough to save them.

But Archer? In the few short hours I'd known him, I felt as though he understood me. Like maybe he fought the same demons I did. Callie has it all wrong. Archer wasn't out here for my wellbeing. He went searching for his missing crew members.

"Callie?"

Damn it.

If she's still in there, she's not answering.

Another distant shriek sends a ripple of fear cascading down my spine. I can't stay out here all night without shelter. It's only a matter of time before the aliens follow whatever senses they use to track us and find me. They may have already heard us shouting.

Why didn't anyone else? Is the back of the building that insulated from the other side? Is that why Callie lured me here? So the others wouldn't hear me scream?

The thought bounces around inside my head until it lands on the obvious answer.

Everyone else is in the front.

With only the moon to light my path, I take off through the dark toward the front of the building, praying Callie acted alone—and Thor is a light sleeper.

Staying to the shadows, I stumble over dense weeds and debris, quickly and quietly making my way to the entrance.

In the dark, the cracked and faded facade, with its bedazzled eyes and chipping white-painted bricks, reminds me of a decaying corpse rotting away in the woods. I shake off the image and run for the door, but when I get there, it's gone. Not *gone*. Boarded up. And by the looks of it, it's not the first time. They must seal the building every night to keep the aliens out.

And I'm locked out here with them.

Chapter 9

The Bunker

Another shriek rends the air, sending an icy chill down my spine. The aliens are getting closer, and out here, in the open, I have nowhere to hide. Keeping the forest in my peripheral vision, I study the simple barricade sealing the building shut. Then, bracing my foot against the bricks, I grasp onto one of the thick boards and pull with all my strength.

A bead of sweat rolls down my face as I struggle to gain entrance to the impenetrable fortress. Muscles straining, I twist and tug, expending every bit of energy I have left. But it's no use. It won't budge. With a sob caught in my throat, I abandon the effort. I'm simply not strong enough to pry the boards loose. Even if I somehow managed to extricate the heavy-duty screws from the brick wall, I would still have to get past the tempered glass door.

"Thor!" I frantically pound on the solid barrier, panic seeping from my pores.

A high-pitched, wholly inhuman sound pierces the sky, and my pulse skyrockets. Adrenaline rushes through my veins as I shift my attention from the heavy boards to the painted eyes, hoping like hell the plywood canvas covering the windows is thinner.

"Damn it, Thor! Let me in!" Desperate to get inside, I slam my fists against the rigid surface until my knuckles split.

Despite the stillness all around me, the forest groans and creaks, the giant pines standing guard in the distance swaying and bending against an unseen force in the windless night.

"Oh, that can't be good," I mutter, searching the darkness for the source of what I know damn well is out there, hunting me.

She may have been wrong about everything else, but Callie was right when she said I needed to keep it down or risk drawing every alien in the area to me. It would appear I've done exactly that. And for nothing.

The sound of branches cracking and leaves rustling as something large moves through the forest sends my stomach into a death spiral and my pulse into overdrive.

"Are you waiting for an engraved invitation? Run!" Coach shouts in my head.

"Shit..." The word tumbles past my lips.

With my heart in my throat, I abandon my attempt to gain entry to the old brick building, darting around the back toward the giant dumpster. I scramble over the rusted steel, landing on top of a pile of torn canvases and rotten tarps. Roaches scatter as I dig through the debris, unearthing God knows how many years' worth of useless junk and funky odors. I don't know exactly what I thought I would find, but I'd hoped for something more substantial to work with than ripped cloth and broken furniture.

Damn it. I couldn't have chosen a worse place to hide.

A series of barking cries call back and forth across the surrounding woods as the aliens seem to coordinate their attack like a pack of rabid coyotes. Then the shrieks come to an abrupt halt, and an eerie quiet settles over the woods. I don't move... don't even breathe... the steady thud of my heartbeat echoing inside my skull.

Slowly, the forest rumbles back to life—and my stuttering pulse along with it, picking up speed until it thunders in my ears. The ground vibrates, and thick trunks snap like toothpicks, taking out smaller trees as they crash to the earth, one after the other.

My thoughts race as I hurdle the side of the open dumpster, self-preservation propelling me forward but my concern for others driving me away from the building. As much as I'd like to see Callie punished for putting me in this position, I couldn't live with myself if anyone else was hurt.

I reach my bike at the front of the building, but before I can climb on, someone grabs me around the waist, lifting me from the ground.

"Let me go!" I scream, grinding a foot under my heel and throwing an elbow into a hard gut.

While my attacker is doubled over, I spin, pulling my saber from its sheath, ready to finish the job.

"Archer?" Relief sweeps through me as I take in his less-than-amused expression. "What the hell? Are you suicidal? I could've killed you!"

"Get in line." He darts his gaze toward the shadows and mutters a curse under his breath.

I turn toward the clearing, and my mouth drops open as three snarling aliens break through the tree line, charging toward us. I barely have time to take a breath before Archer grabs my hand, pulling me in the opposite direction. His fingers slip through mine, gripping my hand like his life depends on it as we fly through the forest, drawing the aliens away from the Dixon House and his friends... and farther from our only source of shelter.

My pulse flutters wildly, but I manage to keep my feet under me as we stumble over rocks and downed limbs, making our way along a muddy footpath through the thicket on the other side of the clearing.

Archer pulls me deeper into the forest, and a million questions pop into my brain like cartoon thought bubbles. *Where have you been? How are you still alive? Where are you taking me?* But I catch sight of another monster slicing through the trees, and my breath catches, the words dying on my lips before I can get them out.

With aliens bearing down on us from all sides, my chest tightens to the point of pain. Air rasps in and out past my lips, but I can't seem to drag enough oxygen into my lungs for a full breath. My fingers go numb, then my toes, the sensation spreading through me until I'm sure I'll lose consciousness at any moment.

"Don't give up on me now, slayer. We're almost there." Archer's voice cuts through the fog.

Clinging to Archer with one hand and my saber with the other, I summon every drop of strength I have left, ready to go down swinging if it comes to that. But true to his word, we reach a stone doorway cut into the hillside, and Archer drags me inside then slams the door behind us.

He barely seals the entrance before something large rams the heavy door, sending a layer of dirt raining down on us. Even with the thick wooden slab between us, there's no ignoring the angry alien on the other side. Each bloodcurdling shriek acts like a sliver working its way under my skin, and I tighten my grip on my saber until my fingers ache. "What the hell were you doing out there?" Archer whirls around, his silhouette bearing down on me in the dark cavern as his voice lashes out in a low hiss.

"*Me?*" I instinctively snap, not about to let him chastise me when I was only trying to help him. "What were *you* doing out there? If you hadn't vanished, I wouldn't've come looking for you!"

"I can take care of myself," he grumbles.

Suppressing a shiver, I fold my arms to hold myself together. "So can I."

Archer snorts, his silence taunting me with all the times he's saved my ass. But with the creature stepping up its attack, he shifts into crisis mode again, leading me deeper into the cavern until darkness wraps us like a heavy blanket, threatening to smother me.

In the pitch-black, my eyes have nothing to adjust to, giving me no choice but to rely on my other senses. Every breath draws in the earthy scent of rot and decay as I listen to the slow, steady trickle of something dripping down the walls. But nothing is more present than the danger just outside... and the agitated man beside me.

The door vibrates with another violent impact, and I flinch, colliding with Archer. My alert senses shift focus to him as he lays a steadying hand on my back, air rasping in and out of his lungs.

"Where are we?" My voice quivers as I whisper. Even as a kid, I never liked the dark—my vivid imagination conjured monsters in every shadow. But back then, I had no idea monsters were real.

"An old storm cellar," he whispers, and I wait for him to pull away, to step back, but he doesn't.

With his hand still anchoring me to him, I fight the urge to lean in and let his body heat chase away the dampness seeping into my bones.

Like a cat determined to pull a mouse from a hole in the wall, the alien frantically claws at the entrance until the faint glow of moonlight seeps through cracks in the frame. I don't know how much more the old cellar can take.

Fear spikes through me with every passing second, and I focus on the almost imperceptible motion of Archer's fingers as he rhythmically presses each one into the ridges of my spine, repeating the pattern every few seconds.

"Did you know this was here?"

"One of the guys stumbled onto it a few days ago. Guess it came in handy."

"Is this where you were hiding? Before—"

"Rescuing you?"

Again. The word pops into my head, but I don't say it.

"Yes. They sealed the building before I got back, so I didn't have much choice. It's not the Marriott, but it'll do in a pinch."

What I wouldn't give for room service and clean sheets... and a long, hot bath. I release a breath, forcing my fantasies back where they belong. "How did you know I was out there?"

"Pretty sure Dr. Dixon's ghost heard you." He chuckles, and my finely tuned senses note the sound of his free hand whispering through his hair.

"Very funny." I roll my eyes. A wasted effort since he can't see me. "Did you find your missing friends?"

"No." His fingers flex against my back, and his somber tone speaks volumes.

"Will you look for them again in the daylight?"

"I don't know." He lets his hand fall away, taking his warmth with it. "I didn't see a single trace of them. No hint of their car either. Maybe they ditched us and headed north."

Of the handful of his friends I'd met so far, only one struck me as the disloyal sort. "You think they'd do that?"

"Maybe?" He lowers his voice until I can barely hear him over the sound of my pulse thrumming in my ears. "Part of me hopes they did. It would mean they're alive."

"You really care about them, don't you?" Matching his whisper, I step forward, bringing our bodies close enough for his heartbeat to blend with mine. I don't know what I'm doing, why I'm so drawn to him, but god help me, I am.

"I do." He exhales in a gust, ruffling my hair. "I never asked to be the leader of our group, but most of them look to me anyway."

My skin tingles, acutely aware of his presence in the cramped space. His every breath, every coiled muscle making my heart beat faster. I should step away while I still can, slam the door on this crazy fantasy before I get more than my heart broken. But I don't. "You have a way of making people feel safe."

"Do..." He clears his throat, and I sense rather than see the quizzical tilt of his head. "Do I make *you* feel safe?"

"You do." The darkness pressing down on us makes me brave, and I reach out, taking his hand. "I can't begin to tell you how relieved I was when you found me tonight. I thought I was saving you, but instead, you saved me. That's three times now."

"Save me?" Archer slips his fingers through mine, rhythmically smoothing his thumb over my battered knuckles. "Why would you think you needed to save me?"

"When Callie said you were missing, I-I tried to ignore her accusations, but I couldn't leave you..." I shake off the unpleasant thought.

His entire frame goes rigid. "What did you say?"

"It's nothing." I try prying my hand free, but his grip tightens.

"It's not nothing." The angry edge to his voice rumbles through me. "Callie accused you of something?"

"She was obviously... *concerned* about you." *Obsessed with* would be more accurate, but I hold my tongue, choking back a snicker.

"Stop defending her," he snaps, and his frustration washes over me in waves.

A bitter laugh works its way out of me. Just thinking about her makes me angry again. "Trust me, I'm not. After giving me a nasty tarp for a blanket and making me sleep in a creepy old examination room, she's the last person I'd defend."

Flinching, he releases my hand. "What?"

"You don't know the worst of it." His reaction spurs me on, and the truth comes flying out of me of its own volition. "She said you were in trouble. Said you needed my help. At least she told me to grab my saber before leading me to the back door and locking me out."

He goes completely still for what seems like forever, sending my anxiety into the red zone.

"She's gone." The deadly calm in his voice sends a shiver through me. "If we make it through the night, she's out. I won't have her putting people I…" He shakes his head. "She's not going to endanger my guests."

Thor's words pop into my head. "She's just a stupid kid."

"I don't care." He lets out a breath and fumbles for my hand, threading our fingers together again. "You could've been killed."

"I wasn't." I cling to his hand like a lifeline.

"No thanks to Callie."

"No," I agree in a whisper. "No thanks to her."

Another impact rattles the door, scattering thoughts of Callie like dust fragments as I drift closer to Archer.

"Will that door hold?"

He squeezes my hand. "I sure as hell hope so."

Huddled with Archer in the dark cavern, I have no concept of time anymore. Seconds, minutes, hours… they all rush past at the same pace. The alien battering the door continues its attacks at random intervals, and I have no clue how long before sunrise. The darkness pressing in around us has taken on a life of its own. I almost don't know which way is up anymore.

"I don't suppose you have a flashlight or a candle on you, do ya?" My voice shakes along with the rest of me. Partly from fear. Partly from the dampness soaking through my clothes.

"Come here," Archer whispers, prying my saber from my tense fingers. He eases the blade into the sheath strapped to my back as he coaxes me to sit on the dirt floor beside him. "We may as well get comfortable."

Comfortable? I choke out a laugh. "I think that's highly unlikely."

"We should at least conserve our energy."

In case the alien gets through the door.

He doesn't say it, but the thought hangs between us just the same. Archer shifts his weight to unstrap the bow and arrow from his back and rests it on the floor beside him.

"I don't think I've ever seen you without that thing attached to you."

He chuckles. "You can't see me now."

"You know what I mean."

Even in the dark, he must feel the heat of my stare because he laughs louder. "Did you think I slept with it on?"

"Don't you?"

"It hogs the bed." His feet slide through the dirt as he draws up his knees and wraps his arms around them. "What about you? Do you sleep with that thing on your back?"

The blade weighs heavily against my spine. "No."

The silence between us spreads until his fingers brush the strap holding my saber, then he eases it over my head and places it on the dirt in front of me.

"There. Doesn't that feel better?" His breath whispers across my neck, making my pulse flutter.

The sound of my racing heart seems to echo all around us, but he either can't hear it or he's being polite.

"So... when you weren't spinning flags and blades on the football field, what did you do?"

The subject change relieves some of the tension, and I laugh. "The usual things... classes, studying, the occasional frat party."

"Boyfriend?"

His question takes me off guard, making my heart skip a beat. "Not anymore."

"Did he...?"

"Die?" A bitter laugh rolls out of me. "He was alive last time I saw him. But he's lucky I didn't kill him myself."

"I'm afraid to ask."

"After the aliens attacked campus, my roommate and I managed to get out of the building, and we headed for Smith's dorm. He was one of the few people we knew with a car. But when we got there, he decided his best chance of survival was to take my saber."

"Ouch."

"Trying to kill me to save his own skin was a deal-breaker for me."

"I'm sorry." Archer finds my hand again.

"Don't be. Good riddance to that guy. The coward would've only slowed me down." I shake off the cloudy memories of my ex and focus on the very real person sitting beside me. "What about you? Girlfriend? *Boyfriend?*"

Callie's face flashes into my thoughts, and a twinge of something resembling jealousy catches me off guard.

He laughs. "Neither."

It isn't the answer I was looking for, but I grasp onto it with both hands. Before I do something stupid, like act on the attraction between us, I change the subject. "Thor said you were training for the Olympics. I'm not surprised. I've seen you shoot. You're amazing. How did you get into archery?"

He shifts his weight. "My dad was a marine. He trained me on weapons from the time I was old enough to hold one. Guns, bows, you name it. The plan was always for me to join the Corps when I turned eighteen."

"But you didn't."

"No."

His clipped answer doesn't satisfy my curiosity. "What happened?"

"Dad died in Afghanistan, and Mom couldn't stand the idea of her only child going anywhere near the military. She had me refocus my training on the competition side." The sadness in his voice guts me.

I squeeze his hand. "I'm so sorry."

His hair brushes my cheek as he nods.

"And college?"

"That's where I met Thor and the guys. We crossed paths in the weight room. Lived in the same dorm. When the shit hit the fan, I was the only one with a vehicle."

"Which one of you had the guns?"

"We *acquired* a few on our way here." He snorts. "The rest we got from Chucky's place."

"And the rest is history?"

A laugh bursts from his throat. "I guess you could say that."

"Thor said you were on your way to the safe zone?"

He hums in the affirmative, and his hand twitches in mine. "We have just about everything we need ready to go. Once Winnie's good to travel, we'll pack up and head north. Come with us."

His invitation knocks the wind out of me, leaving me speechless.

"We could use someone with your mad skills, especially now that Bonnie and Clyde vanished."

"My skills, huh?" I laugh, slipping my hand from his. "What's in it for me?"

"Don't do that." He slips his fingers through mine again, and his warmth races up my arm. "You *know* we make a great team." He leans into me, invading my personal space. "I can't stand the thought of you out there all alone."

"I can take care of myself." The lie burns on the way out. I may be perfectly capable, but I'm tired of being alone. Tired of feeling empty.

"Maybe I can't." His breath washes over me, short-circuiting my brain.

"You... you've done okay so far."

"Come on, slayer." The rough sound of his voice rumbles through me, and my limbs go weak. "Don't make me beg."

"I-I dunno, I might like if you—"

His warm lips collide with mine, cutting me off.

His tongue slides along my bottom lip, and a million tiny electric jolts ripple through me, lighting me up from the inside as my brain short-circuits. I straddle him, and his hands slide into my hair—like a couple of kids copping a feel in the back of a piece-of-shit car at the drive-in. I can't remember the last time someone held me... touched me... *kissed* me. But much like the rest of my life, the minute things start getting interesting, a loud crack vibrates through the door, spoiling the mood.

Chapter 10

Consequences

As the attack on our hiding place begins anew, Archer tears his mouth from mine, leaving me cold. Afraid to move, I cling to him, holding my breath while I count off the seconds in my head. Before I reach twenty, the alien lets out a bone-chilling shriek, but despite the sliver of moonlight seeping through a new crack, the door holds.

Archer exhales, and the words tumble out of him in an awkward rush as he helps me off his lap. "I'm sorry."

"For what?"

"For kissing you." He scrubs a hand down his face. "I shouldn't've done that."

"No! You were good. I mean, *it* was good. I mean..." I groan and shake my head, struggling for the right words. "I, uh... I wanted you to."

He surges in for another kiss, putting a stop to the verbal diarrhea. This time, he pulls his lips away before I can reciprocate and presses his forehead against mine. I can almost make out his features in the faint wash of light coming from the cracked door. "I've wanted to kiss you since I watched you take out those two aliens at the gas station."

"You have?"

He groans. "Hands down, sexiest thing I've ever seen."

His confession reignites the flame in me, and aliens at the gate or not, my anxious lips seek his in the dark.

Instead of kissing me back, he puts a little distance between us. "As much as I hate saying this, can we maybe pick up where we left off when we're not in danger?"

A low groan rumbles out of me. "When *aren't* we in danger?"

"*Less* danger." Chuckling, he drapes his arm over my shoulder and pulls me closer. "We should at least pay attention to the monster outside the door, just in case it figures out how to get past the barrier."

Snuggling closer to him, I lay my head on his shoulder. "Fair enough."

We stay like that for what seems like hours—attached at the hip on the dirt floor, waiting for another attack that never comes. The light seeping through the cracks changes from a faint blue to a pale pink, and I wonder if it's safe to leave the shelter yet.

"The sun should be up soon." Answering my unspoken question, he coils a lock of my hair around his finger then lets it drop. "If you want to get some sleep, I'll keep watch."

"You've been awake as long as me... longer even. If you can stay awake, so can I. At least I managed to sleep for about an hour on that uncomfortable exam table."

I shudder at the memory, and Archer stiffens beside me. After taking advantage of my exhaustion and compromised emotional state, Callie deserves whatever punishment he plans to dish out.

"I still can't believe I let her get one over on me like that."

"Trust me. She won't get another opportunity."

Curiosity gets the best of me, and I ask the question that's plagued me since I first met Callie. "Were you two ever—"

"No." His clipped response speaks volumes.

"I didn't mean..." I shake the unpleasant images from my head. "She seems to think she has some sort of claim on you."

"Not at all." A dark chuckle rolls out of him. "She's Chucky's little sister. I was nice to her... told the guys to keep their hands to themselves. Jesus, she was barely eighteen when the aliens first arrived."

"I guess she interpreted your kindness as you wanting her for yourself."

He flinches, and I bite back a grin. I knew a lot of girls like Callie. All a guy had to do was smile at them, and they had the wedding planned.

He shifts at my side, taking my hand and bringing it to his chest. His heart races under my palm. "I guess I'll have to do a better job of making my intentions clear next time."

His clear intentions have my stomach doing backflips. I really hope I live long enough to explore more than a few innocent kisses in a damp cave with this man.

After who knows how long in the dark, my eyes finally adjust to the burgeoning light seeping through the cracks. Over the past hour, the shelter has grown deathly silent. No shrieks. No pounding. Nothing but the steady flow of water dripping down the walls and our combined heartbeats fill the space.

I clear my throat. "Do you think it's safe to leave?"

"I don't know."

"I know you're being cautious, but we can't hide in here forever." The words come out more harshly than I intended. Between my stomach and my bladder, I'm anxious to get back to what little civilization we have left. "Not that I wouldn't love to spend uninterrupted time with you, but Thor has to be wondering what happened to me by now, and it would be dangerous for anyone to leave the group to hunt for me when I'm perfectly safe with you."

"You're right." Archer kisses me quickly before rising to his feet and stalking toward the exit. He presses his ear to the door and waits for several seconds before whispering, "I don't hear anything."

With the taste of him still on my lips, I scramble to my feet, eager to escape our tomb. "Let's get the hell out of here."

With a sharp nod, Archer hands me my saber then grabs his bow and nocks an arrow. "Stay close in case we have to fight our way out of here."

With the two of us armed and ready for battle, Archer eases the door open.

We barely get past the threshold before the intense glow of the rising sun blinds me, and I throw a hand in front of my face to block the light. My heart kicks, sending a ripple of panic through my tired bones while my eyes adjust. Even the slightest hesitation could be our downfall.

When nothing but the stillness of the forest greets us, I release a breath. "I guess it's gone."

"It would seem so." Archer relaxes his stance and slings his bow across his back to study the shelter's entrance. Deep claw marks score the door and the frame where the alien repeatedly slashed the heavy wood, nearly digging its way through. "And not a moment too soon."

"Where do they go?" Whispering to myself, I run my fingers over the deep grooves. A shudder runs through me as I realize how close we came to becoming alien chow. "In the daylight? Where do they hide?"

Archer takes my hand, spinning me away from the battered shelter. "If we knew that, we could set fire to the hive."

Nodding, I tuck the thought away for later as we hurry toward Dixon House before Thor organizes a search party to find us.

We reach the edge of the clearing, and a sharp prickle crawls down my spine. The scene in front of me sends my pulse into overdrive. The sparkly eyes have been completely gouged out, leaving nothing but shredded plywood in their place, and the boards I'd been unable to budge just hours ago have been torn from the entrance as if they were nothing but cardboard. In front of me, Archer stops cold, freezing in place as he stares at what remains of the care-fully constructed barricades.

Tears blur my vision. Air rasps in and out of my lungs, and I bring my fingers to my lips to get my breathing under control. *What have I done?* "This is my fault. I brought them here."

"No." Archer squeezes my hand a little too hard. "You did noth-ing wrong. This is all on Callie."

I nod, but deep down, I know better. If I'd kept my mouth shut—if I'd just run, accepted my fate—the aliens wouldn't have been drawn to their door.

As if he can read my mind, Archer turns and grips my face in both hands, locking his gaze on mine as if he can see all the way to my soul. "If she hadn't locked you out, none of this would've happened." Once he's satisfied with whatever he sees in the depths of my eyes, he releases me and marches toward the destroyed door. "You coming?"

Before he gets the words all the way out, I rush to his side. As if we've done this a thousand times before, we watch each other's backs, scaling the scattered debris and toppled tables to enter the light-filled foyer. The arts and crafts that once lined the walls have been shat-tered and strewn across every inch of the space.

My heart pounds out a steady rhythm as I study the claw marks etched into the old plaster. "Where is everyone?"

"I don't know." Archer crouches to inspect a fresh blood trail, dipping his fingers into a small drop and rubbing them together.

"Is that...?"

"Human?" He stands, wiping the blood from his fingers with the hem of his shirt. "Yes."

My insides clench as I consider the ramifications. "We need to find them."

Nodding, he takes off, following the bloody trail down the hall and into the shadows.

"Archer, wait," I call after him, wishing I had the flashlight I'd left behind when Callie dragged me from sleep.

Light streaming from the broken doors illuminates the floor ahead of us, where a dark liquid pools beneath the mangled, headless body of an alien. Beside the dead monster is another, smaller, puddle of fresh red blood.

The grim discovery sets a fire under Archer, and he takes off in a full run. I can barely keep pace with him as he weaves through the darkened halls as if he knows the maze like the back of his hand.

We come to a dead end, and he crouches again, inspecting another bloody imprint before pounding on the closed door to his left. "Open up. It's me."

Something heavy scrapes across the floor, and the door flies open.

"Jesus, Arch." Raptor steps into the doorway. "We thought you were dead."

"Came close a few times." Archer shoves a hand into his hair as he peeks around the hulking guy in front of him. "What about you? I saw blood. Who's injured?"

"We're good." Raptor tosses a look over his shoulder. "Lancelot took a claw to the flank. He's pretty dinged up, but he'll live. I see you found Buffy. Did Thor find you?"

My pulse kicks up a notch as his comment sinks in. He's mistaken. "Thor didn't go with me. He's... he's *here*. With you."

"He, uh..." Raptor scowls at something, or *someone*, behind him. "He figured out what Callie did and made her unlock the doors for him. He went out looking for you. Haven't seen or heard from him since."

Archer glowers, his hands trembling as he steps around Raptor to point a shaky finger at Callie. "You did this."

"You have to believe me," Callie whispers, eyeing me as if she expects me to save her ass after what she did to me. "I didn't mean for any of this to happen."

I fold my arms and glare at her, my voice deadly quiet. "What did you *think* would happen when you locked me out?"

"She could've been killed out there!" Fury oozes from Archer's pores as he towers over Callie. "And Jesus. Thor's still out there somewhere!"

"You didn't come back!" she shrieks, eyes wild as she glances toward Chuck, across the room.

His face goes nearly as red as his hair, and he looks as stunned as the rest of them to discover what she's done.

"How was I supposed to know you were even alive? The guys all raved about how she's supposed to be this amazing fighter. I figured if anyone could find you and bring you back—"

"Save it." Archer throws up a hand between them, cutting off her weak excuses. "You know better than that. Even *I* can't take on that many aliens alone."

"I was freaking out… out-of-my-mind worried about you." Callie's eyes fill with crocodile tears, but I'm not buying it. No one's that stupid. "I would've done anything to get you back."

"*You're* the reason the building was breached. And the reason Thor's missing. I've let your childish behavior slide this long because you're Chuck's sister, but you've become a liability. We already lost Clyde and Bonnie. So help me, if anything…" Archer shoves a hand into his already mangled hair, and I know he's more worried about his friend than he's letting on. "Pack your shit. I want you gone before dark."

"What? No!" Callie's eyes widen, and she whips her head around, but not one of them makes eye contact with her. Not even her brother. "You can't let him kick me out! Where am I supposed to go?"

"Arch, let's think about this for a minute." Raptor scratches his head, clearly caught in the middle. He shoots a glance toward Supes then Chuck. "She's a dumb kid, but you can't seriously mean to put her out. She wouldn't last the night... hell, she'd be lucky to make it through the first hour alone out there."

"She should've thought of that before putting everyone in this building in danger," Archer growls.

Callie's the absolute last person I would risk my neck to save, but we have way bigger problems than one bratty little girl, and we're wasting time. I nudge Raptor out of the way and rest a hand on Archer's forearm. "Can you guys sort this out later? We should look for Thor."

He nods, his muscles flexing beneath my fingertips as he shifts into crisis mode.

"Raptor, Supes, you come with me. The rest of you stay here. Chuck, you hold down the fort and do what you can to fortify the doors." He turns his attention to me, taking both my hands in his and pleading with his eyes. "I don't suppose I can convince you to stay with them."

Where it's safe. He doesn't say it, but the thought hangs between us just the same.

"Don't even try it." I snort out a laugh. "I'm going with you. Thor's my friend too." I barely know him, but in a matter of days, Thor has grown on me, filling the shoes of the big brother I never had.

Archer lets out a heavy breath but doesn't press the issue.

"What the hell, Archer?" Callie snaps, pushing past me to grab Archer's attention. "You're holding her hand? I didn't think you even liked girls. You barely acknowledge me when I talk to you, but after one night in the woods with her, you're suddenly a couple?"

"Jesus, Callie. Shut. Up!" Chuck snatches his sister by the arm and drags her away from us. "What the hell is wrong with you? He's right, you know? You deserve to be put out on your ass. You're damn lucky he hasn't tossed your shit on the sidewalk a hundred times already. You done crossed a line this time. You damn near got us all killed—Winnie and the baby too—and what for? What did that girl ever do to you?" He shakes his head. "Momma and Daddy must be rolling in their graves to see you now."

Callie yanks her arm free. "It's not fair."

"Since when is life fair? You'd better shut your damn mouth and pray Thor's alive." Chuck's face screws into a pitiful frown as he turns to Archer. "I can't begin to defend what she's done, but she's still my sister. I promised our parents I'd do what it took to keep her stupid ass alive."

"We'll talk when I get back." Archer nods to Chuck, and I know the conversation isn't done by a long shot. "Come on, slayer. We need to grab a few provisions before we head out."

By provisions, I hope he means food. I haven't eaten since dinner, and my stomach is about to snack on my spine.

We barely make it halfway down the dark corridor when a loud crash echoes down the hall ahead of us. Before my frazzled nerves have a chance to react, Archer shoves me behind him.

"Stay here."

My instincts finally catch up, and I reach for my saber. "We've been through this already. If you go, I go."

Before we can argue the point further, a car alarm goes off, then another, until the sound surrounds us, penetrating my bones.

Archer bolts toward the exit.

With my heart in my throat, I take off after him, fumbling to unsheathe my saber in the narrow hallway. "Archer, wait!" Somehow, the aliens have managed to attack in daylight, and that idiot seems determined to get himself killed, rushing into danger with no backup.

Even running, I can barely keep up. Archer's like a freaking terminator, laser focused on his task as he dodges debris in the main lobby, where the deafening sound bounces off every wall until it feels as if my brain is leaking out of my eyes. It's all I can do not to cover my ears as I follow Archer into the fray. For all he knows, we're diving into what could very easily be a damn ambush, but he won't be deterred.

Archer finally pauses on the front walk, nocking an arrow and catching his breath as he surveys the damage. I don't see any signs of aliens, but someone or something smashed the back window of the old SUV, making the alarms for both vehicles blare in tandem.

I open my mouth, and he brings a finger to his lips to silence me as he creeps around the cars toward the shattered rear window. He reaches the back quarter panel and gasps, dropping his bow to rush forward.

I don't waste a second rushing to his side, where a bruised and bloodied Thor leans against the back bumper.

"Buffy," he chokes out my name on a groan, his face twisting into a gruesome smile and his breath wheezing in and out of his lungs like air leaking from a party balloon. "Looks like I'm late to the party."

Chapter 11

Everything We Know Is Wrong

My breath catches in my throat as I gape at Thor leaning against the back of the old silver SUV. As far as I can tell, the hunk of steel is the only thing keeping him on his feet. With his cheek split open and one eye nearly swollen shut, he looks like he used his face to stop a sledgehammer.

"What happened to you?"

His gaze darts from me to Archer and back again, and he lets out a shuddering breath. "Glad... to see... you found each other." He barely gets the words out before his fragile smile dissolves into a pained grimace.

Before either Archer or I can react, Thor's eyes roll back in his head, and his legs crumple beneath him. He pitches sideways, collapsing into a heap behind the back bumper.

I lunge toward him, barely getting my hands beneath his head before it hits the ground.

Archer crouches beside me, letting loose a string of colorful curses as he lays two fingers against Thor's carotid artery.

"Is he...?" I let the words trail off, unable to bring myself to ask.

Archer locks his gaze on mine, his face grim. "He's alive, but he needs medical attention."

I nod, quickly cataloging Thor's extensive injuries. In addition to his battered face and bloody clothes, he has lacerations up and down his arms, and his knuckles look like he tried to fight his way out of a steel cage.

"Stay with him." Archer rests a hand on my shoulder and squeezes. "I'll go get help."

Before I can reply, he's climbed over the debris and halfway back to the building. I can only hope one of the guys has some sort of medical training.

I wince, smoothing back Thor's hair until his blood coats my fingers. *So much blood.*

"What do I do now?" I mutter to myself—to Coach, hell, maybe to God, I don't know. I'm completely out of my element here. Any idiot can see Thor's taken one hell of a beating, but I'm mostly worried about the damage I *can't* see. *How the hell are we supposed to heal internal injuries in the middle of nowhere?*

It feels like hours before Archer rushes toward me, his gaze locked on mine and Raptor close on his heels. "We need to get him inside."

I scramble out of the way as they each take an end. Archer wraps his arms around Thor's chest while Raptor lifts his legs. All I can do is stand by helplessly as the two haul Thor from the ground and carry him inside.

After transporting the unconscious Thor to a clean cot in a quiet corner of Dixon House, they step aside, and freaking *Callie* rushes in with a plastic first aid kit in her hands. My mouth drops open, but I reluctantly scoot out of her way and take my place beside Archer.

Tearing my attention from my nemesis, I turn to Archer and widen my eyes.

As if he can read the *what the hell* in my expression, he flushes crimson. "She was studying to be an EMT... *before.*"

"In high school?" I cringe at the bite in my tone.

"We, uh, had a tech program." She mumbles as she cracks open the med kit and gets to work assessing Thor's condition and patching his wounds as if she's done this at least a dozen times before. "I was more than halfway through before... you know."

It shouldn't bother me that she actually appears to know what she's doing, but it does. "She's the best you've got?"

Archer jerks his head in a sharp nod.

Great.

Ignoring our audience, he takes my hand and squeezes, bringing his forehead to mine to whisper, "Can you stay here, help her take care of Thor while I give the guys a hand fixing the damage to the building?"

I let out a heavy breath and toss a glance toward Callie as she rips Thor's shredded, blood-soaked shirt open, exposing a nasty gash on his left side. As much as I hate the idea of being stuck with her, I can't abandon my friend. "Of course."

Archer gazes at my lips but, to my disappointment, doesn't go in for the kiss.

"Go." I force a smile and step back, breaking the connection between us. "Do what you need to do."

"Thank you."

The second he leaves, I turn my attention to Thor and Callie. "How can I help?"

"C-Can you press here?" She guides my fingers to the weeping wound on Thor's side, showing me where to put pressure. "I need to try to stitch him up while he's out."

My hand trembles the whole time, but I do as she asks.

"I'm sorry," she whispers, waiting until I'm up to my knuckles in gore to bring up the elephant in the room. "For what I did."

Swallowing the unkind words that keep rising to the surface, I blow out another breath to steady myself. "Can we maybe concentrate on patching up Thor first?"

"Sure." She nods but doesn't make eye contact. *Coward.* "I just wanted you to hear it from me."

"Duly noted." I shake off Callie's apology, mesmerized by the needle sliding through Thor's slippery skin. I flinch, nearly releasing the pressure on his wound, as Thor wraps his meaty fingers around my wrist and squeezes until my hand goes numb.

"You need... to tell them." He chokes out the words, his rough voice rumbling beneath my fingertips.

A second fist wraps around my insides, sending icy ripples cascading through me. "Tell them what?"

"Everything..." His voice cracks, and his eyelids flutter before closing again.

"Shh." I smooth my free hand through his hair. "Don't talk. Save your energy."

His gaze—suddenly focused and clear—lock on mine. "Everything we know is wrong."

The bones in my wrist compress as Thor's thick fingers tighten around it, cutting off the circulation to my hand and making my fingers go numb. His fear is palpable, slithering beneath my skin and twisting my stomach into knots as the weight of his revelation sinks in.

"What do you mean, wrong?" My heart slams against my ribs, stealing my breath as I try to make sense of his current state.

"Tell Arch..." He licks his pale lips and swallows reflexively. The veins in his neck stand out, his eyes stretched wide enough to expose the bloodshot whites all the way around his blue irises.

I wait for him to go on, but he doesn't.

"Tell him what?" I demand, flicking my eyes back and forth between his, trying to pull the answer from their depths.

He gives a weak shake of his head, and his grip loosens. A rush of heat floods my fingers as the blood flows back to each digit, sending hot tingles through me.

"Tell him what, Thor?"

His eyes flutter closed again, his hand dropping to his side as his breathing returns to a slow, easy rhythm.

I resist the urge to shake him awake. "Thor?"

"He's out." Callie keeps her eyes fixed on her task. She ties off another stitch and stabs the needle through his skin again, repeating the pattern.

With every pass, the sting of antiseptic wafts into the air, and the blood oozing from the wound slows.

"What the hell did he mean by that?" I mutter, mostly to myself, as I replay his words over and over, willing my heart to slow. "Everything we know is wrong?"

"He's probably just delirious." Callie shrugs, deftly knotting another stitch. "He's gotta be in pain. And probably hella confused."

"Maybe..." I gaze down at Thor's still form. I don't believe he was confused for a minute. I can't shake the fear in his eyes... the tone in his voice. He was trying to tell me something important. I only wish I understood what he meant.

While I struggle to unravel the mystery of Thor's sudden exclamation, Archer steps into the doorway, eyes hard, frame locked and stiff. "We've got a problem."

"What's wrong?" I attempt to glean meaning from his steely gaze to no avail.

His attention wanders to Thor lying unconscious just a few feet away. Guilt comes off him in waves. "We can't stay here."

Callie's head snaps up. "What? Why?"

Archer exhales a heavy breath, ignoring Callie's outburst. "The aliens ripped those boards off the doors as if they were nothing but Christmas wrap on a package. We've scavenged the whole place, but we don't have anything else to secure them, and—"

"They know we're in here now." I finish his sentence, letting the ramifications sink in. Dixon House isn't safe anymore.

Archer locks his gaze with mine and nods.

"What do we do?" My fingers itch to reach for my saber as I shift into crisis mode.

"Raptor's gonna drive me to where I left the Jeep, just a few miles out. When we get back, we'll start packing everything we can carry. We need to hit the road. The sooner the better."

"We can't leave!" Callie stops stitching Thor's gash to gape at Archer.

"We really don't have a choice." He points his chin toward his unconscious friend. "Finish patching him up, and collect all the first aid gear. We're gonna need everything we've got."

A shaken Callie goes back to tending to Thor, rushing through the last few stitches before grabbing a spool of white tape.

I hope Thor doesn't mind scars.

"What can I do?" I ask.

"I wish we had more time." Archer shoves a hand into his hair. "We've been stockpiling supplies for a while. It'll take all of us to load them up."

I contemplate telling him about Thor's brief moment of lucidity, but it can wait. Archer has more than enough to worry about without trying to decipher a cryptic message. "I can help."

He blows out a breath and flashes a fragile smile. "Thank you."

"What about Thor?" Callie tosses the tape into a clear plastic bin and wipes her bloody hands on a towel. "He can't exactly hang off the back of the Jeep like normal. The minivan is toast, so with Bonnie and Clyde gone, we're down to two vehicles. How are we supposed to fit everyone plus all the supplies, especially with one more person?" She shoots a glance at me.

"Let me worry about that!" Archer snaps. "You're lucky you're the only medic we have, or we'd have one more empty seat."

As much as I hate to admit it, Callie's right. I would effectively be the straw that broke the camel's back if I tried to squeeze in with everyone else. But lucky for her, I wasn't planning on riding in one of their vehicles.

"I have my bike."

Still scowling, Archer jerks his head in a sharp nod. "If you're done here, let's get going. We need to find somewhere safe before dark."

He turns on his heels and marches back the way he came, leaving a cloud of fury in his wake. I'm no fan of Callie's, but I almost feel bad for her taking the brunt of his anger. *Almost.*

Just over an hour later, we've strapped what we could to the roof rack and loaded the last of the boxes into the back of the silver SUV, and the guys transport a still-unconscious Thor to the Jeep, laying him across the back seat.

"Are you sure you won't let one of the guys take the bike so you can ride in the Jeep with me?"

His unnecessary chivalry has me choking back a laugh. "I've been on my own for a while now. I think I can handle it. Besides, if anything happens, you'll be right there to rescue me, whether I need it or not."

"Fair enough." He chuckles, but he flushes until even the tips of his ears turn pink. "But what if *I* need a savior?"

A loud laugh bursts past my lips. "Feel free to ride with me. I'll keep you safe."

"Hey, Raptor!" Archer shouts to the mound of rippling muscles leaning against the Jeep's roll bar. When the guy lifts his head, Archer tosses him the keys and flashes me a knowing grin. "You drive. I'm riding with the slayer."

"You got it, boss." Raptor smiles but doesn't comment on Archer's decision.

Slinging his bow across his back, Archer hops onto the back of the bike behind me, bringing his warmth with him. "Okay, I'm putting my life in your hands."

Chapter 12

Cat Scratch Fever

"*Come on, Eve. Keep your hands steady and steer the damn bike. How hard can it be?*"

My little brother's voice echoes through my memory as I struggle to keep up with the caravan. It feels like an eternity since I've had anyone else on the back of the bike—another lifetime for sure. Basically, a baptism by fire, my one and only riding lesson forced me to navigate the bike with a snarktastic backseat driver. I'd been a few months shy of my eighteenth birthday, and Zack was still a kid—just sixteen and barely a hundred pounds soaking wet. According to my trembling forearms and the sweat rolling down my back, Archer has to be nearly double that.

As if he can hear my thoughts, he leans forward. "Can you get ahead of the Jeep?"

"Sure. No problem!" I shout over the wind, hoping he can't hear the sarcasm in my voice.

Pushing my muscles to the breaking point, I twist the throttle as far as it'll go, and we jump forward, quickly overtaking the SUV. Even with Archer moving with me, my entire body burns from the effort, and it takes every ounce of strength I have left to hold on.

Archer motions to Chuck, behind the wheel, and he responds with an over-the-top salute before honking the horn and falling in behind us. Up ahead, in the Jeep, Raptor seems to take the hint, slowing down and lowering the window as we pull alongside.

"Get off at the next exit!" Archer shouts over my shoulder.

Raptor frowns but doesn't say a word. Instead, he nods and copies Chuck's exaggerated salute. Archer's crew obviously trusts his judgment, even if they disagree with his decisions. I have to admit, I don't understand the unexpected detour any more than anyone else seems to. We already stopped at every gas station between here and the state line, topping off our tanks and filling all four of the spare red plastic gas cans—more than enough to tide us over for now.

Archer squeezes my waist, and I back off on the throttle until we fall behind the SUV again. With the roof rack piled high with boxes and totes, the overloaded vehicle struggles to stay in its lane as we take the off-ramp a little too quickly.

Once we exit the highway, Archer signals the other vehicles to pull into a deserted church parking lot.

What the hell are you up to, Archer?

He hops off the bike before I've shut off the engine and marches to the SUV to root around in the back for something. He comes back with two bottles of water, cracks both of them open, and hands me one.

"Thanks." I barely get the word out before bringing the bottle to my lips and guzzling half the contents.

He nods, taking a healthy swig of his own drink. "You need a break."

I start to protest, but he holds up a hand. "Don't argue. Your muscles have been twitching on and off for the better part of an hour."

A hot flush rushes up my neck, and I avoid his probing stare, dousing the heat with another pull from my drink. I should've known he would pick up on that.

Archer holds out a stick of beef jerky. "Hungry?"

"Yes, actually." I take the offering and quickly make waste of it, not once questioning where it came from. I'd picked up bits and pieces of their plans since I first met them on the highway, and I knew they'd been collecting provisions, but I wasn't prepared for the sheer amount of supplies they'd been hoarding.

With the angry rumbles in my belly quiet for now, I store the last of my water for later. "Did you want to check on Thor before we hit the road again?"

Archer adjusts the bow across his back and flashes a shy smile. "I know you're a total badass, and I'm not trying to take away from that, but maybe I could drive for a while. Even a badass needs a little break now and then."

"That actually sounds great." I don't even try to hide the relief in my voice.

"It's settled then."

He tosses a glance over his shoulder before leaning in until I can't tell his breath from mine. Despite our proximity, the quick kiss takes me by surprise, and his dazzling smile makes my already-wobbly knees weak.

"You need a minute, slayer?"

How is it this man I've known for less than a few days has become everything to me? I don't even know his real name... and he doesn't know mine. "Call me E—"

"Arch!" The sharp bark is like a bucket of ice water.

We jump apart, and Archer tears his attention from me as Chuck runs toward us.

"What's wrong? Is it Thor?"

"It's Lancelot." Chuck runs a hand through his greasy ginger locks. "He's burning up. We checked his wounds, and they look pretty bad—hot with red streaks. Callie thinks it's an infection."

Concern lines Archer's face as he stares toward the back of the SUV as if he can see clean through the layers of steel and molded plastic. "Is she sure?"

Cupping the back of his neck, Chuck winces, and my imagination fills in the blanks. "Pretty damn sure."

"Don't—" I study the carefully stacked boxes strapped to the SUV's roof and mentally catalog the bin of medical supplies Callie used to treat Thor's injuries. They seemed to be well stocked. Along with the assorted bandages and ointments, I remembered seeing several bottles of pain relievers, antihistamines, and other over-the-counter remedies. "Don't you have anything to treat an infection?"

"Uh..." Chuck darts his gaze back and forth between Archer and me as he scratches his sweaty cheek. "We have one of those all-purpose antibiotics. A Z-pack, I think she called it."

"That's better than nothing. Get him started on that." Archer nods before shifting his attention toward the Jeep.

Raptor climbs out of the driver's seat, eyeing us with a curious tilt to his head.

"Already on it, but—"

"Keep me posted..." Archer trails off, patting Chuck's shoulder as he turns to walk away.

Chuck grabs his arm, stopping him in his tracks. "I-I wasn't finished." His gaze lands on me, unspoken questions flickering in his dark eyes.

I wither under the unmistakable accusation in his expression and wish the ground would swallow me whole.

Shrugging off Chuck's grip, Archer glances at me as he shoves a hand into his hair. Guilt washes over me as I once again find myself caught between Archer and one of his friends.

"Jesus, Chucky, she was exhausted. We stopped long enough to grab a drink and swap places. We'll be ready to jump back on the road in five."

"I wasn't gonna ask, man. Seriously." There's no humor in Chuck's dry laugh as he stares off into the distance. "That's the last damn thing on my mind right now."

Archer heaves out a breath. "Then what is it? Spit it out."

"Callie's worried," Chuck whispers, darting his eyes around as if he's afraid there are spies everywhere, listening. "She cleaned the hell out of those wounds right away. *And* used a surgical-grade antiseptic and antibiotic ointment, and the gashes still got infected. It's like the worst case of cat scratch fever I've ever seen. And if Lancelot is this bad..." He locks eyes with Archer and waits for him to catch on.

"Thor." The color leaches from Archer's skin as the pieces finally fall into place.

Chuck nods. "Thor's definitely next."

It doesn't take long for me to figure out what he hasn't said. "You don't have enough meds to treat him."

Chuck exhales a heavy breath. "We need a real doctor... or a least some real meds."

"We need to find a pharmacy," Archer mutters.

"I hate to be the bearer of bad news, but we're in the middle of nowhere." I motion to the vast tree lines on either side of us.

Archer's fingers brush mine, the contact just enough to dispel the residual guilt fraying my nerves. "We're less than an hour from Asheville."

"No. No way." Chuck shakes his head. "That's a bad idea. We're two men down, and those aliens aren't always the worst things out there. I can't have Winnie anywhere near that kind of danger."

"I'll go." The words tumble past my lips before my brain registers what I've said. I may not have thought the idea through, but since I'm the reason they're in this mess, the least I can do is try to get them out of it.

"No." A deep V forms between Archer's heavy brows, and it's obvious he has no intention of budging from his position.

Despite the deep exhaustion seeping into my bones, I fold my arms, creating a wall between us, and stand my ground. "Archer—"

"Not by yourself." He gently cups my cheek as if he's afraid he might break me. "And before you go and twist this into some sexist power play, I wouldn't let Raptor go alone either."

"Where the hell am I going now?" Raptor strolls up behind us, and though I shouldn't be surprised to see him, he startles me.

Archer lets his hand drop, and my skin tingles in its absence. "Nowhere."

"Arch and Buffy are arguing over which one of them is picking up Lance's prescription." Chuck snickers, but I hear the relief in his voice.

"There's no argument." Archer takes my hand and slips his fingers through mine. "We're both going. But not until we get everyone else situated. I don't know how long we'll be gone, and sitting out here in the open isn't safe."

"Agreed." Raptor bobs his head a few times as he takes in the scenery. "It's too damn quiet out here." He throws a lingering glare over his shoulder. "And that damn church gives me the creeps. I don't like it."

"So where to?" Chuck asks. "It's not like we have a lot of options."

"There has to be somewhere nearby we can set up camp for the night." Archer tips his head to the sky as if looking for the answer in the clouds.

"What do you think, Buffy? Where would *you* go?" Raptor locks his gaze on me and waits for a reply.

"Uh." I flick my eyes toward Archer then back to Raptor's penetrating stare. "I hid in a school locker room for three days once. They're usually tucked into the center of the building with no windows, and almost always have two exits—with heavy doors that lock. And they come equipped with bathrooms."

I should probably be insulted by the shock registering on their faces, but instead, I grin with pride as Chuck's mouth drops open.

"That's—"

"Fucking brilliant." Raptor's lips curl up at the corners, and he gives me a slight nod of respect.

A wide smile breaks out across Archer's face, and he leans in, pressing his lips to mine for a quick kiss. "Any idea where we might find the closest school?"

Chapter 13

The Bear Necessities

———◦———

The two-story redbrick building looms in the distance, casting deep shadows across the cracked pavement surrounding it. Built sometime in the late nineteen sixties, the abandoned school looks like it could just as easily house a group of mutant superheroes as dusty old books and rusted lockers.

As soon as Archer and Raptor finish exploring every nook and cranny to ensure the place is safe—and uninhabited—we unload the supplies and get everyone settled inside. But our reprieve is short-lived because, while Lancelot's fever might be coming down, Thor's is going up. And the clock is ticking.

Raptor hands Archer the keys to the Jeep and claps a hand on his shoulder. "Be careful."

"I'm always careful," Archer quips as he climbs into the driver's seat and shoves the key into the ignition.

Raptor barks out a dry laugh, shaking his head and shifting his attention to me. "Keep an eye on this one. He's a loose cannon."

"I will." With a quick smile at Archer, I hop into the passenger seat and buckle up.

"And don't do anything stupid. Get the antibiotics, and get out." Slowly backing toward the building, Raptor directs his last dig toward Archer. "Try to get back before dark this time."

"Save me a seat at dinner." Cranking the engine, Archer tears his eyes from his retreating friend and turns to me. "Ready?"

I nod, peeking at Raptor in the side mirror as he jogs toward the school. Their banter reminds me of countless conversations with my brother, and I wonder if Raptor fills that void for Archer. Instead of voicing the thought, I ask the next-most-pressing question rattling around my brain. "Do you think the doors will hold?"

"I think you were right about the locker rooms being deep enough in the building to provide an extra layer of safety." He puts the Jeep in gear and makes a U-turn on the cracked drive. "But I'll feel better once we get back and find a way to secure the perimeter."

After another glance toward the building, I refocus my attention on the inside of the Jeep, specifically the toe of a tiny sneaker wedged under the seat. *How...?* I pluck Theo's shoe from the floor, wondering how it found its way from the old exam room to the Jeep. I dart my eyes from the worn leather to Archer's flushed face.

"I thought you might want that."

A warm tingle spreads through me as I hug the battered shoe to my chest. "Thank you."

It feels like a dozen years since I met Andrea and her son, rather than a few short days. Time moves differently in the apocalypse. Every day feels like months... or years. As if my next birthday will be my thirtieth instead of my twenty-third. And the people I've only just met feel like old friends. I glance at Archer. Maybe more than friends.

Focusing on my lap, I squeeze Theo's shoe like a stress ball. "What do you think we'll find in the safe zone?"

"Hopefully a resistance. Some sort of plan to take back our plan-et." Archer pulls onto the main road, kicking up gravel as he guns the engine. "What about you? What are you hoping to find?"

My answer comes without hesitation. "My family."

"Where were they? When it, uh, happened."

"Home." I let out a breath, releasing the painful memories from the cage I'd locked them in. "I talked to my mom right after, just before the signal cut out for good."

"You were at school?"

I nod again, the memories flashing back like a video playing at high speed. "I went home after... it took me a while to get there."

He glances at me but doesn't ask.

"They were gone. I assumed they'd been—" I swallow around the lump in my throat. "*Killed*, but now I'm not so sure. Maybe I got it all wrong. Maybe they went to the safe zone."

Staring straight ahead, Archer nods. "I hope they did. I hope you find them."

"Me too." *Are we all wrong? Is Thor actually onto something?* The confession bubbles up, begging to be voiced. "Thor said something strange—before he lost consciousness."

Archer turns toward me, his gaze penetrating my skin until I feel it in my bones. "What did he say?"

"Everything we know is wrong."

"That's it?" His eyebrows jump. "What the hell does that even mean?"

"I don't know. I'm not even sure he was coherent enough to know himself. But he made me promise to tell you."

Archer chews on the inside of his cheek. "Let's hope he can explain when he wakes up."

We ride the rest of the way to town in comfortable silence, but the minute we turn down the main drag, the tension in the air ratchets up a few notches. Just like everywhere else I've been over the past several months, what used to be a quaint little town is deserted. Abandoned cars line both sides of the road. Most look like someone just parked to run into the bank or the dry cleaners, leaving their doors ajar. But a few have smashed windows and doors hanging crooked on the hinges, as if they were cracked open like a dented can of SpaghettiOs.

"Keep an eye out for a pharmacy," Archer says under his breath, gaping at the row of destroyed storefronts and boarded-up buildings.

Scanning the road ahead, past the mangled fast-food signs and the one remaining golden arch, I spot a supermarket and point it out. "What about that?"

"Perfect."

Archer pulls into the adjacent parking lot, winding through the scattered vehicles to the front. He pulls into the fire lane, as close as possible to the main door, cuts the engine, and locks his gaze with mine as he slaps the keys into my hand. "Just in case."

The seriousness of his expression sends a cold ripple down my spine, and I shove the keys against his chest. "Screw 'just in case.' We go in together. We come out together. Got it?" Before he can counter my argument, I unbuckle and hop out.

With an impressive growl, Archer exits the Jeep, wordlessly joining me on the sidewalk.

"No bow and arrow?" I eye the shiny pistol in his hand.

Shoving the gun into his waistband, he glances at the saber strapped to my back. "Too hard to maneuver inside."

The blade weighs heavily against my spine as his words sink in. "I'm good. I've maneuvered in some pretty tight spaces and lived to tell the tale."

He gives a sharp nod, wordlessly taking the lead.

Before he steps through the hole where the glass door used to be, I reach out and grasp his hand. "Together."

Glass crunches beneath my feet as we cross the threshold. Sunlight streams in between the dirty streaks in the remaining windows, illuminating row after row of empty checkout lanes. What would have been a hub of activity at this hour is nothing but a ghost town, and the eerie quiet sends a chill down my spine.

Archer pauses at a rack of reusable green grocery bags and drops my hand to grab a few. Putting a finger to his lips, he hands me a bag before sliding the gun from his waistband.

With a quick nod, I loop the strap over my shoulder and pull my saber free. The building *looks* abandoned, but I know better than to rule out the possibility of an entire army hiding in the shadows.

The rancid smell hits me before we step into the produce department. Instead of the usual bins overflowing with fresh fruits and vegetables, a pile of black bananas and rotting greens greets us. Anything edible has long since been picked through until nothing but the compost heap remains.

Archer's jaw tenses. He keeps his voice low, his attention focused on the shadows in front of us as we weave between the empty bins and abandoned carts. "I guess no one around here has an appreciation for banana bread."

"Heathens," I whisper.

The corners of his lips curl up. "Barbarians."

Like a pair of commandos, we cut down the empty bread aisle, stealthily following the overhead signs for the pharmacy as we make our way toward the back. Nothing but a few boxes of instant stuffing and assorted containers of breadcrumbs are left.

Archer plucks a lonely bag of white powdered donuts from the highest shelf and stuffs it into his bag. I spear him with a look, and he shrugs. Treats weren't on the agenda, but I can't argue with his decision. After months of eating cold canned meat or whatever else I could find, I would kill for a batch of Mom's chocolate chip cookies straight out of the oven.

Darting my eyes from one display to the next, I stick to Archer's side as we head into the belly of the store. The deeper we go and the farther we get from the windows, the darker it gets. Tall racks blanket us in eerie shadows. Wishing I'd brought a flashlight, I keep pace with Archer until we reach our destination.

At some point, someone had the foresight to pull down the metal shutters at the pharmacy counter, effectively locking us out. Archer shoves the gun into his waistband and hops onto the counter. His muscles bunch and strain as he struggles to lift the gate, but he barely manages to rattle the heavy steel.

"Shit!" He hops down again, breathing heavily from the effort.

I check over my shoulder at every creak coming from the old building. "What now?"

"We use the door." Archer grabs my hand and tows me around the corner to a steel door.

"Great. But how are we supposed to open it?"

Frowning, he pulls out the gun and waves it. "I have the key."

"That's gonna draw everyone within earshot to us."

"Then I guess we'd better move fast." He doesn't wait for my next objection before pulling me behind him and pointing the pistol at the lock. "Cover your ears."

A glimpse of red in my peripheral vision draws my attention. "Wait!"

I nudge Archer aside and use the butt of my saber to break the glass and access the fire extinguisher mounted on the wall. It only takes a few tries before I bang the handle loose and open the door.

Archer gapes at me as I brush past him.

"Are you coming?"

Clear plastic bins filled with boxes and bottles line the towering shelves, and the sight brings me back to the task at hand.

I sheathe my saber, and we each take a side, combing through the labels for the names Callie made us memorize—azithromycin, ciprofloxacin, and doxycycline, among others—along with anything else we think we might need. Archer quickly fills a bag and starts on a second while I grab every bottle of Percocet, hydrocodone, or Oxy-Contin I can find, then I grab a handful of sterile syringes and clean out the first aid bins.

The sound of breaking glass freezes us in place. "Did you get everything?"

Archer slings both filled bags over his shoulders like a sexy cat burglar. "Let's get out of here."

With a nod, I follow him, pausing in front of the feminine hygiene aisle to stealthily grab as many boxes of tampons as I can squeeze into my bag. When I can't fit any more, I turn and spot Archer stuffing a few boxes of condoms into his.

As Archer realizes he's been caught in the act, a bright-red flush creeps up his neck and into his cheeks. "They, uh, they're great for camping. To, uh, keep matches—"

"Better grab a few more." My own cheeks burn as I reach for another large box.

His shy grin lights a fire low in my belly, but the sound of cans crashing to the floor douses it with ice water. Archer's eyes go wide, and he wraps his fingers around mine and sets off running with me glued to his side.

We head back the way we came, but a capsized rack of canned goods blocks our path, forcing us to detour the other way. Archer's hand slick in mine, we whip around the next corner and come face-to-face with a huge black bear.

With a chuffing bark, the bear rises on its hind legs, and Archer skids to a stop, making me slam into his back.

"Shit! Shit! Shit!" He releases my hand and pulls out his gun.

I wrap my fingers around his wrist, stopping him. "You can't shoot it!"

"Why?"

"Because it's... it's not one of *them*." The words come tumbling out in a rush as I eye the dangerous beast. "He's one of *us*. This is his home. We can't kill him."

Archer groans and positions himself between me and the bear. "If we get eaten, this is on you."

A laugh catches in my throat.

Tucking me behind him, he nudges me backward. "I guess this explains why no one beat us to the pharmacy."

"You think he's been hanging out here for *six months*, just livin' large in the processed-food aisle?"

"Why not?" He shrugs, keeping his voice low and his muscles taut as we slowly back away. "He's had access to all the bread and honey he could possibly want."

The bear drops to all fours again and sniffs a broken jar of pickles.

I lean in to whisper in Archer's ear, "Maybe you should throw him your donuts."

"The hell I will!"

As if he understood every word, the bear takes a step toward us.

"Hey!" Still gripping the gun, Archer waves his hands above his head. "Go on. Get out of here!"

The bear stops his advance but doesn't retreat.

"I really hope he's alone." I peek around Archer as I back toward the vacant meat section behind me, imagining Mama Bear and Baby Bear hiding around every corner.

Does that make me Goldilocks?

We barely reach the end of the aisle before the bear lunges forward, taking a swipe at us with a massive paw.

With an impressive growl of his own, Archer fishes his bag of donuts from the tote and tears it open. "Okay, you son of a bitch, you want a fucking donut? I'll give you a fucking donut!"

He hurls a few of the white-powdered confections onto the upper shelves lining the aisle, and the bear goes for the bait, quickly scrambling up the side for his treat. The racks wobble under the sudden weight before the entire side of the aisle falls forward, starting a chain reaction.

Archer shoves me out of the way, taking the brunt of the assault as glass jars rain down from above. At least one cracks against the barrel of the gun in his hand, and the rest strike the linoleum like bomb blasts, sending shards of glass and liquid in every direction. I let out a piercing scream as shrapnel hits him from every side, and the sticky contents splatter him from head to toe.

"That worked out well." Archer groans, amber syrup dripping from his hair onto his eyelashes.

"Are you okay?" I do a quick inspection, checking his cuts and bruises to be sure he isn't bleeding from an artery.

He smells like the inside of a Waffle House.

"I'm fine." He touches his tongue to the corner of his lips before using his sleeve to wipe syrup from around his eyes and mouth.

I swallow a snicker. "I'm not sure if I should patch you up or taste you."

"Later." He gives me a crooked grin. "Right now, we need to get out of here while we still can."

I nod. I'd never given much thought to the viral man-versus-bear debate that filled my social media timeline in the time before the aliens, but facing down a very real bear doesn't scare me nearly as much as whatever else might be lurking in the shadows.

With the bear momentarily distracted, we take off running, skirting around another row of collapsed shelves and the dented canned goods strewn across the floor.

I do a quick scan of the labels, hoping to see something we can salvage, but the low chuffing coming from somewhere behind me changes my mind. "Nobody likes lima beans anyway."

With a bark of laughter, Archer grabs my hand, his sticky palm warm in mine, and pulls me down the next aisle toward the exit.

Once we're safely inside the Jeep, I give him a thorough once-over. "You saved me again."

"From a fucking bear." He touches the cut above his eyebrow.

With my gaze locked on his, I shake my head, sliding a finger across his sticky cheek before licking it clean. "From the great syrup avalanche."

"*Slayer*..." His gaze drops to my lips, and he groans. The sound is both a question and a plea.

But he'll get no mercy from me.

"Don't make me beg."

His gaze goes molten, and the intensity liquifies my insides.

Archer slides a hand into my hair, his fingers weaving through my long tresses to cradle the back of my head, and our mouths come together in a desperate, needy kiss. The tension holding my muscles hostage releases its grip, giving way to a shiver of need, as if my whole life has been leading me to this very moment. My lips fall open, and his hot tongue slips inside, caressing mine with slow, deep strokes that set my nerve endings ablaze.

His free hand glides over my ribcage to cup my breast, and all rational thought flies out of my head as my whole body goes up in a column of flame. I've never wanted anything as much as I want him right now.

I curl my fingers in his shirt, dragging him closer—*God, I need him closer*—and a rough sound rolls up his throat as he deepens the kiss, tilting my head for a better angle.

He tastes of salty sweat and maple syrup, and I can't get enough of him. Every sticky brush of his mouth consumes me, every sweep of his tongue has my body humming like a tuning fork. It's been too long since I've been close to another human, too long since I've been thoroughly kissed, and I've missed the intimacy so damn much, I could cry. The whole world could burn down around us as we devour each other in the front seat, and I wouldn't notice.

Without warning, Archer lifts his mouth from mine with a groan and glances toward the deserted street before resting his forehead on my shoulder. "I can't believe I'm saying this, but we need to stop. It isn't safe... not out here in the open."

I follow his gaze to the abandoned cars, and reality comes crashing down on me. The bear isn't the most frightening thing we could run into. "Let's get back to the school. You need a shower."

He untangles his sticky hand from my hair and kisses the tip of my nose. "So do you."

"How fast can you get there?"

Archer guns the engine, squealing tires as he backs out of the parking spot and whips the Jeep around.

We make it back to the deserted school in record time, parking on the sidewalk out front. He grabs the bags we filled at the supermarket, rearranging them to put a few boxes of bandages and ointments, condoms, and what's left of the donuts into one bag and the rest of the supplies into the others. He hands me the bag with the donuts, and we head inside.

We find Callie where we left her, tending to Lancelot and Thor in the nurse's office. Archer places the supplies on a table and turns to leave.

"What happened to you?" Callie's mouth hangs open as her eyes dart from Archer's appearance to me then to the bags. "And why is everything sticky?"

"Not now, Callie." Archer tosses the remark over his shoulder and grabs my hand, towing me out of the office and down the hall.

As we make our way to the gym, it's all I can do to keep my hands to myself. My fingers itch to pull off his clothes, to touch his warm skin, to explore his incredible body. We barely make it through the locker room door before Archer's mouth is on mine, hot and sweet.

We stumble to the showers in a frenzy, and Archer somehow manages to turn on the taps just before I get his T-shirt over his head. I run my fingers down his chest to his abdomen, and his muscles jump at my touch. *God, he's beautiful.*

Dragging me under the spray, Archer peels off my shirt and sports bra and slides my leggings down to my ankles. I quickly kick them off while fumbling with the button on his fly. Not even the cold water can cool the blistering heat building between us.

"So beautiful," Archer whispers as he meets my gaze. "Are you sure?"

Every moment since we met flashes before my eyes as I stand virtually naked in front of him. Maybe a year ago, I would've considered it reckless—*foolish*—to jump into something so intimate with a man I barely know. But after nearly dying at least a hundred times in the past six months and being faced with the very real threat of death lurking around every corner, my perspective has changed. Life is far too short not to live it to the fullest. "I've never been more sure of anything."

A shy smile spreads across his lips, and he hooks a finger under the waistband of my underwear as he leans in to kiss me.

"Archer!" Raptor's voice echoes through the tile shower, and I flinch, covering myself with my hands as Archer steps in front of me.

"Come back later," he growls. "We're kinda busy in here."

"No can do, buddy." Raptor chuckles from just around the corner. "Thor's awake, and he's asking for you."

Chapter 14

The Colony

Before the aliens showed up and gave me something a little more tangible to fear, I used to have this recurring nightmare where I was back in high school again. The setting shifted between the football field and the main hall, but the basic plot played out the same way every time. I was walking in front of the entire school, and everyone was gawking at me—eyes wide, mouths gaping open—because other than the spiral notebook pressed to my chest, I was completely naked.

Standing under the icy stream in the abandoned high school shower, tucking myself behind Archer's unbelievably sexy body while his friend looms less than five feet away and just barely out of view, places me right back in that dream.

Archer cranes his neck to growl at Raptor's profile. "Can you give us five minutes?"

"Dude." Raptor snickers from his spot just past the tile border. "If it only takes you five minutes, you're doing something wrong."

"Naked here." I shiver, goose bumps forming as the cold water runs over my skin.

"Jesus, Raptor!" Archer snaps, his fingers flexing against my waist. "A little privacy would be nice."

"I think it's a bit late for that," I mutter, resting my forehead against his slippery shoulder.

"Fine." Raptor pushes away from the wall, and his voice moves farther away. "I'll finish securing the perimeter. Callie said Thor needs his rest, but he won't let her give him anything until he talks to you, so don't take all day."

"Understood." Archer exhales through his nose. "I don't suppose you found any towels lying around, did you?"

"I guess today *is* your lucky day." Raptor chuckles. "I raided a few of the lockers and managed to scrounge up a thing or two. I'll leave what I found on the bench out here."

"Thanks." Archer waits until Raptor's footsteps fade away before cupping my cheeks in his cold hands and resting his forehead against mine. "I'm sorry about that. This didn't exactly turn out how I'd hoped."

"No. Not at all." I laugh, glancing down my bruised body at my wet underwear. "I really hope he found some dry clothes in those lockers."

"Come on." He slips a lock of damp hair behind my ear. "Let's finish what we started."

"I, uh, know you said we only needed five minutes, but..." I gaze into his dark eyes and catch my lip between my teeth. Five minutes isn't nearly long enough for what I'd like to do with this man.

Archer chokes out a laugh. "We'd definitely need more than five minutes for *that*. I was thinking maybe you could help me wash the honey out of my hair, then we can get dressed and check on Thor."

"Oh." Swallowing a laugh, I grab a bottle of shower gel someone left on the floor and squeeze a glob into my hands. "I can do that."

Archer closes his eyes, moaning under his breath as I lather his hair, massaging his scalp with my fingertips. "That feels really nice."

"I used to love having my hair washed." A low groan slips past my lips at the memory. "I *really* miss the salon."

He leans back into the spray, rinsing his hair before grabbing the shower gel and squirting some into his hand. "Your turn."

He takes his time, following my lead as he works the gel into my scalp, thoroughly washing each strand until it's so clean it squeaks.

Then he tips my head back, sliding his fingers through the length of my hair as he rinses out the bubbles. When he finishes, he squeezes out another dollop of gel and quickly runs his soapy hands over my shoulders, down my arms, and across my stomach, eliciting sounds from me I don't think I've ever made before.

He flashes a shaky grin before taking my hand and squirting gel into my palm. "I think you'd better take it from here. I'm not sure my self-control is up to the task."

While I struggle to keep my eyes from wandering below his throat, he steps under the cold spray again, quickly lathering his skin while I finish washing myself. Once we're both as clean as we're going to get, he turns off the taps and takes my hand, kicking our wet clothes to the side as we make our way to the pile Raptor left for us.

Using what barely passes as a towel, I dry off as well as I can before Archer hands me a worn Raiders T-shirt and a pair of loose gray gym shorts. I quickly dress and slip back into my shoes, pretending not to watch as he steps into a pair of matching gray sweatpants and a larger version of the same shirt.

He pulls on his boots and turns toward me. "Ready?"

I gaze up at him and nod, and the smile he gives me is full of unspoken promises.

"Later," he whispers and crushes his warm lips to mine.

I am so going to hold him to that promise.

We weave through the dark hallways like a pair of naughty schoolchildren sneaking out of class. By the time we reach the nurse's office, a small crowd has formed around the entrance, and the low rumble of deep voices filters into the hall.

My stomach drops. *Did Thor take a turn for the worse?* Archer must have the same thought because his grip on my hand tightens, and he pushes his way through the crowd, towing me behind him.

"Nice of you... to join us." Thor sucks in a heavy breath as he tries to pull himself into a sitting position. He slowly lets it out again, his eyes tightening and his dry lips twisting into a grimace as he lowers himself onto the pillows again.

Archer's eyebrows stitch together as he mirrors Thor's pained smile. "You're the one who's been unconscious, buddy. How ya feeling?"

"Me? I'm aces." Thor darts his eyes to me and winks.

Archer clears his throat. "I hear you have something you wanted to tell me."

Thor locks his gaze on Archer and leans forward. "You ever use a magnifying glass to burn ants when you were a kid?"

I follow Thor's determined stare to Archer's furrowed brow. I can almost see the gears turning as Archer attempts to decipher the obscure clues. "Probably."

"Burning them didn't do shit, did it? There was always another one to take its place."

Confused, I toss a glance at Callie, trying to figure out if she knows what the hell they're talking about. She shakes her head almost imperceptibly, and I shift my focus back to Thor.

"Why do you think that is?" Thor throws out the question and waits for Archer to respond.

The furrow between Archer's brows deepens. "Because the queen keeps churning out more ants?"

Thor's eyes light up. "Bingo! Because the fucking queen keeps churning out more ants."

"Are we planning a picnic?" Raptor asks with a nervous chuckle, clearly as oblivious as the rest of us.

Thor shakes his head, wincing with every movement. "No, man. Pay attention!"

"Are we still talking about ants?" I murmur to Archer.

"No! Damn it. We were *never* talking about ants." A frustrated Thor growls out the words, struggling to catch his breath.

"I'm confused." Archer drops my hand and cautiously steps toward his friend. "What *are* we talking about?"

Thor pulls in another breath. "Aliens. We're talking about fucking aliens."

"You're talking crazy over there, buddy." Flashing a snarky grin, Raptor holds up the doorframe with his shoulder. "I can't make a lick of sense out of a damn thing you're saying."

His cocky expression sends my blood pressure shooting through the roof. I'm as confused as the rest of them, but his condescending attitude isn't helping anything.

"I'm making perfect sense," Thor mumbles and drops his head into his hands with a groan. "You're just not paying attention."

Archer turns to Callie, concern stitching across his features as he whispers, "I thought you said you didn't give him any narcotics."

"I didn't!" she whispers back.

I study the cut above Thor's eye and the purple bruise extending from his cheek to his chin. "A head injury can cause confusion, right?"

"He may have a mild concussion." She shrugs. "But that definitely wasn't the worst of his injuries."

"Damn it!" Thor lifts his head, and his face flushes crimson as he roars, "I'm not on drugs! And I don't have a fucking concussion. I'm *trying* to tell you how we fight these sons of bitches, and no one wants to listen to me!"

Pushing down my unconfirmed theories, I shove past Archer and crouch in front of Thor. "*I'm* listening. Tell *me*. How did you make the jump from ants to aliens?"

"They both have a queen churning out drones and sending them out to die on the battlefield."

For the first time since the aliens attacked my dorm, I see light at the end of the tunnel. I stare deep into his eyes, searching for the truth within. "Are you sure?"

"Not a single doubt in my mind." Thor glares at the doubters surrounding us. "My totally *unconcussed* mind."

"So what you're saying is we should be looking for a really big can of Raid?" Raptor snickers.

"Something like that." Thor chuckles.

"Okay, back up a second." Archer squats beside me in front of Thor's cot. "How the hell do you know any of this? I've been out there fighting these things right by your side, and I've never seen a damn queen."

Thor lets out a breath and flops back against the stiff cot. "*You've* been looking in the wrong places."

"Okay, you win." Archer palms the back of his neck. "You have my attention. Tell me what you know."

Thor eyes his dwindling audience, his gaze lingering on Callie before shifting focus to me. "After ripping Callie a new ass for locking you out, I went searching for you."

Blinking back tears, I swallow the growing lump in my throat. I knew he'd gotten hurt looking for me, but hearing him say it ripped the wound open again. "Thor—"

"Don't go blaming yourself. I knew what I was getting myself into." Thor reaches for my hand, wincing from the effort. "But I must've just missed you out there. Trees were down, and debris scattered everywhere, but no sign of you... or Arch."

"He, uh, found me." I dart my eyes toward Archer, and a shy smile spreads across his lips.

"We..." Archer licks his lips. "We hid in a storm shelter."

Thor chuckles. "While you were *hiding*, I was tracking those bastards as they came crawling out of their holes in the ground. Fucking shocked the shit out of me too. I knew they were holed up somewhere but never guessed they were in actual holes like ants. I found a mound of loose gravel so fine it could've been sand. I saw a few of those things slither out, and I waited until it got quiet then followed the tunnel to the end."

"Jesus, dude!" Raptor shakes his head. "With no backup? Are you crazy?"

Thor grins. "Crazy like a fox."

"You should've gone back for one of us instead of going rogue commando on your own," Archer scolds.

Thor fixes his gaze on Archer. "I couldn't let anything happen to her after promising you I'd keep her safe."

"What if you'd died?" Horrified, I gape at him.

Thor lets out a breath, and the weight of the world comes with it. "I didn't think that far ahead. I just reacted. My gut told me they'd dragged you down into their den, and I was determined to get you out."

"Your gut almost got you killed." Archer scrubs a hand down his face.

"It's gonna take more than a few aliens to kill me." Thor's crooked grin dissolves into a pained grimace. "But they sure as hell tried. I damn near got lost in the maze they'd dug down there. It's like nothing I've ever seen. I don't know exactly when it hit me that I was wandering around in a damned ant farm, but when it did, I got the hell out of there—with at least a dozen of the freaking bastards on my tail."

"And the queen?" I ask.

"The queen is something straight out of a horror movie." Thor squeezes his eyes shut.

When he opens them again, I can see clear to his soul.

"She's huge, like, at least twice the size of the biggest one I've ever seen. And she's sitting down there with hundreds of these pulsing gray... *eggs.*" Thor shudders. "I lit a few of them up. That's when the sons of bitches came out of the damn woodwork and went after me. Thank God they made more than one exit, or I'd still be down there."

Archer stands and shakes his head. "You got lucky."

"In more ways than one." Thor grins.

"What's so damn funny?" Raptor's gaze bounces between the two of them as if he can't believe what he's hearing.

Thor's smile stretches halfway across his bruised cheek, but he doesn't say a word.

Archer narrows his eyes. "You figured out how to kill them, didn't you?"

"It's like the man said." Thor nods toward Raptor. "We're gonna need a big-ass can of Raid."

Concern floods me as Thor's smile fades, and his eyes tighten. "Thor?"

Stiffening against the cot, his muscles flex as he sucks in his next breath through his teeth.

Still crouching beside him, I freeze, unsure of what to do. "Are... are you okay?"

"Never better." He flashes a fragile smile, pain reflecting in his features.

"That's it." Callie squeezes between Archer and me, dropping to her knees beside the cot. She cracks open an amber bottle, pours a small round tablet into her palm, and thrusts her hand into his face. "You shared your information. Now take the damn pain pill like you promised."

"I'm good." Thor shakes his head and mashes his lips together like a stubborn toddler.

Snorting out a hollow laugh, Callie leans in until their noses almost touch. "I swear to God, Thor, I'll sit on you and force it down your throat if I have to."

"Damn it, Calico." He groans, shifting his weight under her threat. "I need to keep my head clear."

"Why?" Archer stares down at his friend and folds his arms. "Never have before."

Thor glances from Callie to Archer. "Trust me, I'm gonna need my wits about me when we go down there. Last thing I need is to be doped up on narcotics."

"Are you crazy?" Heart hammering in my ears, I take in Thor's ragged appearance. Bruises cover nearly every inch of his exposed skin. His clothes and hair are still caked in dried blood. Maybe Callie was wrong. Maybe he does have a head injury. "Have you seen yourself lately? You almost died two days ago! Archer, please knock some sense into him."

Locking his eyes on Thor, Archer shakes his head. "You're not going anywhere until Callie says you're good."

Thor holds his breath, wincing as he struggles to sit up. Part of me is ready to knock him down again, to smack some sense into his rock-hard head.

"I'm good."

"The hell you are!" Archer growls, and the vein in his neck pulses in time with my heart. "We can't afford to lose anyone else. Do you understand me? *I* can't lose any more friends."

"Fine." Thor heaves a breath, collapsing against the cot again. "Maybe I'm not a hundred percent... yet. But you have to promise you won't go without me. You haven't seen what I've seen. You don't know what you're up against."

A sudden spark of fear flares in my belly, and I dart my eyes to Archer. The thought of him—of *anyone*—going underground to confront the aliens terrifies me. Maybe they *are* like ants. Maybe there *is* a way to defeat them using that logic, but we don't have enough information to put that plan in motion. We sure as hell won't stop them if we all get killed trying.

"We can't go down there." I shake my head. "Not yet. Not compromised. Not without a solid plan. It would be a suicide mission."

Archer's eyes meet mine, and he nods. "Agreed." He shifts his gaze to Thor. "We'll wait."

"This is crazy." Raptor cups the back of his neck. "How the hell are you even considering this? Tunneling underground? Facing them on their own playing field? You ever seen what happens when you disturb an anthill? They sure as shit don't roll over and play dead."

Memories of stepping on fire ant mounds sting my thoughts, burning a fiery path through my veins. My voice cracks, barely any sound coming out, as I whisper, "They aggressively defend the colony."

"Bingo." Raptor blows out a breath. "I'd love to get on board here, but there isn't a big enough can of Raid on the whole damn planet."

Thor lets out a low groan. "Every day they're down there, their numbers grow."

"I hate to say this, but I agree with Thor." Archer shoves a hand into his damp hair. "The longer we delay, the more impossible it becomes. We'll wait for Thor to get back on his feet, but then we go. We have to at least try."

"You're both nuts." A dark chuckle rolls up my throat as I study their determined faces. Stubborn *boys*. I don't know what the answer is, but I know it's not this. "This isn't your mom's backyard. And we aren't talking about tiny ants. Even if we had the world's biggest can of Raid, we don't have the means to deliver the death blow to a colony that size. We'd need a hell of a lot more than bug spray to exterminate those bastards. I'm sorry, but we're not equipped to fight this battle."

Another pained breath hisses through Thor's teeth. "If not us, who?"

"Not you." Callie shoves her hand toward Thor's mouth again, and I almost thank her for the interruption. "Not today, anyway."

"Fine." He takes the pill and swallows it dry, shuddering as it goes down. He takes a few more breaths before picking up where he left off. "But the clock is ticking. We either act soon, or we're the ones who become extinct."

Exhaling slowly, I let my eyes drift closed and wait for the voice of reason to give me the answer. *Come on, Coach. No words of wisdom?*

"You know what to do, Evie." Coach's chuckle echoes in my imagination. *"Put that brain of yours to use."*

"Have you ever actually used Raid to kill ants?" I scramble to remember what my father did to combat the ever-present ant mounds in our yard each summer. "It's not the most effective method, is it?"

"What?" Thor screws up his face as he looks at me.

"Raid." I sigh. "It's fine for roaches, but not ants. How do you kill ants?"

"I don't fucking know." Thor chokes out a laugh. "I didn't work for Orkin."

"Hang on." Archer's eyes light up. "She's right. You don't spray ants. You *bait* them."

"Exactly." My lips spread in a wide grin. "You get them to do all the work for you."

"Oh, shit." Thor smiles, finally catching on. "We get those bastards to take the Raid to the queen themselves."

I dial up my grin another notch. "How hard can it be?"

Chapter 15

Winnie

"**N**ow that *that's* settled..." Raptor scratches behind his ear, flicking his gaze from Archer to where Chuck and Supes hover just inside the doorway then back again. "Can we go back to shoring up the doors on this place so we actually live to fight another day?"

Archer nods, and the three of them scatter like roaches in the light. "The slayer and I have unfinished business to attend to."

Archer takes my hand, slipping his fingers through mine, and the gentle pressure sends goose bumps dancing up my arm. Our eyes lock, and the heat radiating from his gaze makes my heart skip. One look from him, and the room fades away. Callie clears her throat, and I look up just in time to catch her staring at our clasped hands.

She blinks a few times before quickly darting her eyes back to Thor. "I, uh... I should go check on Winnie." With a backward glance at Lancelot asleep on his cot, she hurries out the door, her eyes glistening with unshed tears.

"Arch." Thor ends the awkward silence. "We need to talk."

Archer draws in a slow breath. "You need your rest, man. I'll come back in a few hours, and we'll talk strategy, okay?"

"No, listen." Thor props himself on his elbow. "It'll be dark soon, and I know having me and Lance out of commission puts the group in even more danger, but this can't wait. We can't hold off on gathering information until everyone is a hundred percent."

"What're you saying?" I let Archer's hand slip from mine as I step toward Thor.

"Callie said we moved locations while I was out."

I nod.

"That means we're most likely dealing with a whole different colony." He presses his lips into a thin line. "My little bit of intel won't do a lot of good in a totally different tunnel."

The thought sends a ripple of unease through me, and my voice cracks as I ask, "H-How many colonies do you think there are?"

Thor flops onto his back and shoves a hand into his tangled hair. "I'm afraid to even guess."

If they really *are* like ants, they've had six months to infiltrate the entire continent, maybe the world.

"We can't take on a handful of aliens with a third of our crew compromised, let alone a whole colony." Archer shakes his head, and a deep furrow forms between his brows. "We need time to figure out the best thing to bait them with. It's not as if we can go raid the closest Walmart for a truckload of sugar and borax. We have no clue what they're drawn to—other than us."

Thor's eyes light up. "That's what I'm getting at. You need to locate the nearest colony. Spy on them for as long as you can without being seen. Find out what they do. Where they go. We've always assumed they eat... well, *people.* But do they? Or are we nothing but collateral damage in their quest to strip the planet of its natural resources?"

A shaky laugh bubbles up my throat. "You've seen too many movies."

"Maybe." Thor's lips tip into a crooked grin. "But just because I saw it in a movie doesn't make it wrong. It wouldn't be the first time life imitated art."

"Fair enough," I agree, my good humor fading as the reality of his words sinks in. I've been so busy trying to stay alive, I never stopped to consider the aliens' motives. "I guess we really don't know *why* they're here."

"We can do a little recon and scope out the closest colony." Archer slips his hand into mine again and exhales heavily. "If you're up for that."

I give a sharp nod. "I'm in."

"Good. That's settled." Thor sinks into his makeshift bed with a grunt. "I think the pain meds are starting to kick in. The gash in my side only hurts when I breathe."

Archer chuckles. "Get some sleep."

Thor mumbles something unintelligible, his eyes drifting shut.

Archer tilts his head toward the door and gives my hand a little squeeze. I nod, and we slip out of the nurse's office. With the door barely closed behind me, his fingers thread into my still-damp hair, and his lips close over mine. The hallway disappears as I eagerly kiss him back as if we may never get another chance. But all too quickly, he pulls away, leaving us both out of breath.

He groans, and his hands fall to his sides. "I'm sorry."

"Don't be sorry." I grab his hand and squeeze. "I'm not."

Chuckling, he rests his forehead against mine. "I'm not sorry for kissing you. I'm sorry for stopping."

"Oh." A slow grin spreads across my lips. "Well, then you should be sorry."

"I wish..." He lets out a wistful sigh, pushing a loose lock of hair behind my ear.

My heart thunders against my ribs as the what-ifs begin to pile up in my thoughts. Time isn't on our side. "I know."

"If we're going to find the entrance and a safe place to observe them as they come out, we need to go before dark."

Swallowing around the lump in my throat, I nod. "When we get back, you'd better find a room with a lock. I'm not letting you off the hook a third time."

His gaze turns hot, his focus shifting to my lips. "Deal." He barely gets the word out before surging in for another kiss.

His tongue quickly finds mine, and suddenly it's like we're back in the shower, with nothing and no one between us. Neither of us mentions the inherent danger in what we're about to do. We don't need to. It's there in every slide of his lips across mine. Every shared breath. Every touch. Every sigh.

He pulls away again, but this time there's no humor in his eyes. "Grab your saber and anything else you might need. I'll meet you at the door in ten?"

"I'll be there."

After leaving Archer's side, I weave through the deserted halls back toward the locker room to collect my saber.

"Buffy, wait!"

The sound of Callie's voice is like fingernails down the proverbial chalkboard. Dread courses through me as I keep walking. She's the absolute last person on the planet I want to talk to. *But what if it's about Thor?* Biting back a curse, I lurch to a stop and turn around.

"Um, I, uh..." Callie blinks as if she can't believe I stopped any more than I can and tucks her stringy red hair behind her ears. "I wanted to say I'm sorry. For what I did. I didn't think it through, and it, uh... it was—"

"Stupid. That's what it was." A young black woman steps out of the classroom across the hall and leans against the doorframe.

I only saw Winnie once before, through the back window of the SUV, but I recognize the thick mane of tight corkscrew curls framing her pretty face.

She crosses her arms, locking her eyes on Callie with a disapproving stare worthy of my mother. "Stupid *and* dangerous."

"Yeah." Thoroughly chastised, Callie shifts her gaze to the floor and draws in a deep breath. "It was."

"And you'll never do something like that ever again." Still focused on Callie, Winnie arches her dark eyebrows. "Will you?"

Callie shakes her head. "Never."

"And," Winnie continues in her smooth Southern cadence, "you'll do whatever it takes to make it up to her."

"Jesus, Winnie!" Callie's mouth hangs open as she gapes at her brother's girlfriend. "I said I was sorry. Isn't that enough?"

"What you did was beyond wrong, so no, it's not. An ordinary apology isn't gonna cut it this time."

"Fine!" Callie turns to me with a sigh. "I'll do whatever it takes to make it up to you. In fact…" She gives my flimsy gym shorts and T-shirt a quick once-over, and her eyes light up. "I have the perfect peace offering. I'll be right back." Callie turns on her heels and bolts down the hall.

"Thanks." I nod toward Callie's retreating form. "For that."

Winnie shrugs. "All I did was give her a nudge in the right direction. What she did was inexcusable, but she's not really a bad kid. She's had it hard since… well, you know."

At a loss for words, I just nod. She's right. No amount of apologizing will fix what Callie did, but at least it's something. "We've all had it hard since then."

"Ain't that the truth?" Winnie rubs the slight bulge in her belly.

The action draws me in, and I can't help wondering. "How far along are you?"

"Five months, give or take." She chuckles. "Not like I've seen a doctor to know for sure."

A dozen questions flicker through my thoughts as I watch her cradle her bump, but I don't stop to think any of them through before asking, "Are you scared?"

Her eyes snap to mine, and I catch a flash of fear reflected inside their amber depths.

"Terrified. But also, you know, excited. Thrilled. All the things you're supposed to be. Then I'll remember we're living through the damn apocalypse, and I'm back to being terrified." She smiles. "But Will has been an angel. That man has already stepped up more than I could've hoped for."

"Will?" I cock my head to the side as I try to make sense of this new information.

She throws back her head and laughs. "Those boneheads call him Chucky."

"Oh."

"Don't get me wrong. I don't care what *they* call him, but I'll be damned if I refer to the father of my child as a murderous doll."

Her laugh is infectious, and I quickly join in. "I don't blame you."

The topic of names reminds me I don't know Archer's real name—and he doesn't know mine—a situation I'll have to rectify sooner rather than later.

"Should...?" I realize Winnie may prefer to be called by her real name too. "Would you rather I didn't call you Winnie?"

"Actually, Winnie's my real name. Those boys tried to give me one of their stupid nicknames, and I put a stop to that nonsense right away." Winnie turns her attention to something down the hall and shakes her head. "Oh, lord."

I follow her gaze to where Callie jogs toward us with a black bundle folded in her arms.

"This is the something you thought would put you two square?" Winnie asks with another shake of her head.

Callie grins. "She can't go on a mission looking like that."

"What is it?" I reluctantly take the bundle from Callie, unfolding and examining each piece—thick black denim leggings, low-cut leather tank top, and matching lightweight black leather jacket—as if they might reach out and bite me.

"It was Bonnie's. She, uh… she left it behind. You look about the same size as her, so I thought it might fit." She glances at Winnie, and the two of them share a look.

Same size? Maybe. Same tastes? Far from it. "Thanks. That's, um, nice of you."

"You don't have to be so nice. That outfit is…" Another loud laugh booms from Winnie's chest. "Let's just say that girl cosplayed *way* too much *Tomb Raider* as a teen."

"She definitely liked to draw attention to herself," Callie agrees with a nod.

I glance down at my less-than-ample chest and let out a breath. "I don't think I have the, uh, assets to cosplay Lara Croft."

"Girl, you have plenty." Winnie waves off my protests. "And besides, it's wear that or go out there looking like you're on the high school badminton team."

If I've learned one thing in the past six months, it's knowing when I'm fighting a losing battle.

"Fine." I groan. "If it fits, I'll wear it."

Winnie's all business as she sizes me up. "It'll fit."

I thank them again and take Bonnie's battle armor to the locker room to change. As I suspected, the heavy cotton jeggings are snug, bordering on tight, and there's barely enough of me to fill the leather tank top, but when I slip on the waist-hugging leather jacket and strap my saber to my back, even I have to admit I look like a badass warrior.

Thankfully, the halls are still vacant when I make my way back to the front door to meet Archer, saving me from the inevitable cracks about my newly acquired attire. Archer has his back to me when I approach, and I clear my throat to get his attention.

He turns toward me and does a double take, the color draining from his face. His Adam's apple bobs as he swallows, but he doesn't say a word as he rakes his gaze over every inch of me. His inspection leaves me breathless, and a line of heat moves up my throat until my whole face goes up in flames.

"Are...?" When he finally speaks, his voice cracks. "Are you ready?"

Despite my current state of badassery, the thought of staking out the aliens on their own turf leaves me frozen with fear. "As I'll ever be."

He jerks his head in a single nod. "Then I guess we'd better get this show on the road."

Chapter 16

Reconnaissance Mission

W ith little more than the weapons strapped to our backs and a rough idea of where to begin, Archer and I say our goodbyes and make our way to the exit. The sun hangs low in the sky, blinding me as we step outside.

"Be careful. Remember, if you get into trouble, try to get back to the field house restroom. It's small but solid." Raptor tosses out his last bit of wisdom before slamming the steel door behind us.

My heart jumps as he seals it shut with a series of hollow thuds and metallic clangs.

Barred from the safety of the school, Archer and I stand awkwardly on the sidewalk—him silently stealing glances as he stealthily checks out my new outfit and me hyperaware of my Halloween-worthy costume.

I fold my arms across my semi-exposed chest. "So what's the plan?"

"Uh..." With one last lingering look, he rolls up his tongue and shifts his attention toward the overgrown meadow that was once a football field. "I hadn't really gotten that far. What do you think?"

I follow his gaze, staring past the rusted goal post and the concrete block field house to the line of trees beyond and finally the blue peaks in the distance. "Thor said he followed them into a hole, but in all the time I've been running from aliens, I don't remember seeing any giant holes in the earth."

"Yeah, me neither." Archer lets out a slow breath. "They're either hiding them fairly well, or we didn't know what to look for."

"Or a little of both?" I wonder if I would've even noticed a loose mound of dirt if I'd seen one. I've had other, more pressing things on my mind.

"Exactly."

"So where do we begin?" I let my hand fall to my side and hook my pinky with his.

He slips the rest of his fingers through mine to hold my hand. "Your guess is as good as mine."

I study the way the trees jut out of the foothills, following the little peaks and valleys leading up the mountain with my eyes.

"Come on now, Evie. Where would you hide if you were a seven-foot-tall alien avoiding the sun?" Coach's words float freely through my brain as I scramble to come up with a plan.

"What about searching natural outcroppings or caves nearby?" I abandon the horizon to probe the depths of his soul through his eyes. "There have to be dozens of them in every direction."

Archer nods vigorously. "That's a good start." He scans the horizon again before pointing his chin toward the tallest peak in the distance. "Let's head that way, try to get to higher ground so we can observe without drawing attention. We're not trying to get killed, just collect intel."

"So the goal is to get above them?"

He jerks his head in the affirmative, tugging my hand just enough to propel me forward. "We need to find a position with an exit plan."

His comment reminds me of the inherent danger lying ahead of us. If we actually find a colony, we need to be prepared to flee *or fight*.

"After you." With my hand still in his, I fall back slightly, letting him lead the way.

We fight our way through the snarled weeds on the football field and stop at the edge of the copse of tall pines just beyond.

Archer squeezes my hand before letting it slip from his. "Let's fan out. We'll cover more ground that way."

Despite the knot forming in the pit of my stomach, I nod my agreement and head south for several yards before slipping into the deep shadows produced by the thick trunks of two southern pines. Insects so small they may as well be invisible swarm in front of my face, getting in my nose and mouth with every breath. Archer stalks forward in my peripheral vision, and I fight a wave of panic every time I lose sight of him.

Dappled sunlight chases away the shadows, but the farther the sun drops toward the horizon, the more nervous I get. The crunch of twigs and dried leaves underfoot reverberates through the forest, dialing my senses to high alert. Every gopher hole, dirt mound, or gnarled tree root is potentially a threat, and I can't help but imagine myself as Alice, falling down the rabbit hole and landing in the enemy's lair. It doesn't take long to realize how completely unprepared we are for the task ahead of us.

What the hell are we doing? We're going to get ourselves killed out here.

A loud snap interrupts the silence, and I whip my head toward the sound, all too aware that I'm essentially alone. Archer may only be a few dozen yards away, but in a true emergency, that's a few dozen yards too far.

"Archer?" My heart thunders in my ears as I search the distance for any trace of him. He doesn't respond, and I hope it was only a deer or a fat groundhog shuffling through the underbrush.

Another crack has the hair on the back of my neck prickling to attention, and I freeze. With the forest pressing in on me in every direction, I can't tell where the sound is coming from.

"Damn it, Archer, this isn't funny!" I hiss through clenched teeth, frantically scanning the perimeter for signs of life.

A flash of white darts through the trees in the distance, sending a ripple of fear down my spine. I take off like a shot, hurdling over downed branches and loose rocks as I flee in the opposite direction, heading deeper into the forest, away from the safety of the school and farther from Archer.

It's not dark enough for them to come out yet! The thought loops inside my head, and I consider all the ways the aliens could be out during the day. *Damn it, Archer, where are you?*

Keeping my eyes on the tangled path in front of me, I attempt to use my peripheral vision to search for Archer, the alien, or whatever else is out here with me.

A twisted root catches my toe, and I go down, hard, knocking the wind out of me. My lungs struggle to pull in a breath as my first time riding a bicycle without training wheels flashes into my thoughts. I was barely seven, but until that moment, I'd thought I had the whole world figured out. For half a second, I feel like I'm there again, cold cheeks, skinned knees, and all. This can't be the way I die—all alone, dressed like Lara Croft, in a forest somewhere in the middle of Nowhere, North Carolina.

"I haven't even had sex with Archer yet." I barely get the words out before they dry up and float away like ash in the wind.

My throat closes, lodging a scream within, as heavy footfalls rush toward my position, vibrating the ground beneath me. I push to my knees and scramble to pull the saber from my back, but before I can get my fingers around the hilt, something—or someone—crashes through the branches and presses me to the ground again.

Facedown on the forest floor, I quickly shake off the shock of being jumped and suck in a breath to let out an epic scream. Archer has to be within earshot. If he can take out an alien from a moving vehicle with his bow, he can nail whatever has me pinned to the ground. All I have to do is give him a target. But before I can fill my lungs, a hand—a very *human* hand—closes over my mouth.

Hot breath warms my neck as my attacker leans in. "Shh!"

The low hiss sends a fresh shot of adrenaline spiking through my veins, igniting my fight-or-flight reflex. Desperate to claw free, I raise my upper body just enough to throw back an elbow. Pain explodes from my funny bone as I make contact with a hard body, and the stranger lets out a low grunt, his full weight landing on my back, pressing me into the dirt again.

Oh, hell no. Taking full advantage of the element of surprise, I shove against the ground, using my hips to throw him to the side and rolling until I manage to pin him under me.

He lets out a low groan, and the sight of him lying beneath me clears the fog permeating my brain. It doesn't take long for the pieces to click together as his familiar scent washes over me.

"Archer?"

"Easy, slayer," he whispers. "As much as I love the idea of you straddling me, I don't think this is the time or place for that."

I cock my head to the side as his words slowly sink in. "For what?"

"Sex." The corners of his lips curve up, and he rests both hands on my hips. "You said you never got to have sex with me, and believe me, I'm willing, but as much as I'd like to—*really, really like to*—we should probably wait."

His words send a tremor through me, my bones turning to jelly as I become all too aware of our intimate position. "You heard me?"

He nods, his fingers flexing against my sides.

"Why did you tackle—"

"*Shh.*" Archer sits up, gazing over my shoulder as he puts a finger to my lips. "I saw one—stalking a deer."

"An alien?" I whip my head around, glancing over my shoulder. "Is it...?"

He shakes his head. "I don't see it now, but let's not take a chance."

"I thought I saw something out there—just before you jumped me—a flash of white..."

"I think it was hunting." He pats my leg a few times.

Taking the hint, I climb to my feet before helping him to his.

He scoops his bow from the ground, where he must have dropped it before tackling me. "As far as I can tell, it didn't see us, but when you called my name, I was afraid it would abandon the deer and go after you."

"Thank you." I lower my gaze to the ground, chastising myself for being careless. I've seen aliens in the daytime with my own eyes—during storms and in dark, shadowy places where the sun doesn't reach.

They aren't just ants. They're vampire ants. *At least we don't live in Forks.*

"I can't believe I did something so stupid." I let out a breath and tip my face skyward.

Streaks of purple peek from between the towering treetops, reminding me we're almost out of time. We can't allow ourselves to be caught out here much longer.

"Come on." As if reading my mind, Archer grabs my hand. "We need to get out of the shadows, where it can't follow us if it does circle back."

Moving as quietly as possible, Archer and I sprint through the forest toward a break in the trees. The horizon glows where the fiery-orange sunset streams through. If we have any chance of finding safety, we need to make it to higher ground while we still have the light.

"There!" Archer points to a large outcropping jutting from the ground just up the hill.

We quickly hike up the rugged terrain, stumbling more than once before reaching a patch of sunlight warming the rocks, and collapse to the ground to catch our breath.

Resting my head on his arm, I peer up at him. "What now?"

"I think we can be fairly certain we're in the right area. The one I saw didn't come from the clearing, not at this hour. There must be an entrance down in the trees. It isn't safe to go down there, but we can watch and see which direction they come from."

"So we're the bait?" I sit up and gape down at him. "We're just supposed to sit out here in the open and hope they don't eat us?"

"We absolutely hope they don't eat us." Chuckling, he climbs to his feet and drags me up with him. "But just to be safe, I think we'd better find somewhere to hide so we can watch without being seen."

I roll my eyes. "Stellar idea."

"And if we live through this?" His eyes sparkle with mischief.

I arch an eyebrow and wait for him to finish.

He brings his lips to my ear. "We'll find a quiet place and make use of those condoms we salvaged from the pharmacy."

Chapter 17

Theo

⸻◆⸻

As the sun finally slips below the horizon, Archer and I hide in the cavernous hole left by the massive root ball of a fallen tree. Filled with withered vines, wispy roots, and countless unseen creepy crawlies, the space is easily big enough to park a small car, giving us plenty of cover while we wait for the aliens to come slithering out of their den.

Archer throws not-so-subtle glances my way as we peer over the top of the dirt wall. "I'm guessing that was Bonnie's?"

Chuckling, I shift my weight, ignoring the sudden urge to change into my own clothes. "Yes. Callie's idea of making up for locking me out."

"It looks very"—he stealthily sneaks another peek—"rugged."

I nearly choke suppressing a laugh. The last thing we need is to draw unwanted attention to our position. "Rugged wouldn't be the first word I'd use."

He covers a snicker. "Did you find anything interesting in the pockets?"

My hand instinctively goes to the seat of my pants, and I slide it around to the front in a demonstration of how snug they are. "I don't think anything would *fit* in the pockets."

"What about those?" He nods toward the angled slits in the front of the leather jacket.

Exploring the jacket pockets wasn't on my mind when I changed into Bonnie's clothes, but curiosity has me slipping a hand into each one. Instead of treasure, I find half a joint in one pocket and nothing but a soft lump that shouldn't be there behind the liner in the other. I dart my eyes to Archer as I excitedly fish into the left inside pocket.

Thrill turns to disappointment when, instead of discovering candy, I pull out a red BIC lighter.

Archer grins. "That could come in handy."

"The blunt or the lighter?"

He laughs.

I offer him the joint, and he shakes his head, so I toss it to the ground and tuck the lighter back where I found it, remembering Thor's comment about using a magnifying glass to burn ants.

"Do you think...?" I let the thought trail off.

Archer tilts his head and waits.

"It's stupid."

"What?" His quizzical expression reignites my enthusiasm.

I draw in a quick breath before I change my mind. "Remember Thor saying something about burning ants with a magnifying glass?"

His eyes light up, and he nods.

"What if we—" I let out a soft snort, regretting the path my thoughts are heading. "Never mind."

"No." Archer squeezes my hand. "Keep going."

"What if fire is the answer? They don't like the sun because it's bright and hot, right? What if we literally burn them out, like Thor said?"

"It's not a bad idea." Archer studies my expression in the moonlight. "But don't you think someone would've figured that out by now? The government? The military? Surely they would've napalmed the sons of bitches and laid waste to every colony they found."

"You're right." I shake my head to dispel the notion, but the thought keeps nagging at me. "But what if they haven't figured it out yet? What if they don't know about the underground colonies—and the queen?"

He arches a brow, and the sympathy in his smile says he's humoring me.

"I know, I know." Feeling foolish, I slump against the wall of dirt surrounding us. "We're basically a bunch of kids playing soldier. But it's possible, right?"

"Anything's possible." He leans in, brushing my lips with his. "It's a good idea. If we find the colony, we can come back with torches and light them up."

I laugh. "Fair enough."

"Look!" Archer whispers, nudging my shoulder.

I peek over the rim of the hole and watch as several of the pale-gray aliens stalk out of the woods, fanning out in different directions.

"Holy shit!" I duck down as the words hiss past my lips and slap a hand over my mouth. *We found them!*

"Come on." Archer grabs my elbow, bringing his lips to my ear as he drags me to my feet. "While they're out hunting, we need to head in the opposite direction and find the opening."

A zip of adrenaline courses down my spine at the thought. "We're not going in, right? We're just finding the opening so we can come back in the daylight."

"That's the plan." As soon as the last of the aliens disappears, Archer rests his hands on the edge of the hole, using his forearms to push himself up and out before reaching down to help me climb free.

With Thor's description of the last colony as our guide, we stick to the shadows, moving as stealthily as possible through the forest. Thick tree trunks serve as temporary cover as we head in the direction the aliens came from.

An owl hooting in the distance has the hair on the back of my neck standing on end. Between leaves rustling in the wind, water rushing over rocks somewhere not too far away, and the crunching of our footsteps, I'm not sure I would hear an alien approach until it was too late. I nearly crash into Archer's back before realizing he's stopped in his tracks.

"What is it?"

"Look!" He points toward a jagged crack in the hillside up ahead.

Half-hidden by rotting logs and thick vines, the small cave doesn't look like much, but as I step around Archer to get a better look, I notice the clawed footprints leading away from the deep shadows.

"Is that…?"

"I think we just found the entrance—one of them at least." Archer clasps my hand, keeping me from getting closer. "We should mark this with something and get out of here before they come back, or more come out."

I nod, but I can't tear my eyes from the mound of what looks like fine sand trickling from the mouth of the cave and a flash of white poking out of the grains. Wrenching my hand free, I inch toward the opening. "What is that?"

"Slayer, wait!" Archer hisses at my back.

"It can't be…" As I get closer to the familiar dirty white leather, the insides of my stomach swirl and churn, and my heart kicks hard enough to steal my next breath.

The voice inside my head screams at me to turn back, to not get any closer, but my legs won't cooperate. I crouch down and grab the small shoe, dusting off the grains of sand as I study it. I'd held the other one long enough to recognize its mate.

"This is—" My throat closes before I can get the words out.

Archer grabs my shoulders and pulls me to my feet. "It could be any—"

"It's not!" I whirl around, swiping an escaped tear from my cheek as I spear him with a look. "It's his. It's Theo's—his other shoe."

Archer meets my frantic gaze and curses under his breath. "We're going in there, aren't we?"

Theo's shoe may as well be made of iron, the way it drags my arm down as if it weighs a hundred pounds. With my gaze locked on Archer's, I resist swatting another hot tear from my cheek, determined not to fall apart at the mouth of the aliens' stronghold. But I'm close—*too* close—to breaking as I finally nod, confirming what he already knows. We are most definitely going in there.

Archer tips his face to the sky and lets out a slow breath before pulling the bow and arrow from his back. "Okay."

"You're sure?" Following his lead, I free my saber from its sheath. While I would never expect him to back me up, if I've learned nothing else in the short time I've known him, I know without a shadow of a doubt, he would *never* let me go in there alone.

Archer's dry chuckle belies the tension swelling between us.

"Absolutely not." He leans in until our foreheads touch, and his warm breath washes over me. "But you go, I go. Isn't that what we agreed on?"

Gripping the saber's leather hilt so tight that every joint in my fingers screams, I nod and blink back the ever-present tears again. I don't actually want to go in there any more than he does, but...

Theo.

I reflexively squeeze the small shoe in my other hand. If there's any chance he's still alive, I have to at least try.

Archer presses his lips to mine in the briefest kiss before shifting into battle mode. His muscles flex as he unhooks the small blue flashlight keychain from his belt loop and switches it on. He sweeps the beam across the entrance, chasing the shadows within, while I place Theo's shoe on a smooth rock and slowly inch toward the cave.

The narrow opening is only wide enough for one of us to go in at a time, and Archer seems determined to go first. Positioning himself in front of me, he barely takes one step through the gap before coming to an abrupt halt and turning to face me.

"If things go south in there, you turn and run. You hear me?" Fear dances in his eyes as he implores me. "Don't stop. Don't look back. And don't wait for me. You run as fast as you can as far as you can. Got it?"

"I'm perfectly—"

He cups my face in his hand, his thumb rhythmically stroking my cheek. "I know you are, but I'm not setting one damn foot in there unless I know you'll run if it comes to that."

Gazing deep into his determined stare, I can't find the slightest crack in his resolve. With a defeated breath, I surrender to his demands. "Fine."

"Promise me."

The raw emotion in his expression sends a jolt of adrenaline straight to my heart, and I jerk my head in a shaky nod. "I promise. But..." I press out a sly smile as a compromise comes to mind. "If I run, you run. Or no deal."

Archer studies me for a few long moments before relenting with a huff. "Fair enough. If it comes to that, we both run. Let's go."

Gripping my free hand in his, Archer shoulders through the opening, plunging us into the unknown.

Inside, the smooth earthen tunnel curves, blurring the line between the walls and the ceiling, as if the entire passage had been carved by hundreds of years of flowing water. We move forward, following the intricate pattern made by clawed footprints along the winding path. The tunnel slopes downward, dropping several feet of elevation for every dozen or so yards, taking us deeper and deeper underground, where a hint of rot and death—the stench I've learned to associate with the aliens—wafts above the musty scent of wet earth.

The tiny beam of light does little to chase away the darkness, and the farther into the main passage we go, the cooler it gets.

My ears buzz in the silence. Other than our combined breathing and my thundering heart, the tunnel is eerily quiet—too quiet—like a sensory deprivation tank or insulated space capsule. I've never been claustrophobic before, but this must be what it feels like. Every breath I take feels forced, as if the air inside is thinner or my head is slipping underwater. I know better—know it's all in my mind—but I can almost feel the imaginary water filling my lungs. My heart races from the delusion, and I suck in a deep breath followed quickly by another, this time catching a hint of sweetness in the air. If I didn't know better, I would think we'd wandered into a honeycomb instead of a hornet's nest.

A rhythmic scratching from somewhere ahead of us interrupts the silence and clears my spiraling thoughts.

"What is that?" I whisper.

"Sounds like rats in the walls of an old house."

I squeeze Archer's hand. If only rats were our biggest worry.

The faint light ahead grows into a soft glow, and we cautiously make our way toward what appears to be a circular chamber with several more curved passageways branching off from the center like arteries. As we approach the end of the tunnel, row upon row of pulsing gray *eggs* exactly like the ones Thor described come into view.

"Jesus," Archer whispers, lowering the flashlight and pulling me to a stop just before we reach the entrance. "That must be where the queen is holed up."

I release Archer's hand and drift forward, using the glow from the eggs to scan the rest of the space.

Where are you, Theo?

Archer reaches for me again, but I slip past him and continue toward the glowing chamber, moving as if drawn by some unknown force. In my search for clues about Theo's whereabouts, I catch a glimpse of something familiar beyond the eggs, tucked into the shadows on the inner walls of the chamber, and fight against my rising panic to take a breath.

"People." I snap my head toward Archer. I can barely make out his features in the low light, but I can plainly see my own horror reflected in his eyes. "They have people in there."

The buzzing in my head intensifies as blood rushes through my veins like a swarm of angry bees, stinging every inch of me along its path. I can't move, can't tear my eyes away from the bodies displayed across the wall like produce in some sort of gruesome farmer's market.

With Archer's body heat warming my side, I scan the faces, searching for anything recognizable. I don't know if I'm hoping I'll find someone I know or praying I don't. *Are you here, Theo?*

A whisper of movement in my peripheral vision draws my attention to a man about my father's age. Even from several yards away, the decades' worth of smiles etched across his dirty face are clearly visible. He doesn't look dead. If I didn't know better, I might be convinced he was only sleeping.

The man's eyes flutter, and I jerk back, bumping into Archer as a jolt of horror zips down my spine.

"They're alive!" The words come out on a whimper as I struggle to take a breath with my heart thrumming wildly at the base of my throat.

"Don't go losing your composure now, Evie." Always the voice of reason, Coach pulls me back from the brink.

Without stopping to formulate a plan, I tighten my grip on my saber and press forward, determined to reach the stranger, as if I can somehow save them all before it's too late.

I don't get far before Archer yanks on my hand, dragging me away from the entrance.

He leans in, and his lips brush my ear. "We need to get out of here."

"No!" My voice cracks like a sheet blowing in the wind. Tearing my attention from the glowing chamber, I lock my gaze on Archer's. "We can't leave them."

He tucks his bow under his arm and takes my face in both hands, imploring me with his eyes. "We can't help all of them, not by ourselves, and not without backup."

"Please." I know he's right. Leaving would be the smart decision. But I gave up on being smart a long time ago. I can't turn my back on those people—not if even one is still alive. "We have to try."

Archer curses under his breath. "Fine, but don't forget your promise."

"Yeah, yeah." I nod. "If things go south, we run." The lie doesn't taste any better the second time.

Archer switches off the flashlight and hooks it to his belt loop before nudging ahead of me. "Stay close."

He grabs my hand, and we creep toward the entrance again, sticking as close to the shadows as possible. Just before we cross the earthen threshold, Archer freezes, blocking my view inside. Riveted on the people within, he doesn't move—doesn't even breathe—for several long seconds.

"What?" The word comes out on a breath.

He tries to shove me backward, but I plant my feet, determined to see our task through.

"Archer?" Anxious for a response, I squeeze his arm, my fingers digging almost painfully into his hard flesh. "What is it?"

He turns his head, his eyes finding mine in the dim light. "There's a little boy."

The whispered words slice through me like a hot blade. "Theo?"

Archer palms the back of his neck, his expression unreadable.

He never met the boy—I only barely knew him myself—so based on my sparse description, there's no way he can know for certain. "Maybe it's not him."

The desperation in his eyes tells me everything I need to know. Acting purely on instinct, I grip the hilt of my saber and push past him, striding through the entrance like the avenging angel Theo's mom believed me to be.

The instant I cross the threshold, my steps falter. The domed chamber is far larger than it looked from outside. Rows of glowing eggs fill the center, and on every inch of the packed-clay walls...

Air wheezes in and out of my lungs as I dart my gaze around the room, taking in the surreal surroundings. *Bodies... everywhere.* Men, women, kids, half-buried and suspended in the hardened earth like Han Solo in carbonite.

"Snap out of it, kid!" Coach shouts in my head.

Licking my dry lips, I try to catch my breath as my eyes land on the small body of a young boy. Even covered in a thin layer of dirt, I recognize his thick dark curls and the long lashes resting across his brown cheeks.

"Theo..." His name tumbles out on a breath, and the boy's eyes snap open in response.

He coughs, and his lips move as if to speak, but no sound comes out.

With Archer breathing heavily behind me, I hurry to Theo's side. "Shh."

A single tear streaks down the boy's dirty cheek. "Angel?"

"It's okay, honey, I'm gonna get you down from there."

"You need to hurry." Archer whispers the obvious, his frame rigid as he steps around the eggs and scans the shadows. He nocks an arrow, keeping watch as I work my fingers into the compressed earth.

"I know." I frantically claw at the dried clay and dirt holding Theo captive, barely slowing as I break several nails in the process.

Our presence doesn't go unnoticed for long, and as others around us awaken, the odds of getting out of here in one piece get trickier.

"Please!" a young woman a few yards away cries out. Dark-blond hair clings to her emaciated face and neck in greasy strings, and her thready voice trembles as she pleads with Archer. "Help me! Before it comes back."

"Shh." Archer abandons his post to sink his fingers into the dirt around her, digging a trench around her slight frame. "They'll hear you."

"What about the rest of us?" The man I first noticed chokes out a plea of his own. Up close, his sunken eyes and hollow cheeks are more apparent. He looks as if he's been trapped here for weeks. "You can't leave us here to rot like garbage!"

Still working to dig Theo free, I whip my head toward Archer. He doesn't say it, but I can read the fear in his eyes. *These people are going to get us killed.*

A loud shriek ruptures the air, forcing me to stop digging and press my hands to my ears. With the sound still echoing through the surrounding caverns, I go back to work. My heart pounds out a rapid staccato as I fight the urge to run, almost more terrified to stop until I've freed Theo from the wall.

I manage to loosen his left arm, and he uses it to help free the right while I dig out his legs.

"We need to go," Archer whispers as he finishes unshackling the young woman.

She stumbles several times before fleeing down the closest tunnel.

"Don't leave us!" The man repeats his plea, louder this time.

Another shriek—this one closer—pierces my eardrums and turns my bones to jelly.

"We'll come back," Archer promises as he guides me and Theo toward the exit.

We don't get far before the biggest alien I've ever seen emerges from the tunnel farthest from us, filling the domed space with her sickly gray complexion like a vision straight from my nightmares. Her milky-white eyes land on me, and my blood turns to ice. *The queen.*

"Holy..." My words dry up before I can get them out.

"Slayer, go." Archer pushes me away from him. "Run! I'm right behind you."

"Forget it." Squeezing the hilt of the saber in a death grip, I wrap my other arm around Theo as we back toward the tunnel we came from. "I'm not leaving you!"

"None of us will be getting out if I don't slow her down." Positioning himself between me and the queen, Archer nocks an arrow, throwing a glance over his shoulder as she gains on us. "You promised."

"So did you." Pushing Theo behind me, I stand my ground, defiantly refusing to leave Archer behind. "You stay, I stay."

Promise or no promise, I'm not leaving him.

Archer holds my gaze. "Eve, please."

My heart skips as my name tumbles past his lips.

"How did you...?"

"Know your name?" He flashes a sad smile. "Thor told me."

"That's not fair," I mutter. "He didn't tell me yours."

"Ask me later, okay?" Archer leans in and steals a quick kiss. "Now go!"

"No!" I snap. "We go together or not at all."

With one last smile, he rushes toward the queen. "Get the kid out!"

Damn it! I want to throttle him for insisting on playing the hero, but I know he's right. Theo needs me right now. "I'm coming back for you!"

"I'm counting on it!" he shouts then disappears into the shadows.

Chapter 18

Inside the Honeycomb

Despite the pressure of Theo's small hand in mine, I struggle to get my feet to cooperate. Every fiber of my being recoils at the thought of leaving Archer behind. For half a second, I consider turning back. Together, we might actually have a chance to take down the queen. *Stubborn fucking...*

"Are we gonna die?" Theo's reedy voice reminds me why I abandoned Archer to begin with.

"No way." I squeeze his delicate hand and pick up the pace. "Not on my watch, kiddo."

"Okay," he croaks, sounding weaker than he did when I first found him.

How long has it been since he's had food... or water? I don't even want to think about what the aliens may have done to him in that time—or why they kept him alive for so long.

An earsplitting shriek from deep within the cavern sends my pulse into overdrive, and I remember what Thor said. The queen's calling for backup, and if we're still in the tunnel when it gets here...

"Move your butt, Evie!" Coach's phantom voice growls in my ear.

With a scream lodged in my windpipe, I grip Theo's hand as tightly as I dare, dragging him through the dark tunnel.

"Are they chasing us?" Theo's voice cracks.

The sound pierces my bruised heart, dislodging the lump in my throat and knocking the cobwebs from my brain. It's a logical question. And he's right. If they aren't chasing us yet, they will be.

"Do you think you can run?"

Theo nods his little head, but instead of waiting for him to follow through, I lift him off the ground and sprint toward the pinprick of moonlight coming from the exit in the distance.

Far behind us, the queen continues to shriek, and I can only hope that means Archer is still alive. *For now.*

We burst through the opening, and I keep running until we reach the edge of the forest. Once we make it to the hollowed-out root cavity Archer and I hid in earlier, I lower Theo into the hole and rest both hands on my knees to catch my breath.

"Fuuuck!" Frustration breaks through my weak attempt to stay calm. My thoughts race as I try to come up with a plan. Torn between staying with Theo and going back for Archer, I pace over the hard ground.

"Don't even think about it, Evie," Coach warns. *"He's just a kid."*

"I know that!" I shout back as my loose grasp on reality cracks down the middle.

I lost everyone I ever loved, then I met Archer. I can't lose him, too, not when I'm *right here*. There has to be a way to rescue them both. I stop pacing and stare down at the little boy who's driven every decision I've made over the past several days. Surely, he would be safe here while I went back and rescued Archer... *wouldn't he?*

Theo's eyes widen as if he can hear my unspoken thoughts. "You're going back?"

"What?"

"You said you're going back."

A breath catches in my throat. "I did?"

He bobs his head several times, and the fear in his eyes pierces my broken heart.

I hop into the hole and crouch at his feet. "I won't leave you."

"Will he die if you don't go back?"

I choke back a sob, doing my best to maintain my composure when all I want to do is break. "He might."

Theo lowers his eyes and nods once. "My mama died."

"Oh, Theo." Tears spring to my eyes as I think of Andrea's fierce determination to protect her son, and I open my arms. "I'm so sorry."

He falls into my embrace and rests his cheek on my shoulder. "I don't want your friend to die too."

"I don't want him to die either. But I can't leave you alone out here. As soon as it's light, I'll take you to the building with our friends. Then I can go back for Archer."

"I wish we could light up the whole forest," he whispers, and his warm breath fans across my neck. "Then you could go now."

"Oh, honey. I wish I could, too, but that's not—" The conversation Archer and I had about coming back with torches flashes through my thoughts.

Theo lifts his head, and his dark eyes probe mine.

"Maybe it's not impossible after all." I pat my jacket pocket, feeling for the lighter inside. I have the means to make fire. All I need now is a way to keep the flame from going out before I get to Archer.

Wishing I'd paid better attention when Dad tried to teach us survival skills on our trips to the mountains, I jump to my feet and climb out of the hole to find something I can use as a torch. It may be a long shot, but it's the only idea I have right now. The notion that it may already be too late pushes its way to the surface, and I shove it back down. I've already lost enough precious time. I don't have any to spare on negative thoughts.

While I scramble to find a suitable handle, Theo crawls out of the hole.

He staggers to my side, reminding me of his fragile state. "What are you doing?"

"Looking for a stick." Thinking of the tiki torches the frat house used to set up on the lawn, I find a low tree branch no thicker than a broom handle and snap it off at the base, leaving me a piece a little longer than my arm.

"What are you gonna do with it?" Theo picks at a glob of dried pitch oozing from a notch in an adjacent pine tree.

"I'm making a torch." I scan the forest floor for anything that might serve as the flaming head.

He pauses to watch me collect a wad of tangled brush then goes back to collecting sap from the tree. "You ever made one before?"

"No."

"Then how do you know how to do it?"

His barrage of questions reminds me of my little brother, and I exhale in a gust. "I'm basically guessing."

He nods but doesn't look up from his task.

I abandon my brush pile to watch him. "What are *you* doing?"

"Helping you make your torch."

"*You* ever made one before?" I toss the question back at him as he finishes with the tree and marches toward me, both hands filled with resin.

"Mm-hmm." He nods and holds out his hands. "Lots of times."

Gaping at him, I reluctantly open my palm for him. "Why didn't you say so?"

He shrugs, dumping the sticky goo into my outstretched hand before walking over to a sapling barely taller than me. Grabbing a limb almost twice as thick as mine, he bends it back and forth until he's able to wrench it from the main trunk. Then he yanks a length of dried vine from the base of the mangled tree beside it and brings them both to me, laying them at my feet. "You didn't ask."

"Well, I'm asking now." I glance down at the limb. "What's wrong with the stick I found?"

"You need a piece of green wood for a handle. Otherwise, the fire's gonna spread all the way to the end and burn you."

"And this?" I settle my gaze on the handful of pine resin he handed me. "What am I supposed to do with this stuff?"

Theo smiles. "It burns for a really long time, longer if you tear up old rags and soak them in it. You wrap the vine around everything to hold it tight while it burns."

My mouth drops open again. "You really *have* done this before."

"Mm-hmm." He bobs his head a few times. "Mama used to make torches and lamps, and she even used the sticky stuff on cuts. She said pine sap is good for lots of things."

"This is good, Theo. Really good." An idea sparks to life as I glance at the sticky sap in my hand. "Can you find me some more of this?"

He nods vigorously, his eyes glistening in the moonlight.

"And can you show me how to make one of your mama's torches?"

"Sure." He scoops up the items he collected. "We just need to find some old rags."

I glance down at Bonnie's skintight black tank. The skimpy top wouldn't burn long enough to make it to the cave, let alone all the way to the queen's chamber. "I don't have anything to use as rags."

Theo glances at the dirty Iron Man T-shirt hanging off his slight frame. "You can use my shirt. Mama said T-shirts make the best torches."

Following Theo's detailed instructions, I split the end of the sapling limb into four sections with my saber while he collects pine cones from the forest floor, using the front of his shirt as a pouch.

"How many do you want?" he whispers, as if he fully understands the danger we're in.

I glance at his growing collection, and my eyes blur as I imagine everything he's been through since before we met. *Of course he knows.*

"As many as you can find. But hurry." Time is of the essence, and I can't forget we're standing out in the open after dark.

Theo nods and goes back to collecting pine cones, meticulously rolling each one in the thick resin oozing from the towering pine until every surface is completely coated in the sticky substance.

A distant shriek fills the sky, and we both freeze. The unearthly sound turns my blood to ice.

"Go!" I nudge him toward the uprooted tree. The alien isn't close, but that could change with little warning.

Without missing a beat, Theo drops the pine cones and bolts for the cavity, sliding down the side and shrinking into the shadows as if he's done this a dozen times already. As soon as I know he's safe, I quickly sheathe my saber and slip off my jacket, using it to collect our supplies before joining him in the hole. We huddle together for several minutes, the hair on the back of my neck standing on end as I listen for movement in the forest.

When nothing out of the ordinary catches my attention, I fish the red BIC lighter from my pocket and wait for my heart to slow to a normal rhythm again while reworking the dangerous plan in my head.

"Suicide mission, you mean!" Coach's disembodied voice growls in my ear.

Shut it, Coach.

Brushing off the nagging doubts, I tuck the lighter into my jeans and dump the pine cones at my feet, offering the jacket to Theo. He quickly tugs the Iron Man T-shirt over his head and hands it to me before shoving his arms into the oversized sleeves of my jacket.

He blinks up at me, black leather hanging off his slight frame, nearly swallowing him whole. "It's a little big."

"Just a little." I ruffle his tight curls before using my saber to slice his shirt down the middle then tear it into several wide strips.

Working side by side in the dirt hole, we coat each piece of fabric in the leftover resin Theo collected in his dirty socks. Once we finish, I loosely wrap a cloth strip around a fat, sap-covered pine cone to create a thick ball and pry open the split end of the stick to shove it between the prongs. Theo tucks the rest of the slathered pine cones into his socks while I fashion a primitive bandolier using a length of vine, lashing the strips of coated fabric and pine-cone-filled socks across my chest with trembling hands.

"Are you scared?" Theo's reedy voice doesn't waver.

His question takes me off guard, and I concentrate on each breath to keep from panicking. "Almost always."

He gives a resolute nod as if I just confirmed his suspicions. "That's because you're brave."

"Trust me, I'm not brave." I clench my stomach, holding back the overwhelming urge to vomit from the near-paralyzing fear coursing through my veins, and a dark chuckle rolls up my throat. "Most of the time, I'm absolutely terrified."

Theo grabs my hand and squeezes. "Mama said it isn't brave if you're not scared."

I crouch beside him and wrap my arms around his tiny body. "Your mama was a smart lady."

He sniffles a few times, nodding into my shoulder.

"Listen, Theo." I release him to cup his cheeks, locking my gaze on his. "You stay in this hole until I come back, okay?"

His head twitches against my grip.

"Don't come out for anyone but me or Archer. You understand?" I lower my hands and wait for him to nod.

"What if you don't come back?"

"I'm coming back." I drag a finger across my chest and back again. "Cross my heart."

The words *I promise* get caught in my throat. *How can I make that promise when there's a very real risk of me breaking it?*

"But if I'm not here by morning, you wait for the sun to climb above the trees, then you run." I point toward the path that leads back to the school. "Cut through the woods and don't stop running until you get to the building. My friends will take care of you until I get back."

"'Kay."

"Stay hidden." I stand and pat the front of my leggings to make sure the lighter is still there.

"I will." He steps back, and the shadows engulf him. "Go save your friend."

Theo's unwavering faith nearly takes my legs out from under me, and it's all I can do to climb out of the hole.

"You heard the kid. Go save your friend."

On my way, Coach.

With my saber in one hand and the primitive torch in the other, I take off running through the dark forest. As I weave my way toward the tunnel carved into the hillside, I work through my shitty plan until I almost believe it has half a chance.

It has to work.

The claw prints marking the hidden entrance to the cave are gone, replaced by Theo's and mine—and Archer's. Just seeing evidence of his existence gives me something to cling to as I fish the lighter from my pocket.

Please, God, let Archer be okay. Please let him be alive.

I repeat the plea over and over in my head as I spark the lighter and bring the tiny flame to the head of the torch. With a whoosh, the pine resin catches, and the fabric-wrapped pine cone erupts in a fiery ball. Orange flames do a primal dance in front of me, scorching the air and giving me the confidence to stride into the shadows.

"Okay, you bastards. I'm bringing the fight to you this time."

Chapter 19

Fire on the Mountain

"Move your ass, Evie!" Coach bellowed across the field, his gruff voice chasing me up the bleachers like a wraith. "Come on! You're not even trying!"

"Easy for *you* to say," I grumbled under my breath, careful not to complain loud enough for him, or anyone else, to hear me.

"You call yourself a captain? My ninety-year-old mother can run faster than that!" he shouted, using his bright-yellow bullhorn to make sure I didn't miss a single syllable.

Spurred on by his harsh words, I took the stadium steps two at a time, leaving the rest of the squad behind as I led the race to the top. My muscles cramped and burned with every step, my heart threatening to claw its way out of my throat as the president's box loomed in front of me.

"You need me to come up there and show you how it's done?" His taunt chased me to the top.

"Ha! I'd love to see you try!" I called back, using my last precious breath before reaching the top rail with a victory lunge and a fist thrust skyward.

"Okay, okay." He chuckled, serenading me with a slow golf clap. "Come on back, show-off."

I choked out a strangled laugh before spinning on my heels and jogging back the way I came, passing my sweaty teammates on the way down.

They knew as well as I did that Coach was all bluster. But the man sure knew how to light a fire under our asses when we needed an extra push.

"Where are you now, old man?" I mutter as I follow the winding tunnel deeper into the earth, holding the flaming torch in front of me like the hand of God lighting my way.

"Right where you need me." Coach's voice ghosts through my head, and I fully lean into the false sense that I'm not alone out here.

As if signaling its agreement, the billowing flame whooshes in the stagnant air, and the bitter stench of creosote clogs my throat. The deeper I descend into the aliens' nest, the harder it is to fill my lungs. *I must be getting close.*

Conflicting emotions, ranging from fear to impatience, sweep through me, and I run through my crazy plan again, mentally calculating how long I have to get Archer out before all hell breaks loose. When the queen figures out what I have up my sleeve, she isn't going to be happy with me.

Hold on, Archer. My pulse quickens as I imagine him in her chamber, pressed into the wall like the rest of them, and the accompanying rush of dread drives me to pick up my pace. *I'm almost there.*

As I get closer, I coil a fresh strip of resin-coated cloth around the end of my torch, and the flame springs to life with a muffled roar, lighting the tunnel like a summer sunrise and setting off a flurry of activity in the nearby chamber. The closer I get to the nucleus, the more frantic the rats in the walls become. The clawing and squealing almost seem to echo down the several other passageways leading to the glowing eggs.

My muscles lock tight as the realization hits me. *Jesus.* Those aren't rats. That's something far worse. And all things considered, I'd much rather take on an army of rodents.

With one last deep breath and a quick prayer, I breach the opening to the chamber, holding out my flaming stick like a talisman. *This had better work.*

As I step inside, the voices all hit me at once, begging and pleading for me to set them free.

"Eyes on the ball, Evie."

With my heart in my throat, I block them out. No matter how much I want to help them, I can't afford to get distracted now. Concentrating on the task at hand, I sweep the flame in front of me. Fire burns across my vision, leaving orange spots in its wake, as I dart my gaze from one contorted face to another, searching for the one that makes my heart flutter.

Where is he? The beginnings of a panic attack build, spreading to the tips of my extremities like current sparking through a live wire. The flame dances with every wild blast of breath hitting it. *Did I miscalculate? Did she take him somewhere else?*

"Took you long enough." His familiar voice cracks, and my heart cracks right along with it.

I spin toward the sound, bringing the fiery trail with me. "Archer!"

"You don't do things halfway, do you, slayer?" His weak chuckle dissolves into a dry cough as he struggles against the packed clay holding him hostage in the wall. "Can you give me a hand?"

Without missing a beat, I rush to his side and use the hilt of my saber like a spade to dig him free.

"I wasn't sure you'd come back."

My eyes snap to his. "That's a stupid thing to say. I told you I would."

"That, you did." His smile falters, his eyes glossing over with emotion. "Thank you."

"Don't thank me yet." Shooting a nervous glance behind me at the darkened tunnel the queen emerged from last time, I manage to loosen the dirt trapping his right arm, and he works his hand free to help me unfetter the left.

"What about *them*?" he whispers, nodding toward the handful of conscious people pleading for us to help them.

"We need to at least try to get them out before..." Another jolt of dread stabs my belly as the reality of what I'm about to do sinks in. Without finishing the thought, I rush to the closest person—the man who begged me to help him earlier—and sink the dull end of my saber into the earth holding him hostage.

"Hurry!" the man croaks. "Go faster!"

"Can you move your fingers?"

He nods, and the dried clay surrounding his hand begins to crumble. I keep digging just long enough for him to jerk his arm free before moving to the young woman beside him, while Archer works his way through the people on the opposite side. As I sink my hand into the wall alongside her, the woman starts to sob, her entire body trembling from the effort.

"I don't want to die," she cries.

"I'm not going to let that happen," I lie. I know we can't save them all, but I'm doing everything I can to give as many as possible a fighting chance.

The wall gives way beneath her, and she slides to the earthen floor in a heap. As I help her to her feet, she wraps her frail arms around me in a weak hug. "Thank—"

A bloodcurdling shriek cuts her off, draining what's left of the color from her cheeks.

"Go!" I shove her toward the exit, waving the others we freed to go with her. "Hurry! Run!"

The floor trembles, and the scratching in the walls intensifies as something large and heavy moves through the closest artery. Abandoning the rescue mission, with several people still caught in limbo, I shove the torch into Archer's hand and yank the vine bandolier from around my body, quickly pulling the resin pine cones from the socks and positioning them around the alien eggs.

Archer collects his bow from the ground and reaches for me. "We need to get out of here!"

"Not yet." Ignoring his outstretched hand, I continue setting up my pyrotechnic show, winding the length of vine around the pine cones, creating a long fuse. After making sure the vine is attached to each one, I tie the sticky sock to the closest end.

Another tremor rocks the cavern, and loose dirt rains down on us as the queen bursts through the opening, mouth stretched wide in another bone-melting shriek.

Archer wraps his fingers around my upper arm, gently tugging me away. "Damn it, Eve!"

"Just a second!" I wrench my arm free, grabbing the torch from his hand and bringing the business end to the pitch-soaked sock. It catches instantly, and the flames roar down the vine, igniting each pine cone with a loud pop, like a Fourth of July finale gone very wrong.

The queen's head whips toward the inferno just as the flames engulf the first of her eggs. Her frantic screams fill the cavern, and the furious scratching in the walls turns my blood to ice.

"Okay!" I bellow over the noise. "Now we can get out of here."

The alien queen's shrieks chase me down the tunnel, and a wave of nausea spreads through me like pervasive vines twisting their thorny tendrils around my insides. Instead of Coach's ghostly voice shouting in my brain, the racing of my own heart echoes through my skull like pounding hooves. The sound propels me faster as I dart through the cavern, refusing to look back, refusing to even consider the phantom cries of the nameless, faceless people I couldn't save. The only life I allow myself to consider is the man running just a few steps behind me, the man I risked everything to rescue.

I glance at Archer as I wrap another resin-coated strip of Theo's shirt around the dimming torch, and the flame swells to life again.

"Go!" he shouts over the roar of the fire, nudging me toward the streaks of moonlight streaming in from the outside.

The closer we get to the exit, the more intense the mysterious scratching in the walls becomes. The sound seems to radiate from every direction until it completely surrounds us.

"What *is* that?" Archer asks.

"Nothing good," I mutter as we reach the narrow opening.

We slip through the jagged crack in the hillside as the first of the creatures bursts through the earthen walls, landing in the tunnel behind us with a high-pitched squeal.

"What the *fuck*?" I come to a stumbling halt, spinning toward the sound as the monster lunges at us.

Loose dirt crumbles away from the tunnel walls as more of the creatures emerge, raining down like hellish gremlins. The sickly gray monsters look like a science experiment gone wrong—a horrific combination of hairless opossums and rabid scorpions, with their tails arching over their bony heads like daggers.

My hands tremble as I grab one of the remaining strips of cloth, ball it up, and skewer it like a kebab with the business end of my saber before lighting it on fire and lobbing it through the opening. If they make it out of the tunnel, they'll surround us, and we won't stand a chance.

The creatures let out a high-pitched wail and scramble away from the flaming ball.

"It works!" I cry. "They're afraid of fire!"

"Hand me one of those," Archer barks as he grabs a dead branch from the ground.

He takes the strip from my hand and wraps it around the limb, using my torch to light it before hurling it toward the mouth of the tunnel.

Following his lead, I dump the rest of the resin strips into a pile of dried brush just outside the tunnel's entrance and set it all on fire.

"Let's go." Archer grabs my hand, dragging me away from the wall of flame separating us from the monsters.

We take off running, stumbling over exposed roots and loose rocks as we hurry toward the clearing. The farther we get from the tunnel, the more the sounds of the forest drown out the aliens' cries. Drained and exhausted, we slow our escape, stopping to catch our breath at the edge of the forest.

"What the hell were those things?" I pant, dropping the spent torch and collapsing against the massive trunk of a giant tree.

Instead of responding to my question, Archer marches toward me and grabs both sides of my face with trembling hands. "You came back for me."

My eyes sting as I gaze up at him through a blur of tears. "Of course I did. The plan didn't go off exactly as I intended, but—"

He closes his mouth over mine, drinking me in like his first sip of water in days. Pressing my back against the rough bark, Archer draws every drop of unspoken emotion from my lips as his mouth makes love to mine.

Time grinds to a standstill as we devour each other under the canopy of trees. His fingers clumsily slide through my tangled locks, catching every knot in my wild mess of hair as I slip a shaky hand under the hem of his dirty shirt, exploring the grooves in his tense muscles, both of us all but oblivious to the threat of danger still looming in the forest.

After kissing me dizzy, Archer rests his forehead against mine, his hot breath washing over me in bursts. "Thank you. For coming back. The kid was right. You are an angel."

"Theo!" I whip my head toward the orange streaks marking the horizon just past the tree line. "I left him out here."

Archer follows my gaze, and his spine stiffens. "Where?"

"The root ball. Where we hid earlier."

"Come on." He takes my hand, towing me cautiously toward where I left Theo.

When we reach the hollowed-out root cavity, we find Theo curled into a ball, asleep inside my leather jacket.

I hop into the hole and lightly shake his shoulder. "Hey, kiddo," I whisper. "I'm back."

Theo jerks awake, his eyes stretching wide as he notices me. "Angel!" He sits up and wraps his slender arms around me, squeezing the breath from my lungs. "You came back!"

"I promised I would." I blink back the threat of tears yet again.

Theo glances at Archer standing on the rim of the hole. "You did it! You saved him!"

"He helped a little." I wink at Archer.

"Don't let her fool you." A smiling Archer hops into the hole with us. "She did it all by herself."

Theo grins, his eyes sparkling in the pale light of the impending dawn. "I helped with the torches."

Chapter 20

Love in the Time of Aliens

<hr>

By the time the sun finally crests over the horizon, the baleful cries emanating from the alien colony in the distance die down, replaced by the low hum of the forest coming to life. Between the deafening chorus of cicadas buzzing in the trees, the joyful chirps of morning birds, and busy squirrels scurrying from limb to limb on a never-ending quest for acorns, it seems as if life somehow went back to normal in the span of a few minutes. My heart slowly returns to an easy rhythm for the first time in hours thanks to the welcome respite from near-constant danger, but I can't quite let go of the tension holding my muscles hostage.

Not until we reach the safety of the group.

"Are you up for the walk back?" I direct my question to Archer, but before he can answer, Theo succumbs to a coughing fit. "You okay, sweetie?"

His tiny shoulders quake with the force of his hacking, but he nods his head as if this sort of thing happens all the time.

Archer glances from Theo's sunken eyes to his bare feet and holds out a hand. "How 'bout a ride?"

Theo nods, and Archer hoists the boy onto his shoulders as if he weighs nothing. If not for the pained grimace, I might believe the unspoken lie.

"Let me carry him." I adjust the saber across my back and reach for Theo. "You're hurt."

Archer shakes his head and presses out a stiff smile. "I'm fine."

He doesn't mention what happened in the queen's chamber, what she did to him after I left him behind, and by his closed-off expression, it doesn't look like he's going to anytime soon.

He leans in, bringing his lips close to my ear. "But the kid needs to be checked out. Who knows how long he went without food or water?"

I nod, and we set off on the long walk back to the school.

As we trudge through the brambles and thick underbrush, Archer finds little ways to maintain contact along the way, from skating his fingers across my wrist as we step over a rotting log to brushing his shoulders against mine as we hike down the hillside. We finally break through the tree line into the clearing, and I let go of the stranglehold on my lungs, releasing a breath in a loud whoosh.

"We made it."

Archer hooks his pinky with mine and presses a quick kiss to my temple. "Never thought I'd be this excited for a locker room shower."

His heated sidelong glance sends a ripple from the top of my head to the tip of my toes.

"Come on." A low groan rumbles up his throat. "We're almost there."

Raptor meets us at the front door as if he sensed we were coming. He gives Theo a once-over as Archer lowers the kid to the ground then goes in for a one-armed guy hug, slapping a cloud of dust from Archer's back. "Damn, Arch. You take a dirt nap out there?"

"Close." Archer lets out a dark chuckle.

"So what's the word? Did you find the colony? How many of those bastards are there? Did Thor's crazy theory about the ants hold water?" Raptor peppers us with questions, eager for information.

Archer holds up his hands. "One thing at a—"

"Not now." I grip Archer's forearm, steering him toward the makeshift infirmary. "We'll fill you in later," I say to Raptor before turning back to Archer. "Theo's not the only one who needs to be checked out."

"Hey." Archer tips my chin to give me another look that makes my heart race. "I'll be fine as soon as I wash the funk off."

I give him a shaky nod, tingles rushing over my skin where he touches me.

Callie isn't in the infirmary when we get there, but we find Winnie lying on one of the cots with a damp cloth across her forehead.

Concern for the girl I'd only just met takes me by surprise. "Winnie? Are you okay? Is something wrong with the baby?"

Winnie's eyes flutter open, and she blinks up at us a few times. "Nothing being born won't cure." When I don't respond quickly enough, she pushes herself upright with a laugh. "I'm just tired of being pregnant is all." Her attention darts to Theo, a smile lighting her face. "Who's this?"

"This is Theo." I run a hand over his curls. "I've been looking for him for a few days, and I finally found him."

"Nice to meet you, Theo." Winnie's brow wrinkles, and her eyes shift to mine. "He hurt?"

"I'm not sure." I raise my shoulder in a half shrug. "We brought him here for Callie to take a look. He definitely needs water and probably something to eat."

"I'd say a bath wouldn't hurt either." Winnie glances at Archer. "You could use a good scrubbing yourself." She smiles at Theo again. "How about we let these two get cleaned up, and I take you to find something to eat? I happen to know the cafeteria has a pot of Spaghetti-Os with the little hot dogs in them. Would you like some?"

Theo slides his eyes in my direction. "I-I don't really like hot dogs."

"You can pick 'em out." Winnie chuckles as she leads Theo through the door. Before following him out, she turns back to me.

"I'll make sure Callie gives the kid a once-over. You take Archer somewhere and clean his damn wounds before they fester."

"I'm fine!" he calls after her.

"Sure you are!" Her laughter echoes down the hall long after she's turned the corner.

"Come on." He shakes his head. "I guess you'd better do as the lady said. Don't want anything to fester."

We wander the mazelike halls all the way back to the gym. My stomach tightens at the familiar stench of sweat and mildew as we step into the locker room. I can't help but remember what almost happened the last time we were in here. Archer turns on the taps, and without a word, we peel off our dirty clothes and step under the cold spray as if we'd been naked together a hundred times before.

Unlike the last time we showered together, Archer is all business, wincing as he washes away the grime and dried blood.

"Does it hurt?" My voice comes out in a faint whisper as I study the numerous cuts and abrasions dotting his skin.

His hand freezes in the center of his chest, and his eyes lock on mine. "Not too much."

The air between us vibrates with sexual tension as we gaze at each other across the stream. He hasn't even touched me yet, but his slow perusal caresses every inch of me as if his hands were doing all the work.

"Eve." Archer's voice breaks on my name. He pulls in a sharp breath, stepping toward me until our breath mingles.

Cold water washes over us, but his warmth sends a burst of heat through me.

"I was afraid I wouldn't make it back in time. I couldn't stop imagining all the horrible things they'd—" The thought catches in my throat, threatening to choke me.

He skims the backs of his fingers along my jaw. "When you first left, I fought as long as I could, but she—*the queen*—must be venomous. I drifted in and out of consciousness. Lost my motor skills. My muscles wouldn't cooperate. My eyes wouldn't stay open. I hallucinated things I knew couldn't be real. When I came to, I was trapped in the wall." His eyes shimmer.

I cup his cheek. "You're safe now."

"Thanks to you." Archer takes my face in both hands and slowly brings his lips to mine, kissing me as if I were made of glass. As if I were the one who got hurt, not the other way around.

"I won't break," I whisper, gliding my hand from his cheek to the side of his neck.

His pulse races beneath my fingertips as he pulls away, eyes darting between mine. "The last time we stood in this spot, I made you a promise."

The electricity between us sends a violent shudder through me. With my heart pounding so loud I'm sure he can hear it, I dart my gaze to his growing hardness then back to his face.

Archer twists off the taps, licking water from his lips. "Is that still what you want?"

"*Yes...*" The word comes out on a groan, and I close my eyes as my face goes up in flames. I don't dare voice how fucking much I still want him for fear of sounding desperate and needy. But I am. Both desperate and needy for him.

Breathing heavily, Archer takes another step forward. He wraps his arms around me, tucking me under his chin and holding me tight against his bare skin. "Thank God."

He brushes a lock of hair from my face and dips his head to kiss me, but his lips never make contact, as if he's waiting for an engraved invitation. My breasts tighten, my nipples pebbling with anticipation as I meet him in the middle, bringing my mouth to his with a ferocity that nearly takes my legs out from under me.

My pulse skips erratically as his warm tongue slips between my parted lips, delving into my mouth to explore the heat within. I loop my arms around his neck and arch into him, crushing my breasts to his hard chest. Even with nothing between us, I can't get close enough.

His length twitches against my hip and my stomach bottoms out, a flash of heat dancing down my spine.

With a low groan, he tears his mouth away, his breath coming out in shaky blasts as he rests his forehead against mine. "Tell me what you want, Eve. I'm at your mercy."

"You." I lock my gaze on his. "All I want is you."

Archer claims my lips again, kissing me with all the urgency and desperation of a man barely hanging by a thread. A man who faced down *death* mere hours ago.

God, I almost lost him today. The thought nearly paralyzes me. It shouldn't be possible to care so deeply for someone I just met, but I do.

As if he can read every thought running through my mind, his kisses become frantic. As if this may be the last chance we'll ever have. He skates his hands down my back to palm my ass and lifts me off the floor.

I wrap my legs around his waist, locking my ankles and cradling his length between my thighs. Heat pools low in my belly, and I rock my hips against him, seeking friction. I've never wanted anything more than I want this with him.

"*Archer*... please don't make me beg."

His eyes flare an instant before my back hits the tile wall. Using his hips to pin me in place, he slips a hand between us to explore my slick core. His wicked tongue invades my mouth again and again, matching each stroke of his fingers until bursts of pleasure spike through me.

My legs tremble, each shallow breath coming out in a staccato blast as the coil of need wrapping around my insides tightens to the breaking point. Sounds I've never made before come tumbling past my lips as he brings me closer and closer to nirvana.

The rough sound crawling up his throat sets my core on fire. "Damn it, slayer."

Without breaking the kiss, we stumble from the shower to the locker room. With me still wrapped around him, Archer drops onto a wooden bench, his lips gliding down my neck as he frantically reaches for something behind us. The sound of paper tearing reaches my ears, and he lifts me long enough to roll the condom over his length before impaling me on every hard inch.

I gasp at the invasion as my body stretches to accommodate him. "Are you all right?"

"Better than all right," I purr as we find our rhythm and shock turns into pleasure.

"You feel so good." His breath is hot against my lips as he guides my hips, his fingers digging into my curves as he pulls me down to meet every thrust. "I could live inside you."

Curling my fingers around his corded shoulders, I cling to him as he drives me higher and higher, filling what had been an empty void inside me. My lips seek his again, desperate to breathe him in... to feel him everywhere and merge his soul with mine.

He swivels his hips, and the delicious knot building inside of me flares until every coiled strand of pleasure detonates at once, and Archer swallows my cry as I shatter.

━━━●━━━

Tingles rush through my veins as each delicious memory floods back to me. My heart flutters wildly as I replay every frantic kiss, and warmth spreads through my liquid limbs as if I'm there again. I shift my hips against the pile of gym mats and threadbare towels Archer pulled from the equipment room shelves to create our love nest—where frenzied touching morphed into unhurried exploration and unspoken promises. *So* much kissing and caressing.

So many condoms.

Simultaneously fatigued and sated, I wake to the sound of Archer's slow, even breathing and the steady thrum of his heart beneath my ear. As we lie in the darkness, the rest of the world fades away, and for a fraction of a second, my life is normal again. Even if only for an instant, I pretend I don't have the world on my shoulders, pretend we're just a couple of kids falling in love. And I've never felt safer than I do wrapped in his embrace—one arm draped heavily across my shoulders, his legs loosely tangled with mine. Despite protests from my bladder, I don't want to move, afraid I'll break the spell, and our stolen moment will turn out to be nothing but a dream.

As if he can hear my desperate thoughts, Archer pulls me closer, nuzzling my neck in his sleep. With the first brush of his lips against my skin, my breath hitches, and my bones turn to jelly. *How can I still want him so badly when he already answered my body's every plea... more than once?*

A hot flush washes up my chest and throat, consuming my face as I scan for empty wrappers or any other proof of what we've been up to. Archer must have disposed of the evidence while I slept.

A warm finger smooths the pucker between my brows.

"What's wrong?" His sleep-roughened voice rasps directly into my ear.

"Nothing." I relax against his chest again, trying to slip back into the fantasy.

"You're a bad liar." He combs his long fingers through my hair, carefully untangling each knot before moving to the next. "You're worried about something."

"Just wondering how long before they come looking for us." It isn't a lie, but it isn't the entire truth either.

"They won't." He presses his lips to the top of my head, sparking another flurry of tingles. "Don't underestimate Winnie's power of persuasion. She'll make sure the others give us some space. She may not fully understand what we were up against out there, but she saw us walk in. I'm confident she can put two and two together." Archer shudders, and I know exactly where his thoughts have gone.

As I feared, the fragile veil blocking out the rest of the world slips away, and *my* thoughts join his, drifting back to the strangers trapped in earthen walls and monsters engulfed in flames.

"We should tell them about the cave." The words tumble out before I can stop them. As much as I would love to hide in our love bubble forever, we can't.

Archer's spine stiffens, and he lets out a slow breath, ruffling my hair. "I know."

With another quick kiss to my temple, he wordlessly slides out from under me and wraps a towel around his waist. The view brings back another flood of memories, and I drag my eyes away before I'm tempted to act on one of them.

Smirking as if he knows exactly what I'm thinking, he tosses me an oversized T-shirt—another one with the school's logo branded across the front—and wanders back to the locker room, presumably for something suitable to wear.

When he finally comes back, several minutes later, he's dressed in nothing but a pair of loose-fitting dark jeans and carrying my duffle bag and the leather jacket I traded Theo.

I squeeze the jacket to my chest. The boy's scent still clings to it. "Is he—"

Archer grins and pulls on the twin to my T-shirt. "Winnie's mothering him half to death. He was scarfing down a plate of instant eggs and dry pancakes when I left them."

I nod, forcing Theo's mother—*Andrea's*—face from my thoughts. None of us can afford to dwell on our losses at this point. We have to keep moving forward if we have any hope of survival.

Archer bends down and kisses the furrow between my brows. "He'll be okay. Kids are resilient. Isn't that what they always say?"

"I hate that phrase," I mutter, pulling on another pair of black jeans I don't recognize. They're a little tight, but I manage to get them zipped without breaking a rib. "Kids grieve as deeply as anyone else. They're just better at hiding it."

"We'll keep a close eye on him, okay?"

My only response is a quick jerk of my head. Archer isn't any more responsible for what happened to Andrea than I am. It's just the new normal, and I hate it.

"I stopped by the nurse's office." He deftly changes the subject. "Lance is on the mend. He's not quite up and around, but he's getting there."

"What about Thor?"

He shakes his head and chuckles. "He's already moved his things into one of the classrooms with the guys."

"So not dying?"

Archer barks out a loud laugh. "Far from it."

"Did you tell them...?" Images of the dark cavern flash through my thoughts, and I swallow back the bile threatening to choke me.

He squeezes my hand, leading me from the room. "Not yet. I was waiting for you."

"We're going back, aren't we?" I gaze into his handsome face, memorizing his thick brows and the faint lines just under his eyes. I already know the answer, but I need to hear him say it. We have to be certain our plan works. We have to take out the rest of the colony.

His nod sends a tremor through me. "Tonight."

Chapter 21

The Best-Laid Plans

"Hot damn!" Thor jumps to his feet, making the gymnasium's ancient wooden bleachers rattle. Other than the fading purple bruises covering nearly every inch of his exposed skin and a slight hesitation in his movements, it's as if he weren't knocking on death's door just a few days ago. "My ant theory was right!"

While Thor paces across the worn floorboards, excitedly congratulating himself for coming up with the initial idea, the rest of the group—minus Winnie and Theo—listen intently while Archer and I fill them in on the details.

Chuck whistles through his teeth. "I can't believe it actually worked. How is it the military, or whoever, doesn't know this?"

"For all we know, they do," Archer says.

Lancelot pulls his elbows from the board behind him and slowly leans forward, his eyes tightening as if the movement takes far more effort than he's letting on. Unlike Thor's rapid recovery, Lancelot's has been slow. "The military is taking its sweet old time implementing the information, if it does."

Thor comes to a stop in front of us, a gruesome grin plastered across his bruised face. "I say we finish them off tonight—burn the whole damn hillside to ash!"

Beside me, Archer shudders, and I squeeze his hand. "It's not as simple as that."

"Sounds pretty damn easy to me!" Thor folds his long legs beneath him to flop onto the bleachers again, making the boards groan

175

and sending another tremor through the whole unit. "The sooner we take this colony out, the sooner we can move on to the next."

"We can't just set fire to the tunnel and walk away," I snap as visions of Theo and Archer buried alive in the cavern wall flash through my thoughts. "We have to check for survivors inside before burning it all down."

"We will," Archer whispers before pressing his lips to my temple, and the intimate gesture sends warm tingles through me. "If anyone's still alive, we'll get them out."

Thor startles me, bringing his hands together with a loud crack and letting out a whoop of excitement worthy of a twelve-year-old. "Now, if that doesn't warm my miserable little heart. It's about damn time you two sealed the deal. I thought for sure I was gonna have to give destiny a little nudge—maybe strand you in the first orchard we passed until you were sufficiently tempted."

Archer silences Thor with a look.

I drag my curious gaze from Thor to Archer. "What is he talking about?"

Archer shakes his head and chuckles, but a dark-pink stain blooms across his cheeks. "A whole lot of nonsense."

"What's the plan?" Raptor steps forward, creating a wall between Archer and Thor and effectively changing the subject.

Archer quickly shifts gears, clearing his throat before responding. "We grab whatever incendiary devices we can get our hands on—from homemade torches and Molotov cocktails to old-fashioned lighters and aerosol cans. If we're going in, we need to be armed to the hilt. We took out a lot of the aliens last night, but we have no idea how many are left."

"Do we know for sure any of the humans inside even survived?" Raptor's dark gaze flicks from Archer to me. "Can we be certain we aren't risking our lives for nothing?"

My stomach flutters, my heart pounding as the memories come flooding back. I can still hear the queen's shrieks as flames engulfed her eggs, but the horrifying cries of the half dozen people I couldn't save will haunt me forever. Clinging to Archer, I swallow back the bile crawling up my throat and shake my head.

Archer wraps an arm around my shoulders and pulls me close. "We freed as many as we could before the egg chamber went up, but there's no way to know for sure who got out and who didn't."

"That definitely complicates things." Raptor's frame goes rigid as he stares at the wall on the other side of the gym as if the faded pep rally posters and state championship banners hold the secrets to the universe.

"That could be any of us in there. It almost was." Squeezing Archer's hand one more time, I straighten my spine and step out of his embrace, determination driving me forward. "If even one of them is still alive, we have to at least try."

"And if we fail?" Raptor turns around, frustration twisting his features as he towers over me. "What then? Like you said, it could end up being any one of us in there. We need to look out for our own."

The hair on the back of my neck prickles as I stare up at the former football player. He has muscles on top of muscles, but I refuse to back down from the challenge. I cross my arms and arch an eyebrow. "So you're fine with leaving what's left of the human race to die?"

He flinches. "I didn't say—"

"Maybe you could lure the aliens out." Callie's voice comes out in a timid whisper. "You could use something they're drawn to as"—she darts her eyes toward me—"*bait*... to get them away from the tunnel."

"Use some*one* as bait, you mean?" Thor crosses his arms over his broad chest, voicing the thought before I have a chance.

"That's not..." Callie's face goes up in flames, and she clears her throat. "I'm only saying it would be safer to check for survivors while the monsters are distracted."

"She's right."

I whip my head toward Archer and bite back a curse-laden tirade from Coach's ghost inside my head. *He can't actually be considering using one of us as bait!*

"Luring them out is a good idea." His brow furrows as I continue to gape at him. "But trust me, we won't be risking anyone's life to do it."

"Other than *us*, can you think of anything that would be enticing enough to draw them away from the nest?" Chuck asks.

Archer's frown deepens, and I can almost see the gears turning behind his eyes. "They seem to have an uncanny knack for sniffing out humans, so maybe we give them what they want."

Frustrated by his backtracking, I throw up my arms. "You just said we weren't risking anyone's life to—"

"We're not." A slow grin spreads across his lips.

I let out a breath. "I'm confused."

His grin widens. "When I took up archery as a kid, I used to sneak off to the farm down the road and use their scarecrow for target practice. That raggedy old thing was barely hanging on by a thread, and I swear, every crow in the county used to flock to it and perch on its shoulders."

"Sounds like a useless scarecrow." Raptor chuckles.

"Or a perfect decoy." Archer tugs on his loose-fitting T-shirt. "We'll dress *our* scarecrow in some freshly worn clothes and whatever else might give off a strong human scent." He nods toward Thor's midsection. "We should have enough bloody bandages lying around this place to draw a coven of vampires."

My own smile widens as his plan begins to take shape in my head. "Reverse engineering the scarecrow?"

"Exactly." He leans in to steal a quick kiss.

I bring my fingers to my tingling lips. "That's so stupid, it might actually work."

⸺●⸺

"I don't like it." Staring at the dirty *Buffy the Vampire Slayer* T-shirt at his feet, Archer shakes his head and slides his hand into his hair.

"Why? It's a good idea." I kick the other donated clothes toward the bleachers behind us and toss my filthy leggings on top of my shirt. "I was the one who destroyed the alien's eggs. I was the one who set fire to the tunnel." I add Bonnie's jeans and leather jacket to the growing pile of clothes I'd recently worn. "If they have any intelligence at all, they'll recognize my scent and go after it."

He exhales a heavy breath and lifts his eyes to mine, pleading. "That's what I'm afraid of."

"Don't look at me like that." I tear my gaze from his, preferring to focus on the task at hand rather than the ramifications of what I'm suggesting. "You're the one who wanted to create a decoy. I'm only trying to give your plan the best chance for success."

"E—" My name turns into an indecipherable groan on the way out, and Archer glances toward the others. He clears his throat and lowers his voice as several sets of eyes watch our interaction with rapt attention. "I'm sorry, slayer. It's simply too risky."

"Risky how?" I scoop my clothes from the floor and attempt to shove them into his arms. "I won't actually be *wearing* them. They're for your stupid decoy. It's no riskier than using anyone else's clothes."

"She's right, and you know it." Raptor steps toward us and holds out his arms. "It would be just as dangerous for those *things* to catch any one of our scents, but hers is the most likely to draw them in."

I relinquish my pile of dirty laundry to Raptor and mouth a quiet "Thank you."

"Don't thank me. I'm not doing you any favors by backing you up here." He throws a smirk my way. "Signing up as alien bait is crazy stupid."

"And probably reckless," Thor adds with a sobering look.

"That too," Raptor agrees with a nod. "But it's also fucking brilliant. You've gotta be public enemy number one to them right about now, so I imagine finding you is their top priority. And like a blood-hound with a bloody bedsheet, they're gonna be all over your scent."

Archer's face crumples as he tugs on his hair and lets out a low growl. "Damn it, Raptor, stop agreeing with her!"

"It's my *clothes* they'll be drawn to, not me." I slide my eyes toward Callie and Winnie.

They don't waste any time grabbing my jeans from Raptor and stuffing crumpled paper into the legs faster than Theo can rip the pages out of old textbooks.

Dragging my attention from the eerie voodoo doll production line, Archer cups my cheek and rests his forehead against mine. "It'll just give them more reasons to track you."

"Trust me." I rise onto my toes and press my lips to his. "They have all the reasons they need."

Winnie winces, and I freeze, everything else forgotten.

"Win?" Chuck drops the pile of lacrosse sticks he's been fashion-ing into torches and hurries to her side. He kneels between her feet and cups the slight swell of her stomach with both hands. "Is some-thing wrong?"

"You okay, Miss Winnie?" The book in Theo's hand slips through his fingers. His eyes stretch wide as he watches Chuck tend to his surrogate mom.

"I'm fine, sweetie. The baby's just being a little feisty today." She glances at me and presses out a stiff smile, and I wonder what must be going through her head. She puts up a good front, but she has to be terrified. I can't even fathom what it must be like to carry another life inside her while the world around us goes up in flames.

"You should go lie down." Chuck slides a hand under her arm to help her up, but she waves him off.

"Stop fussing at me. I need to finish this first. But I wouldn't refuse a little help if you're offering."

"Sure thing, darlin.'" Chuck settles in beside her, and the rest of us take a collective breath.

This is no place for a pregnant woman, or—I glance at Theo—a kid. I have no idea what we would do if either of them needed any kind of real medical attention in the middle of nowhere.

"Back to work, all of you," Winnie scolds as she roughly shoves another wad of paper into my jeans.

She winks at Theo, and he picks up the science book he dropped and goes back to tearing out the pages as if they'd insulted him.

"Callie, go see if you can find anything that'll work as the head. A headless scarecrow won't lure anything to it."

"You got it, Winnie!" Callie scurries from the room while we all pretend we're not watching Winnie like she's a ticking time bomb.

The awkward silence in the gym stretches out like an invisible net, holding everyone captive. No one says anything, but I imagine they're all thinking the same thing I am. We need to get to the safe zone as soon as possible.

"You people had better be too busy building weapons to talk." Winnie wraps a length of string around the bottom of one of the pants legs, tying the end shut before lifting her eyes. "Better not be waiting for me to crumble or something. Cuz trust me, that's not gonna happen. Not today."

"Look what I found!" Callie gallops into the gym, straddling a crusty old string mop as if it's one of those pony-on-a-stick toys, shattering the tension.

"That'll work." Winnie finishes tying off the other leg and starts stuffing my T-shirt for the torso. "We'll have us a Buffy look-alike in no time."

"Arch!" Supes calls from the opposite end of the gym, holding what looks like a gas can in one hand. "Can I have a word?"

"Yeah. Sure." Archer gives me one more lingering look and exhales through his nose before turning and jogging toward his friend.

"That man is terrified something's gonna happen to you out there," Winnie whispers.

"I know."

"Let him be scared. It'll keep him on his toes." Winnie pushes herself to her feet and shoves the mop handle through the neck hole of my stuffed shirt. "Now, would you look at this!"

"Wow." Thor snickers. "Looks just like our Buffy."

With a stringy head of dirty mop-water hair and weird, misshapen lumps on its chest that I *think* are Winnie's idea of boobs, the rickety scarecrow almost does look like me—in some even-more-screwed-up nightmare version of the world.

"Think she'll fool anyone?" Callie helps Winnie put my jacket on the decoy.

"She'd better." Raptor steps up to the scarecrow and lifts one of the gnarled strings. "We're staking our lives on it."

<hr>

The remains of my dinner writhe in the pit of my stomach like a bucketful of worms wriggling their way into every corner of my insides as the five of us—Thor, Raptor, Supes, Archer, and I—make our way through the thick underbrush along the edge of the woods. As much as I would've liked to see her squirm under the pressure, with Lancelot still recovering and Winnie pregnant, Callie got a free pass to stay behind. And someone needed to keep Theo safe, so despite pleading to tag along, Chuck was nominated to protect the others in the event our harebrained plan goes south.

I shoot a glance behind me. Thor has my look-alike scarecrow strapped to him as if it's riding piggyback.

What the hell was I thinking?

A cool gust swirls through the low-hanging pine boughs like a whispered secret, ruffling my hair and making the back of my neck prickle with anticipation... *and dread*. Every crunch of feet against the dried forest floor, every flutter in the trees above, sends another spasm of fear through me. The mere thought of facing down the aliens again has my heart racing.

Archer comes to a stop at the edge of the tree line, and I turn to watch his brooding thoughts play out across his face. He hasn't said a word since before we left the school, and like a brittle band on the verge of snapping, the tension between us stretches to the breaking point. He made his feelings known about me offering my scent as the decoy, and his opinion clearly hasn't changed in the few short hours since then. Even Coach has gone silent on the subject. Not that I blame either of them. With less than an hour before sunset, the sky is already gray and gloomy as the threat of rain hangs over us like a dark omen, and I can't shake the feeling that we're about to make a colossal mistake.

Archer's eyes slide toward me, and he presses his lips into a thin line. "This is as good a spot as any."

"Works for me." Raptor drops the bundle of torches Chuck put together from lacrosse sticks, grabs the red plastic gas tank from Supes, and begins soaking the ends in gasoline.

Supes gazes over his shoulder. "Are we far enough away from the school?"

"We're good." Thor lays the decoy on the ground at his feet and, with his lips curling into a wide grin, reaches for the sharpened pole sandwiched in the pile of torches. "Let's do this."

A shudder runs through me as he drives the makeshift post into the ground, hammering it as deep as it'll go with a heavy mallet before attaching my doppelgänger with a few zip ties. The *thing*—the so-called scarecrow—isn't me, but it's dressed in my clothes, and even with an old mop for hair, it looks close enough to give me the willies.

A shock of dark hair flops across Supes's forehead as he collects the torches from the ground, careful to keep the gasoline-soaked tips far from his body as he passes one to each of us. "What now?"

Tearing my eyes from the decoy with a shudder, I stare into the trees, where the deep shadows could be hiding any number of dangers. "Now we draw them into the open so we can slip into the cave while they're out here."

Thor pulls a lighter from his pocket and sparks the flame to life. "Lemme know when to light these babies."

"Not yet, dumbass." Raptor shakes his head.

My breath hitches as I steal a glance at Archer, wishing there was time to make him understand, wishing I didn't need to explain my reasons. This is bigger than both of us. "Not until they get close."

"I don't like this," Archer mutters. "It's too damn quiet."

With another measured breath, I pull out my saber and take a step toward the scarecrow. "Not for long."

In the half a year since life as I knew it came to a screeching halt and my entire world crumbled in front of me, I'd never attempted to summon the aliens. Not intentionally. Even the thought of doing something so reckless would've stopped me cold.

So much for that plan.

"Come and get me, you bastards!" My throat burns as the sound echoes through the forest.

Archer flinches. "What the hell, slayer?"

"That ought to do it." I force a smile, but inside, I'm barely holding it together. There's no telling how many aliens survived the fire in the tunnel—no telling how many are within earshot.

It doesn't take long before a faint shriek replies to my invitation, followed by another, and another, each one getting louder... and closer. The trees in the distance bend and sway, then a loud crack sounds, and a giant limb topples to the ground with a thud.

"Now." I turn to Thor. "Light the torches."

"On it!" He lights mine first then his own before quickly lighting the others.

Orange flames dance at the end of my lacrosse stick, but not even the heat from the fire can warm the icy shiver that runs through me when the first fat raindrop splashes against my cheek. I pull in a quick breath and tip my head back in time for the sky to open up, pelting my face with rain and making my vision blur. Behind me, Archer mutters a curse under his breath as one by one, our torches go out.

Chapter 22

Lights Out

R aptor stares at the plumes of smoke swirling from his extinguished torch and licks the rain cascading over his lips. "Shit!"

"This is bad," Thor mutters as he frantically slides his thumb across the metal wheel, trying and failing to relight his flame in the sudden downpour. The lighter sparks several times but refuses to catch. "We're screwed."

"What the hell were you thinking?" Archer throws his torch aside and pulls the bow from across his back. He nocks an arrow and shifts his focus to the trees as he sweeps the perimeter.

I drop my smoldering lacrosse stick to pull my saber from its sheath. We should run—*hide*—but with the aliens' bloodcurdling wails multiplying as if the sound is coming from every direction, it's impossible to know which way to go. "I was thinking *one* of us needed to do something."

"And it had to be *you*?" Archer shoots me a dark glare.

"Shh." Supes holds a finger to his lips as he focuses on the trees in the distance. The tall pines sway and crack as if something is pushing through them, moving quickly in our direction. His eyes go wide, and he pivots on his heels. "Run!"

The five of us scatter—Supes and Raptor making a break for the tree line while Thor, Archer, and I head deeper into the forest. Our original plan may have gone to shit, but if we can get to the cave while the aliens are actively hunting us outside, we may still be able to salvage just enough of the pieces to take the bastards out.

Thor and Archer flank me like a pair of overprotective bodyguards as we sprint through the dark woods. Surrounded by shadows and with rain pelting me in the eyes, I can barely see, let alone stay upright without stumbling several times, but I refuse to fall behind—refuse to allow them to see me as anything less than an equal.

Moving as gracefully as possible with mud seeping into my shoes, I dart over an exposed root and lose my footing on the slick ground on the other side. Archer grabs my forearm, steadying me just long enough for me to get my bearings before leaving me to my own devices again. But he doesn't stray far.

Despite getting turned around a few times, we manage to make it to the mouth of the cave. The charred remains of the hellish creatures that chased us down the tunnel litter the opening, reminding me of the danger waiting for us inside.

While Archer and Thor inspect the tunnel, I drift away from the entrance to watch our backs.

Thor nudges one of the burned bodies with his foot. "What the hell are those?"

"Your worst night—" Archer's words cut off at the sound of something falling through the branches overhead.

A large object drops out of the sky and lands on the ground at my feet, and I flinch out of the way with a squeal.

"What the hell? Is that...?" Thor lets the thought trail off.

Archer swears under his breath.

"The decoy." The heat drains from my face as I answer Thor's unfinished question.

A loud shriek blows my hair back as the first of several aliens darts from the trees to tower over me.

"Eve!" Archer calls, but there's too much distance between us and too many aliens to fight.

I reach for my saber, but the monster in front of me knocks it from my hand before I can get into position.

"Duck!"

I drop to the ground seconds before an arrow sinks into the alien's milky-white eye. Without missing a beat, Archer releases another, slicing through the monster's throat. But he doesn't have enough arrows for all of them. And he can't protect himself if he's too busy saving my ass. I know what the aliens are after. They basically shouted their demands when they dropped the decoy at my feet.

A dark chuckle rolls up my throat as the truth hits me. I was always meant to be the bait. Before I lose my nerve, I scoop up my saber from the forest floor and take off running, hoping the aliens will leave Archer and Thor to follow me.

"Damn it, Eve!" Archer screams, and the frantic sound guts me. "Where the hell are you going?"

"Don't worry about me!" My voice trembles as I call back, knowing there's a chance I won't make it. Knowing that what we had in the wee hours of the morning may be all there is for us. Blinking back the sting of tears, I can only hope Theo's mom was right when she said someone up there was looking out for me. "Finish the mission!"

My lungs burn as I run, twisting back down the path we took to get to the tunnel, tripping over rocks and roots, and getting turned around in a giant circle before I plant my feet to face the seven feet of drooling alien bearing down on me.

"Come on, ET." I swallow the fear rising up my throat and raise my saber in front of me. "Let's do this."

⸻ ◉ ⸻

My alarm goes off before dawn, the angry wails dragging me from a dead sleep. I don't even remember coming home last night, let alone setting an alarm, but the persistent screech pierces my eardrums like a dozen ice picks. My fingers itch to hit the snooze button, to quash the maddening sound before it drives me completely insane, but I can't muster the strength to lift those same fingers to shut it off. Again and again, the high-pitched squeals hammer my skull, drilling through my brain until I'm half-sure every ounce of gray matter has turned to mush.

Where am I? The answer hovers just out of my grasp of consciousness. I have the sense that I'm missing something infinitely important, but I can't quite put my finger on what. No matter how hard I struggle, I can't seem to clear the fog infiltrating my thoughts.

"Rise and shine!" Mom's singsong voice carries over the noise as she sweeps into the dimly lit room, far too cheerful for such a dreary morning.

Long shadows follow her as she drops something near the foot of my bed, but instead of shutting off my still-shrieking alarm, she rips the warm covers from my legs, exposing me to the icy chill in the air. I'm vaguely aware of goose bumps breaking out over my skin, but I can't tear my gaze from the woman who brought me into the world. The woman who sacrificed herself for my well-being on more occasions than I can remember. The sudden urge to hug her hits me like a bag of wet cement, leaving me breathless, as if we haven't seen each other in months. *Maybe longer.*

She pats my exposed leg, leaving an unpleasant tingle in her wake, like the pins and needles of blood flowing through a sleeping limb. "Come on, sleepyhead. It's time to get up."

It takes several seconds to peel my tongue from the roof of my mouth, as if I drifted off to sleep while eating peanut butter... or honey. But if the bitter taste is any indication, it was something far less appetizing. I rack my brain to remember if I'd gone to a party, had too much to drink, maybe, but nothing clicks. *What did I do last night?*

A voice in my head whispers, "*pine pitch*," and I suppress a shudder.

Whatever happened, it left me with the world's worst hangover. Bile churns in my stomach, and I swallow reflexively before croaking, "What are you doing up so early? It's still dark."

"Nonsense," she chimes. "It's a beautiful day!"

A dry laugh scorches my throat on its way out. "No, it's not. It's freezing." *Did it rain?*

With the alarm still wailing in the background, I try to sit up, but the signal from my brain to my legs gets lost in translation, because I can't move. I try again, this time concentrating on each muscle group, one at a time, all but screaming in frustration when nothing happens.

My pulse quickens as the implications sink in, and I scan the dimly lit room in a panic. "What's going on? Why can't I feel my legs? Mom?"

She grins down at me, but her smile doesn't reach her milky-white eyes.

My heart stops, everything around me freezing as if someone hit pause on my nightmare. It's way too dark to make out much of anything, but instinct tells me I shouldn't be here. Before I can take another breath, my ears buzz as my pulse comes rushing back to life with a vengeance. A thousand thoughts hit me at once, coming at me from every direction before scrambling for the corners like roaches in the light.

Mom leans in, and the sour stench of her breath surrounds me, chokes me. As the fog permeating my brain slowly lifts, the façade surrounding the thing pretending to be my mother begins to fade. The warm pink of her cheeks melts into a sickly gray. Her dark hair withers like the tall grass at the end of fall until it crumbles and blows away. And her petite frame lengthens, stretching out until she towers over me, mouth twisting and stretching as if she's made of clay. And just like that, Mom is completely gone, as if she was never really here at all. As if my disoriented brain conjured her to torment me.

The alien seems to agree. Its sinister smile spreads wider and wider until its jaws come unhinged, slime dripping from its thin lips as it finishes packing me into the earthen wall. Then it lets out a bone-chilling shriek, blowing my hair back and turning my blood to ice.

⟝⟞

My eyes flutter open, and I swallow a scream.

I'm living my worst nightmare. A nightmare I can't wake from. The aliens buried me alive—suspended in the wall, up to my neck in the hard-packed earth of their underground fortress. Alone. Nothing but a single glowing orb in the center of my tomb to chase away the darkness. This isn't the chamber where I found Theo... rescued Archer. *Am I still in the colony, or did they take me somewhere else?* Somewhere deeper underground, if the thin air and colder temperature are any indication.

Where the hell am I?

My head spins as I sip the stale air, unable to expand my chest enough to fully inflate my lungs, rationing each breath as if the next isn't guaranteed. My heart thunders out a jagged rhythm as every shallow inhale leaves me desperate for the next. I'm drowning. Drowning without a drop of water to soothe the burn in my throat. Every panicked scream echoes through my head on a loop. The actual memories are vague—flashes of eerie lights and surreal faces—but I can't shake the hallucinations plaguing my thoughts.

Mom was here. I *saw* her with my own eyes. Felt her presence. Smelled her floral perfume. But that's impossible.

What did they do to me?

Bitter cold seeps into my skin, reminding me of my dire predicament, and I dart my eyes to the dark corners, waiting for long shadows to expand into real-life monsters. Panic races through my veins as I strain against the tightly packed dirt holding me hostage. I'm as good as dead if I stay here. Dead if I don't find a way to fight back. But I may as well be encased in a block of ice because I can't wiggle as much as a single joint on a single finger. Uncomfortable tingles shoot through my extremities like thorny vines coiling up the limbs of an old tree. The pins and needles wrap around me from the top of my head to the bottom of my numb toes. My teeth clack together, hard enough to crack a molar, but the body-racking shivers have no place to go except within, with every major muscle trapped in the wall.

A whimper works its way up my raw throat, and I swallow it again. There's no way to escape this time. No saber at my side. No Archer to come to my rescue. In my heart, I know he would never give up on me, but in the deep dark recesses of my mind, I'm terrified he won't know where to search, and I'll be left here to rot slowly.

My breath hitches, and I slam my eyes shut as the first wave of tears prickles to the surface.

"Don't let them see you cry, darling girl."

Mom.

My eyes snap open, almost expecting to see her in front of me, but I'm still alone in a dark hole, deep underground. With her melodic voice still playing inside my head, it takes every bit of focus I have left to hold the tears at bay. I know she was only a hallucination, but I would give almost anything to see her face one more time.

Leaning into the illusion, I suck in a strained breath and let out a jagged sob. "I'm scared, Mom."

"I know you are, sweetheart, but you need to be brave. More now than ever."

A flood of emotions steals my next breath as the familiar refrain echoes through my addled brain. *Be brave.* Those were the words my mother whispered as she doctored every skinned knee, soothed every broken heart. I don't know how long I can hold it together with her voice in my head, reminding me of words I'll never hear her say again.

A low rumble coming from a dark corner draws my attention, and I strain to make out the source. The shadows stretch and bend, forming spindly limbs as the monster strides forward, focusing on my paralyzed form. Its rhythmic movements remind me of a cat stalking a bug—almost graceful—and my heart slams wildly as it approaches.

"What do you want from me?" The thready sound coming from my compressed lungs doesn't have the intended impact.

The alien rumbles again, and it cocks its head to the side as its milky-white eyes watch me intently. Light from the orb reflects off the alien's pale form, and the approaching creature begins to come into focus. I've never been this close to one that wasn't actively trying to kill me. This one is somehow different from the others. Less feral. More... *aware?*

It comes closer, towering over my trapped body. Something in its eyes sends a ripple of dread through my stomach. Its mouth moves, and a series of clicks and chirps comes out. The alien's menacing glare laser-focuses on my face as it shouts its foreign language at me.

"If you're going to kill me, get it over with already!" My lips tremble as I spit out the challenge, certain it has other plans for me if it's kept me alive this long yet terrified it might take me up on the offer before I can come up with an escape plan.

The alien's eyes narrow, and it leans in until its putrid breath washes over me in waves.

A familiar tingle spreads through my limbs like warm water, and my eyes drift shut. *What's happening to me?*

A loud explosion in the distance briefly shakes me out of my stupor, and dirt rains down on me from above. The alien brings its face within inches of mine and lets loose with a furious shriek.

"Sounds like someone missed you, Evie," Coach's voice whispers as the tomb erupts into chaos.

Archer's grinning face flickers behind my eyelids as everything around me goes dark again.

Chapter 23

Change of Plans

I'm dying.

That's the only explanation that makes sense to me at this point. The only explanation for why I feel nothing. No pain. No pleasure. No... anything. As if floating in a lukewarm pool in the middle of the black nothingness. And the only explanation for why Thor, of all people, is standing in front of me—blue eyes sparkling, large hands gesturing wildly, and pink lips moving silently, speaking words I cannot begin to comprehend.

Either I'm dying, or my mind has finally cracked. The lack of oxygen to my brain has clearly caused irreversible damage. As if carrying Coach with me wherever I go isn't bad enough, I've begun hallucinating other people I care about. People who matter to me in some way or another. First Mom, then Archer, now Thor. And I can't even begin to unpack the weird out-of-body moment I experienced while a freaking alien spoke to me in a strange language I couldn't possibly begin to understand. *What's next?* If my tear ducts weren't completely desiccated, I would cry.

"Buff... wake... 'kay?" Bits and pieces of sound crackle in and out of my consciousness, as if coming through a broken speaker. Imaginary Thor waves a meaty hand in front of my face, fanning the stale air around me, but I can't muster the strength to react.

Fanning the air? Is he really here?

The act of swallowing has become nearly impossible, but I manage to work my throat enough to force the last bits of dust down so

I can speak. "Thor?" My voice cracks, the rough sound barely registering to my own ears as I say his name, but he must understand me because his face lights up.

"There she is." He doesn't waste another moment on small talk but goes straight to work, loosening the dirt trapping me in the wall and muttering, "I told him you were tougher than he gave you credit for."

He? Does he mean Archer? A loud bang echoes down the tunnel, stopping my heart. "Where...?"

Thor shoots a glance over his shoulder, but instead of slowing his digging, he picks up the pace. "Killing everything that moves. I've never seen anyone more focused on a single task in all my days."

"Why...?" My voice catches, and I attempt to clear my throat.

"You *know* why." Thor's fingers roughly brush my shoulder, and he lets out a dark chuckle. "He blames himself for you getting captured."

"Not his—" A series of bloodcurdling shrieks cuts off my thought, and I dissolve into a coughing fit.

Thor's features twist into a pained expression, and he darts his eyes to mine. "He doesn't see it that way."

Once I get my breathing under control again, I manage an eye roll. "Stupid man."

Thor barks out a hollow laugh and glances toward the shadows. "You can tell him that yourself once we get you out of here."

"Did he...?" I pause, my stomach clenching as I contemplate whether I actually want to know the answer to my unspoken question. *Why didn't he come for me himself? And why is that what I'm focusing on when I should be worried about escaping with my life?* Groaning at my foolishness, I let the words fly. "Did he send you?"

"Nah." Thor grins, a bead of sweat rolling down his temple as he continues to gouge the wall around me with both hands. "I volunteered. I'm stronger than he is, and we weren't sure if you'd be fit to walk out of here on your own two feet, let alone fight off attacking aliens. I wasn't gonna leave that task to anyone else."

His assumption that Archer couldn't carry me has me raising my eyebrows, the only part of me I *can* move.

"Don't look at me like that. Your boy may be deadly with a weapon, but we all know that when it comes to brute strength, I'm your guy."

Thor finally frees one of my arms, unleashing a brutal attack of pins and needles as blood flows back to the numb extremity. While Thor shifts to my legs, I wiggle my stiff fingers, relieved to finally have use of at least one hand again.

"Do you think you can free your other arm while I dig out the rest of you?"

A pained cry reaches our chamber—a very *human* cry—and both Thor and I turn toward the sound. The horrific noises coming from the tunnels surrounding us have my already-frayed nerves on edge. If the aliens break through whatever battle line Archer has set up out there and get to us before I'm free, I won't be able to fight back. And I know Thor won't leave me. We'll both die—me in the wall and him defending me.

"Hurry," I whisper, sinking my fingers into the dirt surrounding my trapped arm while Thor digs out my lower body.

Every inch of me screams with torturous relief as, bit by bit, Thor frees me from my tomb.

"Can you walk?" He watches my face as he lowers me to the ground, clearly poised for me to stumble into his awaiting arms.

First one foot then the next touches the hard-packed ground, and despite a bout of dizziness, I manage to stay upright without help. "I can try."

"But can you fight?" Thor grins, and I catch a glint of steel in the dim light coming from the glowing orb in the center of the chamber.

My hand trembles as I reach for my saber. "I thought I'd never see this again."

"Don't go getting sentimental on me yet. We're gonna have to fight our way out of this place. You up for that?"

The leather grip warms as I wrap my fingers around the hilt. "You don't call me Buffy for nothing."

Holding out his hands as if ready to catch me if I fall, Thor gives me a thorough once-over in the dank underground chamber, sweeping his eyes from top to bottom before returning his gaze to mine. "You good?"

I manage a weak nod, but inside, I'm a damn mess. I can't even trust Coach's voice in my head to lead me anymore. Not when I keep hearing another voice whispering in my thoughts. No. Not words—*ideas*—coming at me in an unfamiliar cadence, as if speaking directly to my mind. Telling me I can't win. Telling me my kind will be eradicated from the earth—the sooner the better. I can't allow myself to pay attention to what it says. Not if I want to get out of here alive.

Thor continues watching me as if I'm a snow cone on a summer day and he's determined to catch every drip before it hits the ground. Well, he can watch me all he wants. I'm not about to break—not with an audience. I make a show of dusting myself off with a dramatic flourish, as if the past several hours didn't faze me in the least. As if being kidnapped and tortured by aliens happens every other day. As if I'm fine.

News flash... *I'm not.*

"Fake it till you make it, Evie girl," Coach whispers under the noise in my head.

As soon as I convince Thor I'm not about to drop to the ground in a sobbing heap, he turns toward the narrow opening carved into the side of the cavern. "Stick to me like glue."

"Like a bad rash." I flash my best surly grin at the back of his head.

Stepping through the exit, he tosses a smirk over his shoulder and chuckles. "Yeah, you're fine."

Staying as close behind him as possible, I inch forward, my legs wobbling as I make my way through the musty tunnel. Shadows dance in my peripheral vision, making the ground beneath me swirl and pitch. I don't know if it's a trick of the eye caused by the glowing orbs lining the walkway, or if I've yet to get my sea legs, but I feel as if I'm shoulder-deep in quicksand and the saber in my hand weighs a thousand pounds, dragging me under the surface. Head spinning, I lean against the damp wall to catch my breath. My throat is so dry, I'm half-tempted to suck the moisture from the packed dirt. I would give my left pinky for a sip of cool water.

"You don't look so hot." Thor reaches back to place a steadying hand on my elbow. "Do you need me to carry you?"

"Not on your life." My weak attempt at a laugh comes out as more of a snort. "I'll walk out of here on my own two feet if it kills me."

Another shriek echoes toward us through the tunnel, sending a violent shudder down my spine.

Thor shoots me a sour grimace. "Let's hope it doesn't come to that."

Blocking out the dire images plaguing my thoughts, I stare into the abyss in front of us. "Agreed."

The sound of metal striking flint pulls my attention from the darkness as Thor holds out a small lighter, nervously flicking it again and again before stuffing it back into his pocket. "We need to hurry. If you can't keep up, I'm hauling you over my shoulder and making a run for it."

Where is Archer? "He's still in here, isn't he?"

"Shh." Thor stills and cocks his head to the side.

My ears perk, and I focus on the commotion farther down the winding tunnel. My stomach rolls as, one by one, the primal shrieks go silent.

"Do you hear that?" Thor jabs a finger toward the sound. "That's your boy taking those bastards out one at a time."

The hair on the back of my neck stands at attention. "We need to help him."

"What we need to do is get out of here before he burns it all down."

I grab Thor's arm and squeeze with every ounce of strength I have. "He needs to know I'm safe so he doesn't do something stupid!"

"Forget it." Thor shakes his head. "We're getting out. That's the plan."

"Thor—" I plead with my eyes, praying he can see the conviction in their depths.

He presses his mouth into a flat line. "I have my orders. We'll reassess when we get topside."

"This isn't the Army! You don't get to order me around." I push past him, another kind of fear burning off the fog in my brain. If he thinks I'm running from conflict, abandoning Archer now, after everything, he doesn't know me at all.

"You want to get us all killed?" Thor chases me down the tunnel, his meaty hand coming to rest on my shoulder. "He said you'd be stubborn, but I thought after..."

His sentence trails off, and I think maybe he'll let it go. Let *me* go. But before I can form the words to sass him, he lifts me off my feet.

The air in my lungs rushes out in a loud *whoosh* as I land roughly across his back, and my trusty saber clatters to the ground at his feet.

I pound a fist into his lower spine. If he thinks I'll go quietly, he's got another think coming. "Put me down!"

"Not happening. He'd have my ass if I didn't get you out of here." More gracefully than I would've guessed, he scoops my weapon from the ground and turns down the tunnel forking off the main artery, taking us away from Archer and the thick of the fight.

I swallow a scream, scrambling for something—*anything*—that might convince him to turn around and go back. "You're both assholes."

"I know." He huffs out a dark chuckle. "Feel free to scream at me all you want… later."

My eyes and nose prickle with the threat of tears. "If he dies, I'll never forgive you."

Thor's chest rumbles with a deep growl. "If anything happened to *you*, he'd never forgive me."

"Thor, please. He needs us. You don't understand. They…" I grip his shirt in both hands. "They'll overrun him."

He redistributes my weight but doesn't slow. "You're underestimating him."

"*You're* underestimating those aliens." Another fleeting memory pops into my head. Another strange conversation that *couldn't* have really happened… but for reasons I can't put into words, I'm beginning to believe actually did. "They're not what we thought they were."

Thor stops walking. "What are you talking about?"

"I can't explain, but I need you to trust me. We need to find Archer—before it's too late."

"Damn it, Buffy." Thor lowers his head. "He made me promise."

A spark of hope lights my insides. "Then go with me. Keep us both safe."

Thor goes silent for several long seconds before blowing out a breath. "If he's pissed, it's on you."

"Deal." Pushing against his shoulders with both hands, I squirm until he releases me.

Thor shakes his head and lets out a snort. "I'm going to regret this, aren't I?"

"Probably."

Catching a second wind, I inch closer to the shotgun-toting Thor as we wind through the intricate tunnels carved into the earth. Since I insisted we abandon the escape route he'd plotted for us, he dragged the weapon from his back, diligently aiming into the shadows ahead. I hope he knows where we're going because I have no idea where that is, other than up. And we must be changing altitude fast because, with every few yards we climb, the temperature rises, and my ears pop as the pressure in my head decreases. *How deep underground are we?*

As we leave the last of the glowing orbs behind, the tunnel grows darker and the smell of rot and damp earth grows stronger, as if we stumbled into a crypt. As long as I live, I'll never get used to the stench of death and decay. But under all that, I catch something else—something that reminds me of the all-too-familiar sweet scent of my mom's perfume. An icy shiver runs through me as I force the thought back into the dark recesses of my mind.

You're losing it, Eve. She wasn't really here.

The metallic scrape of Thor's lighter as he swaps his shotgun for a tiny makeshift torch draws my attention back to the task at hand.

"So what's the plan?"

"Well, it *was* to get the girl and get out." He chokes out a dry snort. "But clearly, you shot *that* plan thoroughly to shit."

I study his features in the wash of firelight. "Please tell me you didn't come waltzing into an alien stronghold with no game plan for getting out again. Did you?" The moment the words pass my lips, I realize that was exactly what he did.

Frowning, Thor nudges past me to take the lead again. "My sole objective was to get you the hell out of here. End of plan. Archer, on the other hand..." He tosses a glance my way, but I can't read the murky message lingering in his eyes before he turns back to the path ahead. "I don't think *he* considered much beyond killing everything that stood between me and that goal post." Putting a few more feet between us, he doesn't say anything more on the subject.

We crest another mound of dirt, giving wide berth to a decapitated alien carcass, and a whisper of fresh air ruffles my hair. The rush of oxygen allows my thirsty lungs to fully expand for the first time since I was taken, and I devour it as if it were my first breath ever.

Desperate to reach the exit, and Archer, I gulp another huge lungful, making my head spin. "Do you have any idea where this tunnel leads?"

"I have an inkling."

Something whizzes through the air between us, and Thor drops into a crouch, pulling me down with him and making me expel all the precious air from my lungs. As I keep my back to the dirt, my heart kicks hard enough to steal my next breath, and I struggle to identify our attacker.

"Jesus, dude." Thor exhales in a gust, dragging me to my feet before yanking the arrow out of the tunnel wall behind us. "It's just us."

Archer's lean form slowly comes into focus. Even covered in dirt, with his eyes wide and mouth hanging open, he's the sexiest thing I've ever seen.

"Eve?" He rushes toward me, wrapping his arms around me in a bone-crushing hug. "I thought—" His words cut off as he nuzzles his face into my neck.

"You're here," I whisper, tears prickling behind my eyes. I slip my hands between us, sliding them over his chest to seek out his heartbeat. We may have only known each other a short time, but I feel as though our hearts have known each other forever.

He rests his forehead against mine, and his breath washes over me, filling my lungs with its sweet warmth. "I thought I'd never see you…" He stops himself, dipping his head to bring his eager lips to mine.

Our mouths collide, and despite our precarious position, I melt into his embrace until I can't tell where he ends and I begin. Lifting my feet off the ground, he kisses me senseless, making me forget we're standing in a dark tunnel surrounded by dead aliens. Despite my head swimming from lack of oxygen, I have no desire to release him, but I don't have a choice when Thor clears his throat and Archer tears his lips from mine.

As if a switch flips inside him, Archer stills, his muscles tightening into steel bands as he directs the full force of his anger toward Thor. "What the hell were you thinking? You were supposed to get her out of here!"

"Believe me, I tried," Thor grumbles. "You should know better than anyone that she doesn't exactly listen to reason."

Archer wraps an arm around me, tucking me tightly against his chest. "She needs—"

"She's right here!" Shaking off the last vestiges of bliss, I step out of his arms and cross mine over my chest. "And what she *needs* is for you to let her speak for herself."

Thor twists his mouth to the side but, to his credit, stays silent on the subject.

Taking Thor's lead, Archer clamps his mouth shut, watching me as if I'm seconds away from imploding.

"Good." I jerk my head in a sharp nod. "Nice to see you can be reasonable after all. Thor's doing what I asked him to do—getting us all out of here. Together."

Raising both hands in surrender, Archer closes the gap between us, approaching me cautiously. "How are you even standing right now after what you've been through?"

"What are you talking about? I'm fine." I release the anger flowing through me and allow him to cup my cheek. "I'm not as fragile as you seem to think I am. If you can handle a few hours stuck in a wall, so can I."

"Eve." Archer's expression softens. "Baby, you've been missing for more than three days."

Chapter 24

The Voices Within

———◆———

Three days?

Archer's words knock the wind from my lungs, leaving me gasping for air. What he's saying doesn't make sense—isn't even possible. *It can't be.*

Head spinning, I stumble sideways as the tunnel tilts on its axis and the ground shifts beneath my feet. "That isn't..."

"Hey. Look at me." Archer takes my face in both hands, holding me steady. "Breathe."

Frantic, I stare into his eyes, trying to untangle the lie within. He has to be wrong. "We were in the woods. With the decoy. It couldn't have been more than three hours ago. Not..."

Three. Whole. Days.

I can't catch my breath. Can't think. A rush of hot tears blurs my vision.

"You're safe now," Archer coos, eyes locked on mine while, somewhere in the distance, another high-pitched shriek echoes down the tunnel.

"No." My attention drifts to the shadows, and I shake my head as the truth sinks in. I've been trapped in this place for nearly half a week. No wonder Thor questioned my ability to walk out of here on my own two feet. I rest my trembling hands over Archer's and squeeze. "I don't think I am—*safe*. Far from it. In fact, I couldn't get any further from safe if I tried."

Like a wisp of smoke swirling up from an extinguished flame, a low hum rumbles at the base of my skull. The sound quickly builds into a loud buzz, like hundreds of wasps swarming around the opening of a hive.

Or an unintelligible whisper in a language I don't speak.

I gently extract Archer's hands from my face and cock my head to the side. "Do you hear that?"

"Yeah." Thor chuckles. "That's what's left of them licking their wounds."

"Not the shrieks." Turning my attention inward, I strain to hear the strange murmuring in my head. Not words—not exactly. But somehow, my brain manages to translate the bizarre crackling in the white noise as *"foolish humans."*

What have they done to me?

My heart skips, stuttering out a few irregular beats before jumping to life again, sending a jolt of adrenaline racing through my veins. "They're... *speaking* to me. How can I hear them?" *How do I understand what they're saying?*

Archer's brows knit, and he darts his eyes toward Thor. "We need to get her out of here. Now."

"Agreed." Thor sparks his lighter, and a small flame whooshes to life, casting an orange glow in the space around us. "Where did Raptor and Supes get off to?"

Archer glances over his shoulder. "Last I saw them, they were taking out a bunch of those little scorpion-looking bastards. Raptor was forcing them down the tunnel, and Supes was picking them off at the entrance."

"Let's hope they're near the exit because we're about to light this place up." Thor pulls a wad of frayed yellowed cloth from his pocket and holds it up. "You have the stuff?"

"Yeah." Archer unhooks a leather pouch from around his midsection and unzips it to reveal several miniature liquor bottles inside.

Despite the various labels, the contents all have the same cloudy-reddish cast.

"Cocktail hour?" Blocking out the whispers in my head, I nod toward the assorted bottles.

"You could say that." Tearing off a piece of the dingy cotton, Thor lets out a loud bark of laughter. "But I wouldn't drink it if I were you. Not unless you wanna take a page out of Daffy Duck's playbook and blow yourself sky high."

My eyes snap to his face. "Then what's in them?"

"A little of this." Thor uses his teeth to unscrew one of the bottles then shoves the cloth into the opening, plugging it again. "A little of that."

"And a whole lot of eighty-seven octane." Archer gently takes the first bottle while Thor repeats the steps on the next.

Thor shrugs. "Basically, a homemade Molotov cocktail."

"Great." My blood cools as a shudder runs through me. "Glad I asked."

"Story time's over." Archer takes two more bottles from Thor and fishes a bright-blue lighter from his pocket. He slides his thumb across the strike wheel several times before the flame ignites. "No matter what goes down, don't let her out of your sight."

"Of course," Thor agrees with a sharp nod.

"Enough of this chivalry crap." Pulling my saber free, I exhale loudly and roll my eyes. "We walk out of here together."

Laser focused on Thor, Archer acts as if he didn't hear a word I said. "Not for a second. I mean it, Thor."

Unfazed by Archer's intense stare, Thor winks at me. "I'll stick with her like a bad rash."

Seemingly satisfied, Archer brings the small flame to the cotton fuse. "We go on three."

"One..." Lighting his own bottle, Thor starts the countdown. "Two..."

"Three!" Archer doesn't wait for the bottles to land before grabbing hold of my hand and yanking me in the opposite direction.

We don't get far before heat from the blast singes my back and blows my hair into my face as it chases us down the tunnel. Completely taking me off guard, a second explosion comes from within me as a cacophony of voices, all screaming at once, detonates inside my brain. My back bows, my legs folding beneath me as I grab my head in both hands, desperate to keep my skull from breaking apart.

"Eve!" Archer scoops me up, lifting me off my feet.

The warmth of his arms is the only thing tethering me to reality as the buzzing in my head builds, shifting frequencies again and again until it settles into something dark and familiar. Like giant puzzle pieces, the crackling static in my head falls together as a fully formed sentence.

"Running only delays the inevitable."

Archer's mouth moves as he shouts at Thor. "Grab her saber! She'll have both our asses if we leave it."

With my head resting against his chest, I'm able to read the words on his lips, feel the vibration as he barks the command, but I can't hear him. The sound of his voice doesn't carry over the shockwaves reverberating through the tunnel—or the warring voices raging inside my head, competing for dominance.

Like an old radio searching for a reliable signal, my muddled brain continuously shuffles between Coach's voice and my mom's, with the aliens' unearthly whispers providing the ever-growing static white noise in the background. The rapid-fire conversations batter my thoughts, overlapping to the point where I can't discern one voice from the next. The near-constant chatter borders on maddening, but no matter how hard I try to block it out, I can't seem to quiet the incessant droning.

"Let's get the hell out of here." Archer shifts his weight, adjusting me in his arms and tightening his grip before taking off running.

My head pounds with every long stride, every impact of his feet against the hard ground, until I swear my soul is mere moments from splitting apart. *Doesn't he know I'm being slowly destroyed from within? Can't he feel the life slipping from me, inch by agonizing inch?*

My mother's ghost lets out a low wail. *"Hold on, darling girl. You're almost there!"*

"Come on, Evie, don't lose hope now!" Coach barks a gruff order, and I can almost hear the decades-long cigar habit lingering in his voice.

"Run, run, little rabbit." The low hiss of the pervasive static slithers and shifts until the pieces fall together in the form of a taunt. *"Wear yourself out. We'll wait."*

"Shut up!" I scream, pressing my hands over my ears to no avail. The disembodied *thoughts* implant themselves straight into my brain as surely as if I'd formed them myself.

"Who are you talking to?" Archer's chest rumbles again, the soothing vibration like a balm to my battered soul.

"Everyone," I murmur, retreating further into myself. I don't know how much more of this torture I can take. If the pressure between my ears keeps rising, it won't be long before my head explodes.

Archer nods, picking up his pace as if he can hear my internal rantings.

We burst through the cavern's opening, and almost immediately, the voices quiet and the pressure shifts as fresh air floods my lungs with the fragrant scent of the forest. Of *life*.

Overcome with emotion, I bury my face in his chest, muffling my sobs and letting my tears soak his shirt.

"What happened in there? Is she hurt?" Raptor rushes toward us, reeking of gasoline and sulfur.

"I don't know." Without slowing, Archer tosses out a stiff reply, and the concern in his voice manages to shake me out of my incoherent state.

"I think…" I lift my head and clear my dry throat, my forgotten thirst coming back with a fiery vengeance. "They're telepathic—the aliens. I hear them talking. Inside my head."

Archer loses his footing, barely recovering before we topple over. "What?"

"*Jesus.*" Supes lets out a low oath under his breath. "Are you sure?"

"I don't know what else it could be."

"Do they even speak English?" Thor asks.

"Not exactly." I cock my head and listen, but thankfully, nothing but eerie silence remains. "Their language sounds more like the static you get between radio stations. With a lot of clicking and whispering mixed in."

"So how can you be sure they're talking to you and you don't just have a concussion? You probably took a solid hit to the head." Supes asks a perfectly logical question.

"Because, for some reason, I understand what they're saying, as if they've planted the thoughts straight into my brain."

"How is that even possible?" Raptor's intense gaze picks away at the fragments holding my head together.

"They gave me something. In the cavern." Memories of the twilight state I lingered in, apparently for days, come back to me, piece by piece. "Maybe that's why?"

"Why can you hear them when I can't?" Archer's brow furrows as he gazes down at me. "They knocked me out with the same thing, and I don't hear any static whispers."

"I don't know. Maybe…" Heat rushes to my face as I divulge my deepest, darkest secret. "Maybe because I was already hearing voices."

The four of them gape at me but thankfully don't say a word.

"I know what you're thinking, but I swear I'm not crazy."

Archer squeezes me tighter against him. "No one's saying you're crazy."

"Yet," Raptor adds with a pointed look.

"Listen... back when the aliens first arrived, I was terrified. And all alone. After months of being on my own, I started talking to my coach—in my head. At first, it was just me thinking out loud as if he were really there, but after a while, I opened myself up to 'hearing' his reply. Things he'd said to me at one time or another. Or things I figured he *would* say if he were really there. Hearing his voice, even if it was all in my imagination, gave me a mentor to guide me—and a huge dose of comfort in a dark world. Despite his constant presence in my thoughts, I knew he wasn't real, but pretending helped me focus on what I had to do so I didn't fall apart."

"I get it." Thor nods. "He was like the imaginary friend I had that got me over being afraid of the dark."

I let out a breath. "Like that times a thousand."

Archer's lips curve up at the corners. "You did what you had to do."

"That's nice and all, but what does your imaginary mentor have to do with talking aliens?" Supes jogs alongside us.

"Maybe I'm able to hear the aliens because I was already open to listening to voices that weren't actually there."

"Do you know what they want from us?" Thor palms his neck. "What are they saying?"

"They're not afraid of us. All we've managed to do is piss them off."

——⬦——

By the time we reach the safety of the old school, other than the persistent ringing in my ears that I fear may never go away, the competing voices in my head have finally quieted. No more Coach. No more Mom. And blissfully, no more strange whispered threats or taunts working their way deep into my brain like splinters. But after days of listening to the aliens' cryptic messages, I still don't know the first thing about what they want from us. Other than total extermination.

While Thor and the guys relay what little new information we discovered to the others and make plans for our next move, Archer and I head to the locker room to clean up. After an all-too-brief shower, I drag him to the equipment room for a few stolen moments alone. As exhausted as I am, after being buried in the wall—numb from head to toe—my desperate need to *feel* wins out over sleep.

His gaze rakes over me, settling on every bruise, every superficial cut. "Eve..."

"You won't break me," I whisper as I rise to my toes and claim his mouth.

His ragged exhale speaks volumes as he gives in to my demands.

We collapse onto the gym mats in a desperate tangle of limbs and lips, barely pausing to tear open a condom.

A deep sense of relief floods my senses as Archer pushes into me inch by glorious inch. Once he's fully seated, he takes his time, rocking into me slowly, worshipping every inch of my body, loosening my battered muscles and soothing my addled mind. Every touch, every stroke is a balm to my weary soul. It doesn't take long to find my release... and again a second time almost immediately after.

Once we're both thoroughly sated, Archer drags me straight to the infirmary, giving me a direct order to rest.

"I'm not an invalid." I cross my arms, wobbling slightly as I attempt to stand my ground. "I can pack up. They'll need all the help they can get."

Despite bone-deep exhaustion oozing from every pore, I almost feel like myself again for the first time in days. Maybe not strong enough to head into battle, but definitely well enough to pull my own weight.

Cupping my cheek, Archer brushes his lips across mine before leading me to the cot Thor had occupied just over a week ago.

My fingers itch to smooth a wrinkle in the stiff sheet. *Has it only been that long?*

He grips my shoulders and squeezes. "You were all but buried alive for the past three days. You need rest."

I let out a frustrated sigh, but exhaustion wins out, so I don't fight him as he gently guides me down onto the mattress. But instead of walking away after tucking me in, he slides in beside me, wrapping me in his arms, clutching me tightly to his chest, as if he fears I might vanish if he lets go.

The last thing I want to do is hurt his feelings, especially after he risked everything to rescue me, but after being trapped in the walls of the underground cavern, I can't bear to be held so tightly. I crave his touch like oxygen, but after my ordeal, his unyielding embrace borders on claustrophobic and threatens to trigger my fight-or-flight response.

Desperate to put a little breathing space between us, I shift away from his grasp. "If you don't go help Thor, he's likely to send the cavalry."

Instead of picking up on my subtle hint, Archer apparently interprets my weak attempt to wiggle free as a reason to tighten his grasp. "They can do without me for a little while."

"I'm okay, you know." The rising pitch in my voice belies the confidence of my words, and I struggle to shove the panic down before he senses it. "I won't break. You can go help the others."

Archer tenses, his muscles coiled like springs. "I'd rather stay with you if that's okay."

"But you don't *need* to." Despite my growing feelings for him, he has to understand I won't be a burden to him or anyone else. I'm no one's damsel. "I'm perfectly capable of being alone for a little while."

He nods but instead of releasing me, he rests his chin on the top of my head.

"Hey..." I turn in his arms until our gazes meet, only half believing the words forming on my lips. "I'm safe here."

His chest rumbles with a low groan. "I know that, but—"

"No buts. You won't let anything happen to me." This time, when the words roll off my tongue, I actually believe them. Archer has proven more than once that he would risk his life a hundred times over to protect me—whether I need it or not. A sense of warm comfort washes over me, and I settle into his arms, resting my head in the crook of his shoulder.

"But don't you see? I already did. You were taken on my watch. You were gone. I..." Archer's breath hitches. "I couldn't find you."

"But you did. I'm right here."

He stares at the blank wall across the narrow room, seeing things I can't begin to imagine while I study the sharp set of his lips, the tightness in his eyes, and the deep furrow between his brows.

"It took us days. We combed the entire woods, every inch of that damn cavern, killing everything that moved. We only found a few stragglers, as if the rest of the aliens had picked up and cleared out without a trace," he rambles on, but nothing he says makes any sense.

Didn't we walk out of the same cavern I pulled Theo from? And Archer after that? "But I thought that's where you found me."

He turns and locks his gaze on mine. "It was."

"I don't understand. You just said the tunnels were empty."

"*Those* tunnels were." He nods. "The caverns go far deeper than we realized. And I think they might connect several different colonies like some sort of subway system that runs between them. For all I know, they're all connected. That has to be why the government hasn't been able to smoke them out yet."

I sit upright, pulling him with me. "Archer, if that's true, we need to tell someone! The government... or the military, maybe."

"I know. That's what Thor and Raptor are discussing now—whether it's safe for us to travel to the safe zone in the morning."

"Safe or not, I vote we go."

Chapter 25

Race with the Devil

———◦———

"Stellar plan you had there, buddy," Raptor mutters, sarcasm dripping from between his clenched teeth as he aims his shotgun, fires, then quickly racks another round.

The charging alien's head explodes in a sloppy mess before its headless body drops to the forest floor like a bag of wet cement. Before any of us have time to celebrate the kill, two more rush forward, taking its place.

"Abso-fucking-lutely brilliant." Thor squeezes off a shot and then another, stopping them both in their tracks. "Seriously. Best plan ever, dude."

Archer releases an arrow before tossing a dark look over his shoulder and locking his steely gaze on me. I'm pretty sure his unspoken anger is going to leave a permanent mark. "It wasn't mine."

"I said I was—"

The high-pitched squeal of a fast-approaching alien hurdling through a break in the trees cuts off my apology. My *third* apology since insisting we abandon the highway for the road less traveled.

Me and my big mouth. I should've just taken Archer's first no for an answer. Even the second. But no... I had to stand my ground. For reasons I don't understand myself, I just *knew* we had to cut through the woods and take the little road running along the river. The plan didn't even make sense to me, but I couldn't shake the feeling that following the water was the right decision.

The aliens don't like rushing water.

I have no clue where the information came from or why—even with the truth staring me straight in the face, I still inexplicably believe it with every fiber of my being.

Chuck inspects the underside of the SUV. "This isn't going anywhere."

"What's wrong with it?" Archer asks.

"Busted axle."

A chorus of curses lights up the forest.

Clearly, my misplaced confidence has screwed us all, and the so-called *truth* I staked our lives on was apparently part of an elaborate hallucination or fevered dream. *But even if my instincts can't be trusted anymore, how was I supposed to foresee the SUV hitting a massive pothole? Or how the combination of cloud cover and a canopy of trees would make our location as dark as a cave, landing our entire group in the middle of an unwinnable situation?*

The still-shrieking alien lunges forward, and I swallow my scream as I swing my saber through the air, slicing through the creature's slender neck. The body drops at my feet, thick, syrupy blood staining my shoes as I finish my sentence. "Sorry!"

"What the hell made you think off-roading in the middle of the North Carolina wilderness was a good idea?" Supes barks as he scrambles to reload his weapon from his perch on top of the crippled SUV.

Telling him it was my mother's idea is out of the question. The mere suggestion sounds insane, even to *my* ears. She wasn't there. Not really. *So why does it feel like she told me secrets—wanted to protect me from just this occasion? Or was it because someone—something—else wanted me to believe I would be safe so I would fall right into their laps?*

"I'm an idiot," I mutter as our little group spreads out, forming a circle around the two vehicles as Chuck ushers Winnie, Theo, and Callie from the hobbled SUV into the already overcrowded Jeep.

"What did you say?" Archer steps closer as if waiting for the next shoe to drop.

I groan. "Nothing you don't already know."

Chuck tosses an army-green duffle out of the Jeep and lets a few choice four-letter words fly. "We're gonna have to dump most of our stuff."

Archer pulls his gaze from mine and nods. "Do what you need to do."

"I can keep the first aid kit, but even with ditching everything else, it's still gonna be tight." Chuck scratches his neck as he surveys the situation.

"Whatever you do, do it fast! I'm almost out of ammo!" Thor bellows as he reloads and fires into the line of incoming monsters.

One by one, they drop, but it doesn't take long before another row pops up behind them as if they're reproducing on the fly.

"Where the hell are they coming from? How did they even know we'd be…?" The answer comes to me before the words are past my lips. *Me. I'm the reason.* Whipping my head toward Archer, the air rushes from my lungs. My head spins, making me sway on my feet. "They can hear my thoughts."

"What?" Archer grips my shoulders to steady me.

"I don't know how they're doing it, but… I think they can read my mind."

"Damn!" Thor glances my way but doesn't stop firing. "That's bad."

"Really bad," I agree.

"How long?" Raptor snaps, trading his spent shotgun for the loaded revolver in his waistband.

"I don't know." My eyes well with tears as the truth sinks in. Not only did I steer our whole group into disaster, I gave the aliens a fucking map to our location. "Maybe since before we left the school."

"Chuck! Take the Jeep, and get everyone out of here. Head for the main road." Archer turns to me, either sympathy or pity shining in his eyes. "The slayer and I will take the bike and meet you at the next town. We'll give you a five-minute head start. Don't wait for us!"

Chuck throws a glance at me but holds his tongue.

"Get out of here. Now!" Archer barks over his shoulder, and the guys jump at the order, each of them scrambling over the underbrush toward the Jeep idling on the narrow road.

As his words sink in, my steps falter, and my breath catches in my throat as I bring my saber down to separate another alien's head from its shoulders. My third—*or is it the fourth?*—since ending up in our current predicament. I've lost track of how many I've killed since our little convoy ran aground. Since I *drove* us into the ground. *My fault. All my fault.* Whatever they did to me in their tunnels seriously screwed me up, leaving all of us vulnerable to their mind tricks.

Before the latest creature's head hits the ground, I whip my gaze toward Archer, desperate to talk some sense into him. "We can't hold them off ourselves! Not with these bastards coming out of the wood-work like roaches!" *Not when I can't even trust myself to make the right call.*

"We're gonna have to." Laser focused on a pair of aliens bolting toward us through the trees, Archer nocks two arrows, letting them fly and miraculously taking both monsters out at once. "At least long enough to give the others time to get out of here."

"Fuck that!" Thor storms toward us, shoving two shells into his shotgun. "I'm staying."

Archer fixes his gaze on me, and I can feel the tension bubbling out of him from where I stand.

He exhales a heavy breath, which somehow steals the air from my lungs, and shifts his attention to Thor. "We'll be right behind you."

"No way." Thor shakes his head and steps around me to flank Archer, the barrel of his gun pointed toward the shifting shadows. "You're crazy if you think I'm leaving you two out here unprotected."

Without missing a beat, Archer angles his body to block Thor's advance and spears him with a dark look. "I need you to stay with the others in case they follow the Jeep. We can't risk them getting close to Winnie... or the kid. And we don't have enough room for three on the motorcycle."

Thor curses under his breath, but he lowers the gun a fraction as the fight drains from him. "You'd better be *right* behind us. Don't make me come back for you. I've rescued your asses enough for one week."

Archer lowers his chin in a resolute nod.

"I mean it, Arch. Five minutes." Thor jogs the rest of the way to our only functioning vehicle, hops onto the running board, and bangs on the frame. "You heard the man, Chucky. Get us the hell outta here."

Chuck guns the engine and takes off, leaving a thick dust cloud behind him as the Jeep races down the gravel road with Thor emptying his last few rounds into the handful of aliens giving chase.

Blocking out the sounds of gunfire in the distance, I assess the danger right in front of me. At least half a dozen aliens—maybe more—emerge from the edge of the forest, avoiding the narrow slits of daylight streaming through the trees.

"Now what?"

Archer slings his bow over his shoulders, swapping it for a pair of pistols tucked in his waistband. "We need to get to the bike."

"You couldn't've suggested that before dismissing our backup?" Holding my saber in front of me like a shield, I swallow a hysterical laugh and slowly step backward toward the bike, praying I don't trip.

Archer's lips twitch, briefly twisting into what I swear would be a smirk if it hadn't vanished just as quickly. "Stay close."

"I'm sorry," I mutter as we close the distance between us and my motorcycle. "For putting us in this position."

"It's not your fault."

"It is."

"Fine. It is," he agrees.

I suck in a breath, but he cuts me off before I can stutter another apology.

"But that's only because of what they did to you. You're not responsible for what happened. It could've just as easily been any one of us."

Hot tears prick my eyes, and I blink them away. "But it wasn't."

"And that's *my* fault."

"Archer..." His name comes out on a groan.

"So you see, we're both to blame, which is why we're still here, while the others—"

The closest alien lunges, and Archer puts a bullet into its brain, dropping it to the ground in a heap.

"If it's all the same to you," he whispers, "I'd like to get on that bike and get the hell out of here."

Glancing over my shoulder at the keys still dangling from the ignition, I can almost taste the exhaust on my tongue. "Sounds like a plan."

We reach the back fender, but before I can wrap my tingling fingers around the handlebars, Archer clasps my hand and brings it to his chest.

"I have an idea, but it won't work if you don't trust me."

Our gazes meet, and his heart races under my fingertips.

"Archer, I trust you with my *life*."

After stealing a quick kiss, he releases me and pulls his shirt over his head.

My thoughts scramble as unease gives way to confusion. "What are you—"

"Trust me." He wraps his sweaty shirt around my eyes, effectively blinding me.

"Is this really necessary?"

"You said it yourself. They're watching everything we do through your eyes."

Once he's certain I can't see anything under his makeshift blindfold, Archer settles me onto the bike and climbs on in front of me. With my eyes covered, my other senses have no choice but to take over. Giving in to the sensations, I cock my head, listening for the inhuman gait of the monsters moving through the underbrush behind us. I can't see them anymore, but I know they're out there. Their telltale stench—the unlikely combination of sickly sweet syrup and death—wafts above the earthy loam of the forest. But between the crackle of twigs snapping in the distance, the rushing river, the loud hum of cicadas singing in the trees, and my pulse thundering in my ears, I can't tell which direction they're coming from. I'm literally flying blind here, and I don't like it.

"Get us out of here," I mutter.

Archer folds my arms around his bare midsection, giving my hands a firm squeeze. "Hold on tight," he growls, shifting his weight to kick the bike to life.

We take off like a missile, flying through what feels like a wet sponge as we escape down the narrow river-access road. Hot wind whips my hair into a wild tangle around my face as the dense forest air claws at my clothes and threatens to unfurl the shirt tied around my eyes.

Archer leans to the right, throwing his whole body into a sharp curve, and I follow him over, pressing my chest to his back. I barely get my bearings again before we're banking to the opposite side, dipping so far to the left that my bare skin makes contact with the steam rising from the road. And with every change in direction, flashes of daylight strobe through the blindfold like lights in a rave club, making my heart race to keep up with the imaginary beat.

"Are they following us?" My voice breaks as I scream over the growl of the engine.

"I can't tell you."

"What? Why?"

"You know why!" he barks back.

The very real threat of having to pick bugs from my teeth is the only thing keeping me from letting my mouth hang open. *What kind of* Bird Box *bullshit is this?*

"Shit!" Archer's muscles go rigid, his whole body tensing as he swerves hard to the right.

Choking on the cloud of gravel dust hanging in the air, I cry out, "What's happening?"

He doesn't respond, instead letting out a string of four-letter words as we skid across the road, the back tire skating over a patch of loose gravel.

Disoriented and head spinning, I desperately cling to him as the bike lurches over the rough terrain, dragging us sideways. "Archer!"

"Hold on!" he bellows as an earsplitting shriek rends the air directly behind us.

Too close.

My fingers itch to reach for the saber strapped to my back, and I dig them into his waist to keep from going for my weapon. *I can't fight what I can't see.*

"Step out of the dark, little rabbit. Show yourself." The low buzz of the alien tongue echoes through my skull, planting thoughts in my brain and turning my blood to ice.

I can't breathe—can't *think* with them inside my head.

"It's back." My grip loosens as I mutter the words, my voice dissolving like ice chips on my tongue.

"Hang on, slayer!"

"He can't save you. No one can. You're already dead." The buzzing continues, forming more jumbled thoughts and confusing words.

My scalp prickles with an unspoken warning, and the message comes through loud and clear.

"Go faster!" I scream the words over and over until my throat is raw.

Archer cranks the throttle, and the bike jumps forward, rocketing over the uneven pavement like a stone skipping over a pond.

Just when I think we've made it—finally gotten away from the unseen threat—pain explodes through my shoulder, and fire rips through my veins.

"Eve!" Archer's voice comes from somewhere far away, like the bottom of a deep chasm—or a tomb.

I'm floating on a raft in the middle of an unforgiving ocean. Surrounded by sharks. Blind. My skin blistering. Burning.

"Hang on, baby. I'm here," he coos, his voice filled with panic. "Don't let go."

I feel Archer's presence in the darkness, but when I reach for him, he slips through my fingers as the last stitch of light goes out.

Chapter 26

Welcome to Zombieland

Everything is dark. Dark and *way* too hot, like the inside of a bakery oven. I'm burning up, my skin on fire—as if I fell asleep on a tin roof under the summer sun and fried to a damn crisp. *Where am I?*

Using every bit of strength I have left, I try to sit up, but at the slightest movement, intense pain stabs me everywhere. A cry lodges in my throat as I struggle to connect the dots floating in my head. Something is very wrong, and I need to figure out what's happening. Why I'm all alone in the dark. Why every single inch of me hurts.

Did I die? Is this hell? Freaking figures.

"Eve! Baby, can you hear me?" Archer's panicked voice tumbles toward me, down what feels like a deep well.

Why is he so far away? Is he burning too?

"Archer?" My voice cracks as it rips from my throat, and the sound is foreign to my ears. "Where are you?"

"I'm right here."

Something cool—*his hands?*—cups my cheeks, and his touch grounds me, pulling me back from the brink.

The familiar scent of honeysuckle floods my senses. And the sounds of nature rush back to fill the vacuum—birds in the trees, the rustling of dried leaves blowing in the breeze... *a goat?*

Archer slides his fingers into my hair, probing my skull gently, and I greedily lean into his caress.

"Am I dead?" I ask, choking on a sob.

"No." He heaves out a breath and presses his trembling lips to my forehead. "You're alive. Thank God."

Still too afraid to move, I blink against the darkness, and an icy jolt of fear stabs my heart, stopping it cold. "Why can't I see anything?"

"Shh." Archer rests his forehead against mine, and his warm breath is a soothing balm washing over me. "It's okay. You're just blindfolded."

"Oh. Right." I cautiously reach up and hook a finger under the sweaty cotton T-shirt wrapped around my eyes.

Before I can drag his shirt over my head, he grabs my wrist and brings his lips to my ear. "Don't take it off yet."

A shudder runs through me as the implication sinks in. We're not alone—not when I've basically been turned into a spy for the enemy. "Are they...?"

"I don't know." He slips his fingers through mine and squeezes. "Maybe."

"What happened? Why are we...?" I let my free hand drop to the rough pavement beneath me. *I'm on the ground? No wonder I hurt.* "Did we crash?"

"Kinda." He pulls his hand free, and I imagine him nervously sinking it into his tangled hair. "One of them, uh, swiped your shoulder with its claws."

The ungodly burning sensation suddenly makes sense. I've been infected with alien venom, and based on what happened to Lancelot and Thor, I only have so long before infection sets in. "How bad is it?"

"Bad enough. I stopped the bleeding, but..." His voice drifts off, and I can *feel* the intense scrutiny of his scorching gaze.

Frustration rolls off me in waves. There's something he's not saying. Something crucial. "But what?"

"We need to find the others before nightfall."

Behind the blindfold, I can barely tell the difference between day and night, but I don't need to see to know the aliens can move within the shadows no matter what time of day it is. And the thought of being trapped under a heavy tree canopy on the edge of the forest makes my blood go cold. "Where are we? Is it even safe here?"

"We, uh, should be safe. At least for now."

Using all the strength I can muster, I ignore the pain radiating from every fiber of my being and shove against the pavement to push myself upright. "What are we waiting for? We should go while we still can."

Archer doesn't respond. He gets so quiet that I'm not sure he's even breathing.

"What is it? What aren't you telling me?"

"The bike is..." He clears his throat. "It's pretty banged up. I don't think it'll even run anymore, let alone carry us. I'm sorry."

That damned motorcycle has been my lifeline for over half a year, and now it's gone. The unexpected loss brings tears to my eyes, and I'm thankful he can't see me cry. "It's not your fault. What about you? Are you hurt?" I run my hands up his arms and over his shoulders, using my fingertips to probe for injuries.

He clasps my face in his hands and kisses me, hard. "I'm fine. Just worried about you. That cut is..." He exhales slowly through his nose. "As soon as you're able, we need to catch up to the Jeep and pray they didn't leave the antibiotics in the forest."

"How are we supposed to catch them without the bike?"

"I have an idea, and it just might work."

"I'm afraid to ask."

Archer chuckles. "How do you feel about tractors?"

Visions of *Old MacDonald's Farm* swim through my thoughts, and I can't help but conjure images of trash-talking roosters and stuttering pigs in overalls from the cartoons I watched as a kid. The colorful pictures clash with the dire reality of our circumstances, and I sweep them aside like soap bubbles floating through the air. Replacing Loony Tunes with actual memories, I shuffle through the handful of farms I passed along my travels to pick out a foggy image of a real tractor.

"Like a rusty old red one with great big tires and a huge steering wheel, dragging a giant plow thing behind it in a corn field?"

"Yes! Keep picturing it." Archer oozes excitement, and I can't begin to understand why.

Despite the makeshift blindfold covering my eyes, I tip my face toward the sound of his voice and let my mouth gape open. For what has to be the hundredth time since Archer wrapped his shirt around my eyes, my fingers itch to yank it off so I can properly glare at him. "Are you crazy?"

"Like a fox." He squeezes my hand. "Picture us perched on that tractor, crawling down the road at a snail's pace with the sun slipping behind a cloud bank and the sky turning dark."

"Are you *trying* to get us caught?" I choke out, my pulse racing as the frightening picture he painted sends chills down my spine.

"Something like that." He brings his lips to my ear, and the grin in his voice warms the chill spreading through me. "Are you picturing it?"

Despite my better judgment, I do as he asks, imagining the two of us jammed together in the single seat while giant tires rumble over the rough pavement. "Against my will."

"Good. Hold onto that thought." Archer's good humor dissolves into concern as he slips a hand under my elbow. "Do you think you can get up?"

"I can try." Ignoring the pain, I let Archer help me to my feet. "Where are we—"

"I can't—"

"Tell me that. I know." I lean into him, allowing him to take the lead—in more ways than one. I'd almost forgotten how both our lives depend on me placing my trust in him, yet again.

Archer glides his fingers over my injured shoulder, checking the makeshift dressing. "Ready?"

"Not even a little." I chuckle darkly.

He gives my hand another firm squeeze. "Just don't let go."

Before I can form a reply, he tucks me under his arm and sets off like a shot. I stumble a few times, but Archer doesn't let me go, barely managing to keep me upright as we tear across the hard pavement, destination unknown.

"Still picturing our tractor? Can you hear the engine growl? Feel the wind in your hair? Smell the fresh-cut hay?" Archer rattles off the scene for me, keeping the vision alive in my head. "Do you see those dark clouds rolling in? Looks like it's about to storm again."

His vivid description sends a shudder through me, and I swear I feel the distant echo of thunder rumbling up through the soles of my feet.

"Step up." Gripping me around the waist, Archer lifts me off the ground until my feet contact a solid surface. He quickly guides me to a soft seat and folds my hands across my lap before releasing me. "Stay put. Keep thinking about that tractor ride. And don't touch anything!"

A loud creak to my right draws my attention before a heavy steel door slams shut, startling me and leaving me in silence. "Archer?"

He doesn't answer, and I can't hear him breathing anymore, but I pick up the muffled sound of footsteps not far away.

The low groan of another set of rusty hinges creaking open sounds to my left before he lands on the seat beside me with a bounce. He doesn't speak but goes straight to work, and I can only imagine what he's fiddling with over there. Instead of focusing on things I shouldn't be, I drift back to the vivid portrait he painted and concentrate on the tractor ride toward the dark horizon.

A growling engine breaks my concentration as our escape raft roars to life, and Archer lets out a low whoop. "Hot damn! This thing may have a little life in it yet."

"Is it...?" Afraid to hope, I struggle to keep the imaginary tractor alive in my head. "Are we safe yet?"

"Almost..." He trails off, and I hold my breath while I wait for him to say more.

Archer throws the ancient vehicle into reverse, grinding the gears as he pulls onto what feels like pavement.

"It's working," he whispers as we speed away. "I can't believe my plan is actually working."

⎯⎯◈⎯⎯

"**O**uch!" I flinch as far away from Callie's probing fingers as I can in the confines of the diner booth.

Of all the people in our ragtag little group, *she* had to be the medic. I reluctantly forgave her for locking me out of the shelter after we first met, but I sure as hell wasn't planning on hugging it out or inviting her to be my new bestie. Our "relationship," if I could even call it that, was tenuous at best.

Callie's cool hands still on my injured shoulder, and she mutters, "Sorry."

"No, you're not," I grumble under my breath, instantly regretting the bite in my voice. Regardless of my complicated feelings toward her, I should be more grateful she's even willing to stitch me up.

My guilt quickly evaporates when she stabs the needle into my skin with a little more vigor than before and mumbles something that sounds a lot like "maybe not." I can't help but imagine she's enjoying my pain at least a little.

"Play nice, you two." Thor tosses three dusty foil bags of potato chips and an ancient Snickers bar onto the cracked Formica table before sliding into the red vinyl bench across from me. He nods toward my wounded shoulder. "Does it hurt?"

His ridiculous question has me rolling my eyes. "Only when I'm conscious."

"Touché." Thor bobs his head a few times, understanding shining in his dark eyes as he gazes into the deserted parking lot outside the window.

Archer and I finally caught up to the rest of the group not long after the Jeep gasped its dying breath on the outskirts of the quiet little mountain town. With no gas in sight, everyone piled into the back of the rusted-out pickup, and we limped to the closest safe harbor to lick our wounds and come up with a new plan. The little diner situated on a corner lot right in the middle of the deserted town fit the bill as well as anywhere else.

Thor cocks his head, shoving the chocolate and one of the bags of chips toward me while he studies me in a shaft of sunlight streaming through a clean streak in the dirty picture window. "I kinda miss the blindfold."

"I don't." I snort, picking up the candy bar and flipping it over to search for the sell-by date before deciding I don't really want to know. I can't remember the last time I've eaten, and we're far from the first people to ransack the place in search of supplies. Other than a few bottles of ketchup and artificially flavored maple syrup, the place was cleaned out. Or so I thought. "Where'd you find these?"

He hooks his chin toward the back of the old diner. "The safe."

Arching an eyebrow, I wonder how he accessed what I assume was a locked safe and why anyone would stash treats in there. It's as if they knew how valuable sweets would become in the apocalypse. "Is there more?"

His lips curve at the corners. "Maybe."

With a shake of my head, I tear open the wrapper, saluting him with my Snickers before taking a big bite.

"So..." Thor rips open his bag of chips and shoves one between his lips. After a few quick crunches, he finishes his thought. "Arch says you can hear them."

"Kinda. It's more like they force images into my head." Just thinking about the mental invasion makes me shudder.

"And it's a two-way connection, so they can hear your thoughts too?"

"Unfortunately. If they're close enough, anyway. We were able to trick them into thinking we were in the shadows so we could get away, but once we were out of range, and in the daylight, the connection appeared to be severed."

"That's freaky." He leans in, bringing our faces within inches of each other. "So we basically have an enemy spy in our midst."

My skin prickles, and I fidget in my seat. "Or a double agent, according to Archer. That is, if we plan our next steps carefully."

Thor nods, stuffing a few more chips into his face and chewing with his mouth open.

Avoiding the disgusting display, I scan the room, but other than Winnie and Theo playing a game of paper football at a table across the little diner, we're alone. Theo waves his small hand, and his innocent smile wrecks me all over again. *We saved him, but for what?* This is no kind of life. But if we have any hope of survival, it may lie in my ability to connect with the aliens. *Awesome.*

"Where is he?" I don't say his name. We both know who I'm talking about.

"They took that hunk of steel you dragged out of the woods to look for gas for the Jeep. We can't stay here forever." He eyes the dirty glass with contempt. "That window won't keep anything out."

I follow his gaze, realizing for the first time that we're essentially sitting in a fishbowl. "No. I don't suppose it will."

Callie slaps a wide bandage over the stitches, a little more roughly than necessary. "You're all set. I cleaned the wound as best I could, but you're gonna need at least a few rounds of antibiotics to make sure you don't end up with an infection."

"Thanks, Calico." Thor flashes her a wide smile and slides a bag of chips toward her.

She frowns at the chips but takes them anyway, shooting a dark look my way before glaring at him. "What? I'm not good enough for chocolate?"

He rolls his eyes and pulls a half-melted KitKat from the side pocket of his cargo pants.

"Fine. Whatever." Callie makes a face but takes the offered chocolate and wanders over to Winnie and Theo, taking a seat in the booth behind them. "I call next round!"

I tear my eyes from their rousing game and focus my attention on Thor. "She's a ray of sunshine, isn't she?"

"She's a kid. Cut her some slack."

"We're all just kids, Thor. Every damn one of us."

"Yeah." He grins. "But some of us are freaking superheroes, aren't we?"

"I'm no superhero." *And no avenging angel for that matter.* "I'm walking alien bait."

His grin widens. "Then I guess it's time for a little bait and switch, isn't it?"

Chapter 27

Bait and Switch

———◉———

Archer cups my face in his hands and gazes into my eyes as if he can see all the way to my soul. All the way to the truth I'm hiding, even from myself. Behind him, the horizon glows orange, framing him like an impressionist painting as the ever-present threat of nightfall looms.

Across the parking lot, the guys tinker under the hood of a newer cargo van they *acquired* on one of their supply runs—something that will hopefully prove to be more reliable than the rusted pickup—while Winnie ushers Theo into the back of the Jeep, pretending we're on the cusp of a new adventure. In truth, we're running out of time. And resources.

A light gust ruffles my hair, and the cool air carries a trace of autumn, reminding me the days are getting shorter... in more ways than one.

"Are you sure you want to do this?" Archer drags my gaze back to him.

The answer lodges in my throat, but instead of telling him the truth, that the only thing I'm actually sure of is wanting him—wanting all of them—to be safe, I swallow my fears and nod. I'm the key to everything, and I can't give him any reason to stop me.

As if he can hear my thoughts as clearly as the aliens do, Archer's face twists into a pained scowl. He releases me and shakes his head, turning toward Thor, perched on top of the ancient pickup. "I don't like this. It's a bad idea. We can't protect her… not if they attack from within. I can't believe you signed off on this madness."

"It's a solid plan. And you said it yourself…" Thor grins at Archer before cutting his eyes to me. "The aliens can't read her thoughts unless they're close."

"We hope." Archer heaves out a breath. "It's only a theory. We don't know anything for certain."

Thor shrugs, seemingly unaffected by Archer's growing unease. "They haven't shown up here, have they?"

"They can't. It's sunny." Archer glances over his shoulder to the fading horizon. "But that won't last long either."

After shooting Thor a death glare, I force a smile for Archer's benefit and drag his attention back to me. "I'll be fine."

"Why do I feel like we've had this exact conversation before? Oh, right." He snaps his fingers. "Because we have. Taking foolish risks is precisely how we ended up in this position to begin with."

I grab Archer's hands and squeeze, willing him to listen to the subtext floating beneath my words. "This time will be different."

"No, it won't!" He stares over my shoulder at the line of purple streaks stretching across the sky.

How long do we have before sundown? Before we risk our lives yet again?

"It'll be the same as every other time we thought we were invincible." Archer shoves both hands into his hair. "Jesus, what the hell were we thinking, taking on an entire race of alien beings on our own? We should've headed straight for the safe zone when we had the chance, instead of putting ourselves in the line of fire again and again as if we might actually make a difference."

Thor rests his hands on the hood and leans forward. "We were trying to save the world."

"Well, we can't." Archer shifts his attention to his friend and lowers his voice. "Contrary to popular opinion, Eve isn't unbreakable. You of all people should know that."

The grin melts from Thor's face, and he slides down from the truck. "I won't let anything happen to her."

"Heard that one before." Archer cups my cheek in his hand. "I've already lost too many people I care about. I can't stand the thought of losing you too."

"Arch—"

"No." He cuts me off before I can argue. "Listen to me. We both know you're an amazing warrior. I'm in awe of what you can do—what you've done for us. For Theo. But you've already risked way too much. What they did to you in the tunnels... you're too vulnerable now. I couldn't live with myself if anything happened to you."

"Hey." I pull his face to mine, kissing him soundly before pressing our foreheads together and willing the words I can't speak—can't even think—to sink into his brain. "I'm putting my complete trust in you. Just like I did on the tractor. Do you understand what I'm saying? I trust you, Archer. Completely."

He lifts his eyes to mine, understanding dawning within them. "Like on the tractor?"

"Like on that old rusty tractor," I whisper, grinning up at him.

He wraps his arms around me, pulling me in for a tight hug. "You're crazy, you know that?"

"Like a fox."

"No time for that nonsense, you two!" Raptor shouts across the lot as he slams the van's hood and jogs the short distance to the Jeep. "Time to roll!"

Everyone but Thor climbs into the Jeep, leaving the cargo van for the three of us.

"We're up." Thor climbs behind the wheel, cranking the engine to life.

"Are you—"

I press a finger to Archer's lips. "Yes. I'm sure. Now, let's get out of here before it's too late."

"Fine." He concedes with a deep scowl. "But I'm driving."

⎯⎯⎯◉⎯⎯⎯

"You good back there?" Thor asks from the front passenger seat of the *borrowed* cargo van.

Huddled on a dusty old moving blanket on the floor of the windowless cargo area like illicit contraband, I draw my knees to my chest and rest my forehead on their peak. "I wouldn't use the word *good*."

Thor chuckles. "Just hang tight."

"Not like I'm going anywhere," I mutter, eyeing the pile of coiled hose and rows of red plastic gas containers leaching fumes throughout the enclosed space.

Despite the payload we're hauling, Archer guns the engine, and I wonder if his knuckles are white on the steering wheel, wonder if he's still pissed off at being left in the dark. *No more in the dark than I am.* Hopefully, Thor clued him in—explained what I haven't... what I can't.

I focus my attention on the white enamel walls surrounding me, imagining intriguing backstories for every scratch—every smudge—while Thor's words float around my brain like sad party balloons.

Come up with the craziest plan you can think of. Something really out there. Don't hold back. It can be as dangerous or reckless as you like, but it has to make sense. Has to be doable. When you have something, lay it on me. Don't worry. I've got your back.

Famous last words. Not that I doubt his intentions, but I'm not quite convinced he'll be able to nail the execution. I did exactly what he suggested, coming up with something crazy, reckless, and most definitely dangerous. Which is why we're returning to the scene of the crime, as they say. Back to the winding river road to retrieve our supplies. Back to where I know the aliens can hear me. Where they'll be lying in wait for me. Where escape will be difficult, if not impossible. But if I die—*when* I die—at least Theo and Winnie will be safe. At least I will have done something right.

The static in my head buzzes quietly, the way it has since we first rolled onto the highway, heading south again. Farther from the safe zone. Farther from our friends, giving them time to put as many miles between us as possible. The hum, a constant reminder that the aliens are out there somewhere, grows louder the closer we get to the outskirts of the colony.

"Hold on!" Archer's warning echoes through the cavernous vehicle, barely giving me enough time to grab the wood side rail before the bulky van swerves hard to the left, leaving the smooth blacktop. He hits the gas again, and we jump forward over rough terrain, jostling me like a pan of Jiffy Pop on a hot burner. With every violent jolt, the sealed gasoline jugs bounce into the air, landing hard enough to slosh fuel at my feet.

Keeping my death grip on the side rail, I slide as far away from the splash zone as possible. "Can we at least *try* not to blow ourselves up before we get there?"

"Working on it!" The strain in Archer's voice makes me almost as uneasy as the oily spill soaking into my shoes.

Thor lets out a string of obscenities, but before I can ask him what's going on, the bottom drops out of my stomach. My sweat-slick hand slips from the handhold, leaving the other one to support all my weight as we hurtle down a sharp incline. The hell with the aliens. *This* is how I'm going to die, and there's not a damn thing I

                    ERICA LUCKE DEAN

can do about it. My pulse races, counting down the seconds until the van rolls over and the whole thing turns into a giant fireball. If we're lucky, we'll take out a few aliens along the way.

But instead of crashing, flipping over a dozen or more times, the steel frame groans, and the van comes to a shuddering stop. With my hand still frozen on the rail, I crane my neck to see out the windshield, but I can't make out anything but a sea of green. *Nothing but trees.*

"Are you okay?" Archer unbuckles and rushes back to where I sit, still dangling from one arm.

Dazed, I gape up at him. "Where are we?"

"The mouth of the alien tunnels."

At least a dozen questions flicker through my thoughts like a faulty lightbulb as Archer gently pries my fingers from the wood rail then massages the tension from my aching shoulder.

"Can you stand?"

I see his lips move—register the words he's saying—but all I hear is the low hum of static building between my ears, buzzing like a nest of angry hornets living inside my head.

He doesn't wait for an answer before gripping my elbow and helping me to my feet.

With Archer's hand resting on my lower back, guiding me forward, I stagger toward the door and climb out of the van on shaky legs.

"Why are we here?" The hair on the back of my neck prickles as I gaze into the shadows lurking beyond the mouth of the cave.

Archer raises his eyebrows. "You know why."

I nod, forcing down the unpleasant memories this place dredges up. I hate that my own thoughts hold me hostage. Hate that we're forced to keep so many secrets. "Maybe—"

"The less you know the better." He furrows his brows and releases a breath, glancing toward the van where Thor slings a coiled hose over his shoulder. "Stay here."

Archer presses a kiss to my open lips before jogging back to Thor, leaving me alone under a withering pine while the two of them pull the five-gallon jugs from the cargo area and line them up outside the cave.

It's all I can do to keep from stomping my foot like a child. I want to argue, to demand they clue me in immediately, but the inhuman chatter inside my head is all the proof I need. He's right to keep me in the dark, but that doesn't mean I'm useless. I march toward them, determined to do my part. "At least let me help."

"You *are* helping." Archer carries the last two jugs toward the tunnel while Thor unrolls one of the hoses.

"He's right, you know. Just the fact that we didn't have a welcoming committee when we got here means the plan worked and the aliens were waiting for us at the river. By the time they catch on..." Thor lets the thought trail off with a sly grin. "Let's just say, it'll be too late."

"That's all well and good, but I can't stand here and do nothing while you two..." I glance at the hoses and jugs of gasoline. "Do whatever it is you're doing."

"Sure you can." Thor pats my back a few times as if I were a puppy in need of reassurance.

"So much for being a damn superhero," I mutter, surveying the damage to the van. With two flat tires and a plume of smoke billowing from under the hood, the odds of driving out of here are slim to none. A twinge of unease sends a ripple through my insides. It's a good fifteen- to twenty-minute walk back to the school from here. And easily twice that to the highway, not to mention wherever the rest of our group is. "Are we *walking* back?"

"No." Archer doesn't even look at me as he threads the ends of two hoses together.

Frustration seeps out of my pores, and I kick a deflated tire with the side of my foot. "This thing won't be going anywhere."

"No. It won't." Archer reels in the far end of the hose and drags it into the dark cave, the rest of the length trailing behind him. As his silhouette fades into the darkness, the realization of where we are and what we're about to do sinks in, and my stomach plummets. Even *my* crazy idea doesn't compare to the suicide mission we've apparently committed to.

The buzzing inside my head morphs into a thunderous roar that threatens to split my head in two. Desperate to block out the deafening sound, I press my hands to my ears. My knees buckle beneath me, and I let out a desperate scream as I fall to the forest floor.

Thor's wrong. They've already caught on. *They already know we're here.*

While I crumble under the barrage of mental attacks, Archer wraps his arms around me from behind, cradling me to his chest and effectively preventing me from curling into a ball on the forest floor.

"What is it?" He brushes the hair from my sweaty neck and brings his lips to my ear. "What's happening?"

Despite my best attempt to focus on his heartbeat to ground me, the clicks and whirs of the alien language continue to come at me from every direction, battering me with sound. They have me caught in the current, and no matter how hard I swim, I can't escape the pull.

"Time to die, little rabbit."

The words unleash a fresh swell of panic. Wave after wave rolls over me, holding my head under water until I'm certain I'll drown.

Archer scrambles to his knees and grabs both sides of my face, commanding my attention and allowing me a second to catch my breath. "Eve, baby, are you okay?"

Despite the scream clawing its way up my throat and the angry sea churning inside me, I redirect my attention to the sound of his voice. "They found us."

Chapter 28

War Games

Archer pulls me into an embrace, hugging me so tight I can feel the words rumbling from his chest as he yells for Thor. "Get ready! They're coming!"

"On it!" Thor drops everything and bolts for the van. He rummages around the back, tossing out the moving blanket and a few empty containers before jogging back carrying a white plastic garden sprayer and a wide nozzle.

Archer nods at the items Thor retrieved, and I can only imagine what they have planned.

After a brief staring contest with Archer, Thor grabs the hose and screws the nozzle onto the end as he marches back into the cave.

With Thor out of sight, Archer closes his eyes and rests his forehead against mine, his hot breath washing over me as we huddle on the ground in front of the alien cave. Tension ripples between us, and I can't help but wonder if this will be our last moment together. Our last moment *alive*.

Emotions raw, I draw in a sharp breath, tasting the declarations resting on the tip of my tongue, begging to be heard. But before I can get the words out, Archer crushes his lips to mine, stealing my next breath and snatching every thought from my head. Nothing matters anymore. Nothing but the blissful sensation of Archer's unyielding mouth.

I kiss him back frantically, feeding him every word I couldn't say, every emotion I've been too afraid to express. I'm drowning again, but this time, I surrender willingly—eagerly—to his onslaught.

All too soon, he tears his mouth from mine and breathlessly holds my gaze. He squeezes my hands, his eyes brimming with emotion. "I love you, Eve."

Tears clog my throat, and I have to swallow several times before I can choke out a response. "You aren't just saying that because we're about to die, are you?"

With a shake of his head, he chuckles. "No. I really do. I love you with every fiber of my being. And I know you're probably thinking it's too soon. We've only known each other a few weeks, but—"

Pressing my fingers to his lips, I put a stop to his rambling and give him a watery smile, conveying my feelings as best as I can with the constant chatter in my head. "I love you, too, Arch—"

"Adam." He clears his throat. "My, uh... my name is Adam."

"Adam?" The irony isn't lost on me, and despite the seriousness of the moment, I swallow a giggle. "Really? So we're..." I can't bring myself to say the words.

"Adam and Eve?" He shifts his gaze to his hands, and a bright-pink stain colors his cheeks. "Yeah."

"I love you..." Joy seeps from my pores as I tip up his chin until our eyes meet. "Adam."

His lips curl up at the corners, but the tears welling in his eyes tell me he's anything but amused. "No one calls me Adam. You can if you want to, but I'll still answer to Archer, if you'd rather. Or you can come up with a new name. I don't care. You can call me anything you want."

"Well, I love you, Archer. Or Adam. Or whatever name you decide to go by."

With a gentleness that makes my soul ache, he feathers his lips across mine. "I love you so much."

"Promise me you'll tell me again later. When we're safe."

He kisses me one more time then pulls me to my feet. "If we live through this, I'll say it so often, you'll be begging me to stop."

"I'm already begging you to stop." Thor groans from behind us. "If you two are quite finished, we have a few hundred aliens we need to kill."

"He's right," I agree. We have at least a few hundred aliens to kill. If they don't get to us first.

With loud static still buzzing between my ears, I plant a forceful kiss on Archer's open lips and push to my feet. Ignoring the chatter isn't easy, but I'm determined to be an active part of this team, not a liability.

My hands tremble, my knees still a little unsteady, but if this truly is our last stand, I'll be damned if I sit on my ass while Archer and Thor have all the fun. "Where's my saber?"

Archer's shocked expression melts into a wide grin, and he points with his chin. "In the van."

"Glad to have you back, Buff." Thor claps a hand on my shoulder, squeezing my aching muscles before nudging me toward the disabled vehicle. "Now, go! We're about out of time."

Don't I know it!

While they finish implementing their game plan, I jog the short distance to the van. The inhuman growls and clicks only I can hear increase in volume until the forest fades into the background again.

"Run, run, little rabbit. You won't be fast enough this time."

Maybe not, but if I go down, you're going with me.

As the war of words inside my head rages on, making it impossible to hear the thundering of my own racing heart, I grab my saber from where Archer had tucked it under the front seat.

The leather grip warms in my hand as if it missed me. The feeling is mutual. That stupid piece of steel has become another appendage, a vital piece of me, and I feel oddly lost without it.

An overwhelming sense of peace spreads through me as I lash the strap to my back and slide the blade into the sheath. With my weapon slung across my back where it belongs, I turn back. Every quaking muscle—every shaky breath—reminds me of a ticking clock as the passing seconds count us down to the eventual confrontation. I can't allow myself to think about living or dying. I have to concentrate on the here and now.

As my feet make contact with the ground, I realize the tremors aren't coming from inside me, they're coming from somewhere deep below. Something big—several somethings most likely—scramble underground. I press my hands over my ears, desperate to block out the unbearable noise while I get my bearings, but all I manage to do is trap the sound in my head.

"Archer!" I take off running, my fingers itching to draw my saber from its sheath. Instead, I scan the perimeter for Thor and Archer. They were just at the mouth of the cave moments ago, but now I don't see them anywhere. "Guys! They're coming!"

The rumbling beneath me grows more intense until I'm certain the aliens will start erupting from the dirt at my feet.

A new roar fills the forest as a massive fireball shoots from the mouth of the cave. The powerful explosion throws me backward, knocking me to the ground as a wave of intense heat singes the baby hairs on my exposed skin. My chest seizes—my lungs won't inflate, my heart won't beat—as I realize the entire cave is engulfed in flame.

"Archer!" I scream his name again, jump-starting my frozen heart.

Blinking back tears, I drag myself from the ground and gape at the embers floating through the air, igniting every bit of dried timber in their path. If Archer and Thor were inside, I can't help them. *They're not dead, damn it!* I beg the universe to listen.

They can't be dead. They wouldn't leave me behind. They had a plan. I have to believe they knew what they were doing. *Come on, guys. What the hell were you doing?*

Pulse racing, I start forward again, but I don't get far before something hooks me around the middle, dragging me down just as another wall of flame bursts from the tunnel.

Lips brush my ear, sending warm tingles through me. "Are you trying to blow yourself up?"

Relief washes over me, and my breath catches. "I was about to ask you the same thing."

"Not yet." Archer chuckles. "Too busy trying to kill aliens."

"You could've warned me."

"No." He pulls me tighter against him and rests his forehead on my shoulder. "I couldn't have."

He's right. Of course he is. Like it or not, I would be a liability if I knew the plan. But that doesn't mean I'm going to sit back and watch. I've never been much of a spectator. Not even *before*. Not when there's a chance I can be in the thick of things.

"So is that it? Your whole plan?"

He lifts his head and shrugs but avoids eye contact, keeping his secrets to himself. "Most of it."

With nothing but the crackle of dried leaves catching fire, the forest is oddly quiet, and the absence of sound is almost louder somehow. Ominous. Then the chatter in my head picks up again, the clicks and whirs reminding me of a sea of typewriters busily clacking away in unison. *We may have slowed them down, but we haven't stopped them. They're still coming.*

High-pitched shrieks rip open the sky, the battle cry echoing in my war-torn brain as the queen bursts from the tunnel, tearing the opening wider, her milky-white eyes filled with rage.

"There you are, little rabbit. Are you ready to die?"

Shaking free of Archer's grasp, I stand tall and draw my saber, giving it a twirl like in the old days, before holding it in front of me like a shield. "Bring it on, bitch!"

"Eve, no!" Archer shouts as he lunges for me, but I'm too fast for him.

Acting purely on instinct, I dart forward, and his fingers barely skim my arm as I put myself between him and the approaching danger. I've made so many mistakes, watched too many people I love die when I could've done something, even if the only thing I can do is play decoy. "Let me do this."

"Fuck!" Archer lets out a pained cry, his voice breaking as he pleads with me. "Don't you dare die."

"Not planning on it." My skin still tingles with the ghost of his touch as I focus my attention on the creature plaguing my dreams.

With patches of her sickly gray skin charred and smoldering from the blast, the queen towers over me, more terrifying than even my worst nightmares could conjure. Slime oozes from her gaping mouth as she tosses back her head and shrieks, almost as if she's laughing at my feeble attempt to look ferocious.

She won't be laughing when I remove her nasty head from her body.

The queen narrows her eyes, barely containing the pure rage simmering beneath the surface, and she lifts her head and sniffs the air. She lets out an angry wail and gnashes her stained teeth at Archer.

Her mouth never moves, but I hear her thoughts as if she's speaking out loud. *"I smell his fear, and I will savor every drop of his sweet nectar when I kill him slowly."*

Visions of Archer helplessly spread on the ground while the alien tears him apart flicker through my brain, and my stomach roils from the disgusting images. "Enough!"

"What is it?" Archer comes up behind me, and his body heat warms my back.

With a shudder, I shove the disturbing thoughts down. "Trust me, you don't want to know."

"Tell him, little rabbit. He deserves to know how he will die."

No! Clenching my jaw hard enough to shatter bone, I shift my weight and tighten my grip on the hilt of my saber, letting the heavy blade lead me. "Archer, get out of here. I need to finish this."

"No, slayer," he whispers, as if speaking softly will prevent her from plucking every word straight from my mind. "You really don't. I have a pl—"

"Don't tell me! Just go!"

Archer chokes down his next thought and slowly backs away, taking his warmth with him. "I love you, Eve."

"Later. Remember?"

"That's a promise."

The queen howls, her rancid breath turning my stomach.

Blocking out the sound of Archer's retreating footsteps, I stand my ground, hot tears streaking down my face. "What do you want with me? Why me? I'm nobody special."

The queen tosses back her head again, and another ragged shriek cuts through the air. *"Why, little rabbit, don't you know? You're one of a kind. You're our eyes and ears in the human world."*

The truth makes my knees buckle. Like it or not, they've turned me into an unwitting spy.

"We're connected."

Her words echo inside my head. *We're connected.* If we're connected, that connection should work both ways. I don't know why I hadn't thought of that before. With a deep, cleansing breath, I force myself to relax for the first time in what feels like forever. My eyes flutter shut, my heart rate slowing as I slip deeper into the shadows, concentrating on widening the connection I'd been so determined to sever.

And then the veil lifts, and I see myself standing in the trees, my saber limp at my side. *Holy shit! Is that me? Am I really seeing myself through the queen's eyes?*

"*Clever girl.*"

An uneven thrumming rattles through me. A sound—*a feeling*—I've never felt before. *Is that...?* I let the sensation wash over me until the rhythmic sound resonates through every fiber of my being. *Is that* her *racing heart?* With my eyes still shut, I crawl farther into her thoughts, unearthing another room filled with rows upon rows of glowing eggs, all of them thrumming with the same uneven cadence.

My eyes snap open as the queen advances on me, something akin to terror flickering in her milky eyes.

Is she afraid? Of me? I tighten my grip on my saber, positioning my fingers in the permanent indentations in the leather as I imagine Archer standing behind her, his bow at the ready.

The queen flinches, turning her head just long enough for me to attack.

Tensing every muscle in my body, I bring my saber up and around, swinging it clean through the tendons and sinew of her neck, separating her head from her shoulders with a sickening squelch.

Chapter 29

The Queen Is Dead, Long Live the Queen

The unbearable buzzing inside my head quickens, the sound increasing until the wild thumping resembles a pair of rogue helicopter blades, smashing through my skull. I drop my saber at the feet of the slain queen and press my hands over my ears in a futile attempt to escape the sound. Thick brown syrup spills from the alien's slender neck, spreading toward me like an oil slick.

She's definitely dead, so how can I still hear her?

An irrational laugh bubbles up my throat as a flock of headless cartoon chickens runs circles through my thoughts.

"Eve?" Archer's voice filters through the noise—a distant echo, leading me from the darkness.

The thundering beat amplifies, ticking off the passing seconds until the intensity has me doubled over.

How the hell is her heart still beat—

Before I can get the thought all the way out, the droning stops, leaving me in blissful silence. I almost don't dare breathe for fear I might trigger something, starting the pattern all over again.

"Dude, that was badass!" Thor lets out a whoop, chasing a flock of birds from the treetops.

"It's so..." I scan the perimeter, studying the shadowy opening to the tunnel. I don't know what I expected to find, but there's nothing there. "Quiet."

Archer wraps his arms around me from behind and brings his lips to my ear. "Don't ever do that again."

I gaze at him over my shoulder and grin. "Save your ass again, you mean?"

He plants a rough kiss on my temple. "Risk your life for mine."

"Duly noted." I nod, but we both know I'll do it all again if it comes to that.

Thor nudges the queen's head with his foot, widening the gap between her skull and her narrow shoulders. "That was the trippiest thing I've ever seen. She was afraid of *you*!"

"I'm told I can be terrifying." I flash my teeth. "Keep that in mind for the future."

Archer gives me one more squeeze before releasing me. "Let's not get ahead of ourselves. This queen is dead, but I doubt we got the whole colony."

"Oh, we definitely didn't," I agree, picturing the glowing egg chamber in my head as I collect my discarded saber and sheathe it across my back.

"But if these bastards are like ants, without a queen, it won't take long for the rest of them to die." Thor kicks the decapitated head into the underbrush like a deflated soccer ball.

"What if they're not like ants?" A quick image of Ms. Frizzle from *The Magic School Bus* flashes through my brain as I spin to face Archer and Thor. "What if they're more like bees?"

Thor cocks his head to the side. "Bees?"

"I can't believe I didn't think of this before." As I pace back and forth in front of the tunnel, bits and pieces of old memories begin to fall into place. "My brother did this science project in elementary school where he spent weeks on end reciting the life cycle of bees. We watched the beehive episode from *The Magic School Bus* so many times I started seeing Ms. Frizzle in my dreams."

"What does your brother's science project have to do with us?"

"Maybe nothing." I press out a stiff smile. "Or maybe everything. You see, bees might get pissed off when the queen dies, but they don't just give up and die. They..." I let my thoughts trail off to swat at a swarm of gnats buzzing around my ear.

"They what?" Thor raises his eyebrows.

"They..." The persistent insects drag my attention away again as I continue my attempts to shoo them.

Archer's brows knit together as he gazes down at me as if dissecting his own science experiment. "What's wrong?"

"Stupid bugs," I mutter, flapping both hands around my face.

Thor scratches his head as he studies me. "What bugs?"

"Damn gnats... or mosquitoes or whatever they are." I still, hands raised to my ears, and focus my attention on the two of them gaping at me. "Why aren't they after you too? Do I stink or something?"

Archer shakes his head slowly. "I don't see any bugs swarming around you."

"Well, they're there!" I step up my campaign to rid myself of the tiny nuisances. "They're just *microscopic* or something—my mom used to call them no-see-ums."

Archer steps forward, capturing my face in his hands to inspect the space around me. "Nothing's here. No bugs."

With an exasperated grunt, I pull free of his grasp. "Not possible!"

"Hey, uh, Buff?" Thor backs away from the dead queen, putting distance between him and the mouth of the tunnel. "What were you saying about bees?"

Doing my best to ignore the *no-see-ums* buzzing around me, I let out a breath and redirect my train of thought to the subject at hand. "They regroup. Rear a *new* queen from the larvae in the hive."

"So the, uh, bugs you say you're hearing... ya think they might be, uh"—Thor taps his temple—"in your head?"

"I'm not imagining it!" I stomp my foot like a toddler having a tantrum.

Archer shoots a dark look toward Thor before turning back to me. "I don't think that's what he's saying."

"Oh." As their meaning slowly sinks in, I close my eyes and turn my attention inward to focus on the low hum. The deeper I allow myself to go, the more intense the building vibrations rattle my brain. The darkness slowly lifts to a faint green glow, as if I were looking out from inside one of the glowing eggs. A breath catches in my throat as I realize I *am* seeing the inside of an egg. And that egg is cracked right down the middle.

Fuck!

I open my eyes, flicking my gaze from the guys to the tunnel then back again. "Run!"

Archer and Thor stare at me as if I have two heads.

"Did I stutter?" I grab the front of Archer's shirt, dragging him forward. "I said run!"

As we race toward the disabled van, the ever-present buzzing in my brain swells again, reaching a crescendo that radiates in every direction and permeates every cell of my being until I can't tell what's real and what's coming from inside my head.

As if he senses my anxiety rising along with the sound, Archer tightens his hold on my hand, steadying me as another tremor rocks the earth. The jarring vibrations rumble up from deep beneath my feet, as if we're hurdling across a thunderhead in the throes of a storm.

With the earth mere moments from opening up and swallowing us whole, everything screeches to a halt, and the forest falls silent again.

"What the hell?" Thor mutters, drifting into a defensive position so he and Archer flank me while I catch my breath.

"No clue." Archer's grip loosens, but he doesn't release my hand.

"Do you hear that?" My gaze darts from Archer to Thor then to the stillness of the forest, where the shadows stretch beyond the trees—where it's *too* still. Too quiet.

"Hear what?" Thor does a cursory check of his pistol's magazine.

"That's the point. *Nothing.*" I stare into the treetops. "No birds, no bugs. Not a damn thing."

Thor shoves the pistol into his waistband. "Maybe the fire chased them off."

"Maybe..." I want to believe it's as simple as that, as simple as a little smoke and flame clearing the forest. But in the back of my mind, I'm not convinced.

A deep furrow forms between Archer's brows. "We should get the hell out of here regardless."

"Agreed." Thor nods.

A loud crack shatters the air, and the ground convulses as if an unseen force knocked the Earth off its axis.

Letting loose a string of obscenities, Archer drops my hand and drags the bow from his back to nock an arrow. At the same time, Thor pulls out his pistol and levels it toward the rock outcropping behind me.

I follow their horrified gazes to the mouth of the cave as dozens of newly hatched aliens explode from the shadows. Less than a third of the size of the adults, the sickly gray arthropods look as if they could've used a few more weeks gestation to reach their full potential—like dozens of crescent rolls pulled from the oven too soon. A handful succumb to what's left of the inferno burning at the opening, but at least twenty more rush toward us, exactly like the swarm of angry bees I'd imagined.

"Shit!" Thor fires, unloading half his magazine at the oncoming assault.

My breath rasps out in shaky blasts as I unsheathe my saber, finding stable footing on the quaking earth before bringing the blade in front of me.

Another tremor nearly knocks me off my feet as the ground opens beneath me, and more monsters crawl out of what looks like a giant gopher hole. There are simply too many of them, and it doesn't take long for us to get overrun.

"Get to the van!" Archer shoves me back, abandoning his bow for a pistol and taking the brunt of the assault coming toward us.

I drop one... two... then a third as I back toward the vehicle, but they keep coming. Without their queen to guide them, the newborns' attack is anything but coordinated, but their sheer numbers have us outmanned.

Thor takes several more creatures down before exhausting his ammo and switching to a flame thrower. Those fucking *things* keep coming and coming, crawling out of the earth like demons.

Andrea's words at the cabin loop through my thoughts, knocking the wind out of me.

They're the harbingers of death, the four horsemen from the Bible.

I laughed when she said it, but the Biblical ramifications don't sound as impossible anymore.

You're an avenging angel doing God's work, striking them down where they stand.

I'm no avenging angel. Hell, I'm not an angel at all, but if I hadn't seen the spaceships with my own eyes, I might be inclined to believe a door to hell just opened up beneath us.

With my gaze laser focused on my own battle, I momentarily lose sight of Archer and Thor fighting their attackers. I can't see him, but I know he's close. Somehow, I'm always aware of Archer's presence, as if his soul calls out to mine when we're near. But I can't shake the feeling of dread coursing through me. As if the threads that connect us are moments away from being severed.

"Archer!" I call out, desperate to know he's alive.

"Run, Eve!" he bellows, his voice rough and weak. "Get out of here!"

A chill cuts through me, and I take out two more newborns before abandoning my fight to find him in the melee. "Don't you fucking die on me, *Adam*! If we go down, we go down together, got it?"

"Leave me," he croaks.

"The hell I will!" My blood turns to ice as I fight my way through the sadistic bastards, determined to find him.

Two of the demons have him pinned to the ground, a gaping mouth full of needle teeth lunging for his throat.

A bloodcurdling scream rips from my throat, and every damn one of those bastards whips its sickly gray head toward me as if I held them all on a string. "Stop!"

The aliens freeze at my command.

Archer coughs, freeing himself from the two monsters holding him. Neither puts up a fight as he crawls away and collapses against a tree to catch his breath.

It nearly kills me, but I resist going to him for fear of breaking the tenuous spell I apparently cast. Instead, I assess his condition from where I stand, praying he isn't bleeding from anywhere I can't see.

"What the fuck is happening?" Thor staggers forward.

"Don't move!" I order him through gritted teeth.

Thor stills. "Are you doing this?"

"I don't know." I survey the transfixed horde.

Every damn one of them watches me as if waiting for their next command.

"Jesus. Do you think...?" Thor voices the thought running through my head.

I killed their queen. *By all rights, wouldn't that make* me *their queen?*

Air rasps in and out of my lungs as I work out what this means for us. *If I can command the aliens, what does that mean for the rest of the world?* Letting my eyes flutter shut, I open my mind to them, my pulse slowing as I concentrate on the fragile connection between us. Like wires running through a giant circuit, I connect each thread until I sense dozens of eyes... dozens of scattered thoughts focused solely on me.

Go! Leave us alone!

One by one, the newborns turn, ignoring Thor and Archer as they make their way back to the mouth of the cave and disappear into the shadows beyond.

Archer curses under his breath.

Thor gapes at me as if seeing me for the first time. "What in the ever-living *fuck* just happened here?"

Chapter 30

A New Beginning

As the dark forest does its best to swallow us, Archer locks his gaze on mine and staggers to his feet.

"How...?" He barely gets the word out before dissolving into a coughing fit and dropping to one knee in the dirt.

"Archer!" A jolt of adrenaline spikes through me, and I rush to his side. *No no no.* I didn't risk everything battling through all those monsters just to lose him now.

My hands tremble as I run them over every exposed inch of him, counting at least a dozen blood-soaked tears in his shirt before discovering the slick warmth seeping through the thin fabric. My gaze follows my fingers to the deep gash. "You're hurt!"

He rasps out a jagged breath. "I'm fine."

"The hell you are." Blood oozes between my fingers as I apply pressure to the gaping wound.

Archer sucks in a breath and lets out a curse.

"I'm sorry. But we need to stop the bleeding. Thor, can you—"

"On it!" Thor takes off for the van while I desperately attempt to hold Archer together.

"How did you do that?" Archer exhales sharply and nods toward the last of the retreating horde vanishing into the shadowy depths of the tunnel.

"I don't know." I drag my attention from his injury long enough to meet his eyes. "I—according to the dead queen, we're connected."

"Connected?" Archer pulls in another ragged breath and cocks a sweaty brow. "More than just hearing each other's thoughts?"

"I don't know exactly. It's as if we're of the same mind. We can communicate, yes, but it's more than that... The offspring didn't just *hear* me. They *obeyed*."

"Jesus!" Thor hands me a wad of paper towels and a roll of duct tape, staring down at me as if seeing me for the first time. "So you're some kind of alien whisperer now?"

"I don't understand it any more than you do!" I snap, retreating within myself to listen for the whispers of the survivors as they crawl back into their lair to lick their wounds. The moment their voices go silent again, my thoughts spiral down another path. "But dear god, if I can control them..."

"We might have a fighting chance." Archer finishes my sentence with a resolute nod.

"I'm afraid to get my hopes up, but yes. Exactly." After staunching as much of the blood as possible with the paper towels, I use several lengths of duct tape like makeshift butterfly bandages and seal the gash shut. "This won't hold forever. You need stitches—and antibiotics. We need to get back to the rest of the group."

I haul his arm around my shoulders and help him to his feet. He's heavier than I anticipated, and he weighs me down as we stagger forward.

"Not a problem." Thor flanks Archer's other side, lifting most of his weight from my shoulders.

I glance toward the beat-up van's broken axle and snort. "Looks like a big fu—" An engine growls in the distance, stopping me cold. "Is that...?"

"Our ride." A wide grin splits Thor's dirty face.

Disbelief steals my breath as a pair of headlights crests the top of the hill. The familiar vehicle accelerates toward us, its tires crunching over loose gravel, and I whip my head around in time to catch Thor's smug grin. If Archer weren't wedged between us, I might've kissed him. "Part of your plan?"

"Don't look so surprised." Thor chuckles. "I'm chock-full of good ideas!"

Archer groans and motions toward the silver tape holding his side together. "I beg to differ."

"But did you die? No." Thor snickers.

The Jeep lurches past the van and comes to a screeching halt just a few feet from us, cutting off Thor's laughter. With the engine still running, the rear passenger door flies open, and a small boy leaps from the vehicle.

"Angel!" Theo races over the underbrush to my side. He throws his arms around my middle, dragging me from Archer to squeeze the life out of me.

"Jesus, dude!" Thor growls. "You brought the *kid*?" He drags his attention from Raptor to me. "For the record, that was *not* part of my plan."

My stomach clenches into a ball, the fury building below the surface a mere breath away from detonating. Tucking Theo into my side, I round on the hulking man. "What were you thinking? Do you have any idea what kind of danger you might have put him in? They could've captured him. *Killed* him."

Raptor heaves a breath and scratches the thick stubble on his dark chin. "Listen... bringing the kid wasn't *my* idea. He *insisted*."

"He's a *kid*!" I throw my hands in the air. "He can't possibly understand the stakes involved. You *do*!"

Raptor's nostrils flare—the only indication my words broke through his rough façade. "We knew he'd be safe. *He* knew."

"How?" I tighten my hold on the little boy. "Please enlighten me. Exactly *how* did you know it was safe?"

"I heard them leave." Theo's little voice rises from below.

I whip my gaze toward him. "You *what*?"

"In my head." He beams up at me. "I can hear them. Just like you."

My breath falters as I try to make sense of Theo's declaration. "How long have you been able to hear them?"

His grin turns into a smirk. "Since the cave."

The cave. It can't be a coincidence that we both acquired the ability to communicate with the creatures after spending time in their colony. And we certainly weren't the only humans held captive. If they did something to *us*, surely there are others.

"Are you thinking what I'm thinking?" Archer lays a hand on my shoulder and squeezes.

My pulse quickens. "We can't be the only ones."

"We might win this war after all." Archer lifts his face to the moonlit sky, his expression unreadable in the dark. "This is a game changer. We have to get to the safe zone. They need to know."

Is it even safe to travel? The thought tumbles around in my brain, but before I can voice it, Theo tugs on my shirt.

"They won't attack us," he whispers. "They're afraid of you. Like Mama said, you've been touched."

Touched... or marked*?* Andrea's scathing words continue to haunt me. *But that marks you—puts a great big target on your back.*

Archer gazes down at me, and a soft smile curves his lips. "Maybe you are an avenging angel after all."

Raptor clears his throat. "I hate to interrupt this love fest you've got going on, but if you don't mind, I'd like to get the hell out of here before something big and snarly proves you both wrong."

Archer nods, stepping away from Thor as he turns toward the Jeep. He only takes a few steps before losing his footing.

"Whoa, buddy. Take it easy." Thor quickly steps in to support his weight.

"Where's Callie?" I scan the dark Jeep for signs of life. "Archer's hurt."

"She's with Winnie. But before you freak the fuck out, Chuck, Lance, and Supes are with them. Safety in numbers and all that." Raptor smiles down at Theo. "I had the kid to watch my back."

"So they're still holed up in the diner?" Archer asks.

"Nah, man. After you left, we *acquired* a mint condition Volvo station wagon on the outskirts of town, but it isn't exactly rated for off-road excursions, so they're waiting a few miles down the highway."

A shiver of unease courses down my spine at the thought of them out in the open after dark. I may have defeated the queen, but there's no telling how many stragglers could be out, looking for revenge. "We should go."

"Let's get on it!" Raptor brings his big hands together in a loud clap then ushers us back to the Jeep.

He navigates the darkness as if he's driven the route a thousand times. The Jeep easily climbs over rocks and logs, taking us back to the highway in record time. As promised, the rest of our group waits for us a few miles down the road.

We barely come to a full stop before Callie hops out of the Volvo and rushes toward us, eyes wide. "Archer!"

Archer grimaces as I help him out of the Jeep.

"What the hell happened?" Callie gapes at me as if I caused every gash in his skin. And maybe she's right.

Archer waves off her concern. "Nothing a needle and thread can't fix."

"Come on." She loops her arm with his and drags him toward the Volvo.

While I scan the horizon for trouble that never materializes, Callie tends to Archer's injuries. After his wounds are clean and stitched up, she administers a dose of antibiotics to stave off infection.

Less than an hour later, we're back on the highway—Archer in the Jeep with me, and Theo riding shotgun in the Volvo like a badass warrior. The two of us take turns scanning the perimeter, listening for the now-familiar clicks and whirs of the alien language as our little band of survivors heads north.

Archer wraps his arms around me, tucking my head beneath his chin. "You okay?"

"I will be." I snuggle into his chest. His warmth soaks into my weary bones, and the rhythmic cadence of his breathing grounds me.

"Eve?" Archer murmurs against my hair.

"Hmm?"

His heart thunders beneath my ear. "I love you."

I lift my face and lock my gaze on his, bringing our lips a whisper apart. "I love you too."

I barely get the words out before he closes the distance between us and kisses me soundly.

⸺◆⸺

Time passes in a blur. Cradled in Archer's embrace, I drift in and out of consciousness, fighting sleep for fear of what waits for me in my dreams.

The vibrations from the Jeep's tires rumbling over smooth asphalt penetrate all the way to my soul, lulling me into a deep calm. But with the weight of the whole world resting on my narrow shoulders, I'm terrified I'll miss the warning signs and our group will fall to another attack.

"Hey." Archer presses his lips to the top of my head. "You awake?"

I curl my fingers into the front of his shirt and nod.

"Look," he says, gently prodding me.

Lifting my head from his chest, I follow the path of his gaze to a line of cars in the distance. I blink, expecting the vision to clear, for the military base looming ahead of us to vanish into thin air... like a mirage. But it doesn't.

My pulse races as I realize what I'm seeing.

Fort Liberty.

The steel gate spanning the entrance swings open, and the line moves forward as the car in front passes through, heading deeper into the base.

I suck in a breath, snapping my gaze to Archer then back to the armed service members searching the next vehicle before opening the gate again and letting it inside. "We made it? It's real?"

"It's real." Archer's smile widens.

"You did it, kiddo! I'm so damn proud of you!" For the first time in days, Coach's gruff voice ghosts through my subconscious, and a lightness I haven't felt in months washes over me.

"We fucking made it," I whisper.

"Thanks to you." Archer pulls me into the circle of his arms, and for the first time since Serenity tore me out of a dream and into this perpetual nightmare, I feel truly safe.

The battle isn't over, but we have the one thing we didn't have before—*me*. For all their brutality and wild unpredictability, the alien race respects the victor. And when I defeated their queen, in some weird way, that made me one of them. We may not have won the war, but knowing we finally have even the narrowest path to victory—a real chance of survival—gives me hope. It won't be easy, but with my help, the human race will carry on, and with any luck, I'll be around to see it through to the end.

Acknowledgments

I'd like to thank everyone who helped bring *Eve Versus the Apocalypse* to life, starting with my go-to beta readers and writer soul mates: Karissa Laurel, Casey Dembowski, Rashida Williams, and Deborah King. Without these amazing women, I don't think I would've survived this book... let alone an apocalypse!

To everyone at Red Adept Publishing for supporting me and helping me grow these many years. I wouldn't be the writer I am today without you.

To my agent, Cathie Hedrick-Armstrong at Marsal Lyon Literary agency, for always being in my corner. I appreciate your guidance and friendship more than I can convey.

To my family for their continued support. I wouldn't want to survive an apocalypse without you. I love you guys.

And to my readers who have been with me from the beginning, thank you from the bottom of my heart. I do this for you!

About the Author

Best known for her engaging and relatable characters, Erica Lucke Dean specializes in crafting stories that explore the complexities of relationships and feature quirky young women navigating the ups and downs of life and love. For over a decade, her novels have captivated readers of romantic comedies and paranormal romances alike, thanks to her ability to blend humor and authentic emotions.

Erica was born in the Twin Tiers of Upstate New York and lived on both coasts before ultimately settling in the scenic North Georgia Mountains, where she and her family live with two ginormous English Mastiffs and a diabolical Frenchie hell-bent on world domination.Represented by: Cathie Hedrick-Armstrong of Marshal Lyon Literary Agency

Read more at https://ericaluckedean.com/.

About the Publisher

Dear Reader,

We hope you enjoyed this book. Please consider leaving a review on your favorite book site.

Visit our site to find more quality books!

Read more at https://RedAdeptPublishing.com.

9 781958 231685